S. R. Harnot's
Cats Talk

S. R. Harnot's
Cats Talk

Edited by

Khem Raj Sharma and Meenakshi F. Paul

Cambridge
Scholars
Publishing

S. R. Harnot's *Cats Talk*

Edited by Khem Raj Sharma and Meenakshi F. Paul

This book first published 2018

Cambridge Scholars Publishing

Lady Stephenson Library, Newcastle upon Tyne, NE6 2PA, UK

British Library Cataloguing in Publication Data
A catalogue record for this book is available from the British Library

ISBN (10): 1-5275-1357-2
ISBN (13): 978-1-5275-1357-0

Dedicated to Elizabeth Paul

CONTENTS

INTRODUCTION

S. R. Harnot is an eminent Indian writer occupying a coveted place in contemporary Hindi short story writing. His stories derive life from the majestic mountains, cascading rivers, and simple folk of the Himalayan region. Written in dialectal Hindi, his stories bring to life the pulse of the people in their everyday reality. With his keen and evocative powers of description and his dispassionate gaze at the deeply rooted social, cultural and religious milieu, he creates a world where the timeless encounters the exigent. In this regard, his stories have often been placed in the storytelling tradition of Premchand.

Harnot dextrously contextualizes the complex overtones and subtle rhythms of society, and succinctly captures the flow of life in a way that is authentic and aesthetic. His short stories present the little joys and unceasing ironies in the life of Pahari people. His narratives explore the absurdities and incongruities arising from political shenanigans and religious hypocrisies, class and caste discriminations, corruption and unbridled development, and self-centeredness in human relationships. While the mountains, forests, water, land, flora and fauna of the Himalayas are present as melodic resonances in them, his stories bring focus to issues of women, caste, class, nature, ecology, democracy and development as central concerns. Within the framework of Pahari culture, Harnot weaves the changing truths of contemporary times. On the one side, he is agitated by the abrasion of spatial significance in his culture; on the other, he creates characters who strive to realize their full humanity. Thus, even though his stories are embedded in the subsoil of Pahari life, they are not limited to the local but are universal in nature.

Many of Harnot's stories are about social changes that have brought loneliness and sorrow to the hill villages. "Cats Talk", "The Twenty-Foot Bapu Ji", "Ma Reads" and "m.com" narrate the experiences of aging individuals, who live by themselves in homes where their children seldom or never return. Akin to the mountains among which they dwell, they watch the exodus of their children in search of higher education and better livelihoods. For these parents, life alone in the hills is as difficult and tiring as age itself. Yet, all of them are self-respecting and socially aware, resourceful and self-reliant, hardworking and stoic.

Harnot joins the dalit discourse obliquely through the stories, "The Saddle", "Savarna Devata, Dalit Devata", "m.com", "Slur", and "In the Name of Gods". These stories deal with characters who are marginalized, deprived, and othered on the basis of caste. He deconstructs the insidious methods through which caste is perpetuated and concurrently delineates the resistance of those who face it. The stories speak for the dignity of all human beings. In them, Harnot strikes a progressive chord and imbues the characterisation of his protagonists with clear strokes of reason and purpose.

This collection includes two stories, "Aabhi" and "The River Has Vanished" which are sensitive explorations of environmental degradation on account of human actions. Harnot is deeply concerned with distorted human sympathies towards the natural world that contribute to ecological imbalance. The very rivers, mountains and forests that gave rise to human civilizations are threatened by them today. Harnot's stories compel us to think where we have come. Where we are going. Where we will reach. And for how long this can continue. Through a bird, a monkey, a dog, a cow, a river, Harnot minutely explores the retreat of nature in the name of development. In "Aabhi", the tireless strivings of a bird to keep a temple lake clean come to naught in the face of careless littering by tourists and the ruthless exploitation of the forest by the mafia. "The River Has Vanished" captures the intense tension between the need for development and the age-old ways of life in the mountains. These stories give voice to the idea of preserving ecological spaces of the mountainous region and its people. Location itself becomes a discursive character in these stories.

Harnot often juxtaposes rhythms of nature and the people who live close to them against the disruptive encroachment of modernity, even as he acknowledges the inevitability, and sometimes the desirability, of change in the social and cultural praxes in society. The crux in his worldview is that of keeping balance rather than the negation of one or the other. Harnot's writings present this aspect of Himachal's milieu and its culture through the precise apposition of incongruities and the resultant ironies. This narrative strategy heightens the impact of his satire on superstitious, casteist, gender-biased, ageist and fundamentalist tendencies in society. Interestingly, his protagonists, more often than not, succeed in transcending their personal and social problems through determined endeavour and clarity of purpose.

Harnot's flair for photography equips him with an eye for detail and mounting a scene with deft touches of contrast, interest points and perspective. His description of action and events is almost cinematic and he draws nature's vignettes with the painter's palette. He writes in a deceptively simple and lucid language that allows for an in-depth unfolding of human nature and relationships. Localisms imbue his language with authenticity and a unique charm in the manner of Chinua Achebe. His mastery is on display, particularly, in his characterisation. His protagonists resonate in our sympathies long after we are done reading their stories. Their idiosyncrasies and existential dilemmas almost become part of the reader.

The rich layers of meaning conveyed through a straightforward narrative technique in Harnot pose a delightful challenge for the translators. Local words and syntactical patterns apart, the anachronistic but lived culture of his world together with the deep ingress of the present times into it, test the translators' agility. An adequate translation of many of his stories cannot be wrought without the translators immersing themselves in the complex cultural matrix of his society. Thus, while his characters are universally human, the field of their humanity is particularly specific. This is clearly reflected in the many translations of his texts, which range from close translations, adaptations and transcreations to inter-semiotic migrations.

The various translators in this collection have naturally interpreted the stories severally and translated them according to their own diverse translating practice and belief. Hence, there are varying spellings of Hindi and Pahari words in different stories, for instance, 'devatas/devtas', 'gur/goor' and 'biri/bidi'. Also, there are varied interpretations and descriptions of cultural ideas and concepts, for example, 'chariot/palanquin' for the 'rath' (open palanquin with a canopy) of the devata and priest/oracle/vehicle for the devata's 'gur'. In our view, these variations add to the richness of the narratives and to the reader's holistic reading experience by adding different strokes of nuance and texture.

While striving for the desired balance between the two languages, the translators have almost always given primacy to the original. For example, relational names have been mostly retained, 'Amma' (mother), 'Baba/Bapu/Pita' (father, grandfather, respectful term for an old man), 'Chachu/Kaka' (father's younger brother, respectful term for an older man), 'Chhote Pita' (father's younger brother), 'Badi Ma' (wife of father's older brother). Even so, they have not shied from accepting precedents set by earlier translators which aid fluency, such as following the English rule for making plurals. In Hindi and Pahari, plurals may be synonymous with the singular, e.g. 'neta' (leader or politician) – 'Ek (one) neta', 'Kayi (many) neta'. Or they may be different, e.g. 'bachcha' (child), 'bachche' (children). Plurals also change with the case, e.g. 'sapna' (dream), 'sapne' (dreams), 'sapnon ka' (of dreams). In these translations, this complexity has generally been avoided by accepting the addition of 's', to make plurals, for instance, 'devatas' and 'raths'. The possessive noun has been used in both ways, with an apostrophe 's', 'panch's' and also in consonance with the first language, e.g. Pahari ('of /belonging to' the 'Pahar' i.e., mountains).

For this collection, the earlier versions of the translated stories: "Cats Talk", "The Reddening Tree", "Daarosh", "Saddle", "Savarna Devta, Dalit Devta", "Slur", and "In the Name of Gods", have been reworked by the editors with the consent of the translators. In doing so, the guiding principles have been those of lucidity and accuracy, especially of cultural concepts specific to Himachal.

"Cats Talk" was published in Hindi as "Billiyan Batiyati Hain" in the collection, *Daarosh Tatha Anya Kahaniyan* and has been translated into English by R. K. Shukla and Manjari Tiwari. The story first appeared in the Hindi magazine *Pahal* in 1995; its English translation was published in the Journal, *Indian Literature* in 2013. The story depicts the harsh reality of the outmigration of people from villages to urban areas and reflects on the varied aspects of motherhood. It is the story of an old alienated and longsuffering mother whose world is now peopled by her affectionate domestic animals and her devoted pet cats. The story is a memorable piece for its rare delicacy and profound simplicity.

The Twenty-Foot Bapu Ji, "Bees Foot Ke Bapu Ji", is also part of *Daarosh Tatha Anya Kahaniyan,* and has been translated into English by Meenakshi F. Paul and Khem Raj Sharma. The story talks about the changing father-son relationship. Harnot skilfully juxtaposes the statue of Mahatma Gandhi with the life of old Chachu to portray the abandoning of old values by the younger generation and the compulsions of economy and social prestige that ensnare it. This abandonment is paralleled by the retreat of Chachu from his son's life, which in turn is mirrored by the elevation of Bapu Gandhi's statue from six feet to twenty feet in order to keep it safe from vandalism. This story is a telling and ironical reflection of our society that glorifies its ancient culture but neglects the teachings and negates the bonds.

The Reddening Tree was first published as "Lal Hota Darakht" in the anthology *Akashbel* in 1988. Harnot modified the story and included it in *Daarosh Tatha Anya Kahaniyan* (2001). The story has been translated into English by Meenakshi F. Paul. It is a powerful and moving story, narrated in almost lyrical terms, about a poor farmer family, torn between their dharma and their means. The unprecedented conclusion of the narrative leaves the reader breathless and wonder struck at the denouement, which is both impossible and inevitable. The story was included in Paul's anthology of translation, *Short Stories of Himachal Pradesh* (2007). The translation of "Lal Hota Darakht" has been reworked by her for the present collection.

"Daarosh" is a fine and subtle delineation of an atypical custom of a tribal area in Himachal Pradesh. It first appeared with the same title in the Hindi magazine *Hans* in 1997 and was then published in *Daarosh Tatha Anya Kahaniyan*. The story has been translated into English by Khem Raj Sharma. Daarosh means 'by force'. A dying custom of that particular area is called "Daarosh dublub" which means marriage by force. The story is about an assertive resistance by an educated village girl against the disempowering patriarchal setup of her society. It captures the eruption of tensions in an ancient society when the light of new knowledge penetrates its strong walls. An upholder of preserving the rich culture of his inheritance, Harnot is also known for going all out in doing away with social evils in the garb of customs and traditions. "Daarosh" posits a counter discourse to these hegemonic forces.

"The Saddle" was originally published in Hindi as "Jinkathi" in the literary magazine, *Kathadesh* in 2005 and was again selected for publication in the special issue of *Kathadesh* on "Ten Years One Choice" in 2007. It was included in Harnot's collection of short stories *Jinkathi Aur Anya Kahaniyan* in 2008. The story was translated into English by R. K. Shukla as "The Saddle" and published in the *Journal of Literature and Aesthetics* in 2008. The story brings out the subtle textures and complexities of 'Bhunda', an ancient and terrifying Himachali festival involving human sacrifice. The insidiousness of caste prejudice is represented in this festival. The central role of the scapegoat is assigned in it to a male from a dalit community of the hills, called beda. It is worth mentioning here that the word 'dalit' is used in this introduction to convey the limited sense of referring to persons belonging to the diverse range of communities traditionally considered as low caste or untouchable. The chosen dalit man is deviously consecrated as a brahmin only for the purpose of the potentially fatal ritual in which a long rope is tied from the top of a hillock to a point below and the beda has to slide down it. While the ritual may have been a way of propitiating the gods for the high castes, but for the beda it spelled likely death. In the story, Harnot employs 'Bhunda', as a narrative device to express his angst engendered by the inscribed hegemony and hypocrisy in the ritual. Saddle becomes the ironic metaphor in the story to convey how, saddled with the risky job of the Bhunda, the dalit protagonist uses it to gain advantage and some form of redressal.

The story, **"m.com"** was published as "Em Dot Com" in *Kathan* (2001) and included in *Jinkathi Aur Anya Kahaniyan.* It has been translated into English by Meenakshi F. Paul. The story is a powerful story about the ironies etched into the transformations wrought by economic development and modern technology in traditional societies. On the one hand, these changes bring about ease and prosperity, on the other, they loosen the ties that keep the community together. Young people are able to find dignified alternatives to traditional caste professions but they also become uncaring of the values of consideration and cooperation. Ma is able to travel on modern transportation but feels helpless and inadequate to deal with the internet-based process of registering cattle. The story strikes a deep nostalgic note for community feeling and innocent bygone times but also accepts the injustices and inequities of those very days. The present is a mixed bag, as indeed are all times.

"Ma Reads" was first published as "Ma Padhti Hai" in the leading Hindi magazine *Hans.* It has been translated into English by Ira Raja, and appeared in the literary magazine *Atenea,* in 2004. It was later included in her book, *Grey Areas: An Anthology of Indian Fiction on Ageing* (OUP 2010). It is the story of a writer and his hardworking independent mother. Her son wins accolades in the city but does not share his literary success with his illiterate mother back in the village. Till one fine day, he realises with a pang that he has gifted his books to many people but has never shown even one to his mother. He carries a bundle of his books home only to realise that all along she has quietly been ordering his successive books and carrying them around fondly as she did her innumerable chores. The dramatic turn accentuates his shame which is overwhelmingly and bitterly felt.

"Savarna Devta, Dalit Devta" was published in Hindi with the same title in the collection of short stories *Jinkathi Aur Anya Kahaniyan* and has been translated into English by R. K. Shukla and Manjari Tiwari. It records the pain and anguish of a dalit boy, who could not reconcile himself to being subjugated and mistreated on the basis of caste. The inhumanity of the practice of caste pollution perturbs him greatly. He questions the religious traditions that lead to the othering of people lower down the caste hierarchy and concludes that these are part of a conspiracy to keep them in perpetual bondage. He decides to honour the lesser deities standing outside the gate of the temple rather than worship the main devata and his attendant deities inside, who he comes to believe are captives of caste. An act that is simultaneously defiant and inadequate, but which nevertheless augurs the beginning of change towards social equity and dignity.

"Slur" was published as "Kaalikh" in the monthly journal *Himprasth* (2002). It was later included in *Jinkathi Aur Anya Kahaniyan* and has been translated into English by Khem Raj Sharma and Meenakshi F. Paul. It is the story of a bold young dalit widow, Shyama, who has a son born a couple of years after the death of her husband. Her husband had died of insanity caused by his dabbling in witchcraft and thereafter Shyama has managed on her own. In a conspiracy to deny her and her son their rightful share of her husband's property and to prevent her son from being educated, she is sought to be castigated by the very men who had exploited her physically and financially. Instead, she exposes their hypocrisy and shames them before the whole village council. Her agency shakes the hegemony of the social, political, and cultural setup of her society. Her son cannot lay claim to his father's name but in the end, there is no cause for him to do so as the name of his mother is sufficient. The epilogue-like ending accentuates the hollow assertion of male supremacy in an already surrendered bastion.

"In the Name of Gods" was first published in *Pahal* in 2006 by the title "Devataon Ke Bahane". It is also part of *Jinkathi Aur Anya Kahaniyan* and has been translated into English by R. K. Shukla and Manjari Tiwari. It is the story of Som, an educated dalit boy, who wants to rid his area of backwardness and underdevelopment. He devises and executes an intelligent political strategy around the egos and influence of the powers that be to ensure that development finally comes to the area. In the end, Som emerges as the leader of the village and is acknowledged by everyone, irrespective of caste or status. Harnot debunks the casteist notions that dub people of the scheduled castes as incapable and unworthy of high office. Harnot presents education and political voice as effective levellers of the field which enable the disadvantaged to shine and contribute meaningfully to society.

"The River Has Vanished", "Nadi Ghayab Hai", was published in the short story collection *Mitti Ke Log*. It has been translated into English by Ravi Nandan Sinha and is part of his anthology of translations, *Great Hindi Short Stories*. A book on Harnot's environment-based stories has also been edited in Hindi by Usha Rani Rao with the Hindi title (2018). In this story, Harnot exhibits his engagement with environmental issues and promotes the idea of development with conservation. In Himachal, as in all of India, rivers are worshipped and have mythological legends attached to them. In the story, the village boy Teekam senses the conspiracy of the rich and the powerful to tame the river for their benefit, which would deprive the villagers of their livelihoods and lay barren the whole area. He intelligently uses the faith of the people in the village devata to thwart the construction of a dam on the river.

"Aabhi" is taken from Harnot's latest short story collection *Lytton Block Gir Raha Hai* (2014) and has been translated by Meenakshi F. Paul. It is the story of a bird, locally called Aabhi. Legend has it that the bird keeps a lake by the name of Serolsar in Kullu district of Himachal Pradesh scrupulously clean, not allowing even a twig to remain on the clear waters. In this age of environmental degradation and unsustainable exploitation of natural resources, the bird becomes a living symbol of interconnected ecological coexistence. Aabhi and the Mother Snake Goddess, who lives in the temple close by, embody the essentially pantheistic aspects of Pahari culture while also depicting people's increasing disregard for nature and the divine. Masterful in its description and personification, "Aabhi" is one of the most loved stories of Harnot. Together, these twelve stories provide a representative canvas of Harnot's oeuvre that we hope will both delight and engage the readers.

Khem Raj Sharma
Meenakshi F. Paul
April, 2018

CATS TALK

BILLIYAN BATIYATI HAIN

Amma's tiffs have begun—with herself, with the match-box, with the earthen lamp, the pieces of cow-dung fuel smouldering in the hearth, and with the cats racing in and out of the house. That's how her day begins. She wakes up at about four in the morning and with her also wake up the cattle in the shed. Birds take their cue from all this and start twittering and chirping in the courtyard. Not to be left behind are the cats who start their racing bouts the moment Amma rises from her bed. Who can say who wakes up first, Amma or the cats!

Many a time Amma quarrels with the dark, her hands measuring its multiple layers. Her hands explore the bed, the pillow but the match-box is nowhere to be found. Sometimes Amma lights her bidi in the night and the match-box drops from her hand and slips under the bed. Half asleep, she takes a few puffs but forgets to pick up the match-box before falling asleep again. When she wakes up in the morning and needs it again, she cannot find it and starts cursing it. After all, she needs it to light the earthen lamp but it takes her a good deal of time to refresh her memory about the match-box lying under the cot. She bends from the bed and moves her fingers over the floor to retrieve it. She manages to find it finally but not before getting fully worked up. Then she straightens up, takes out one matchstick, and tries to light it but to no effect. This works her up even more and she starts cursing the matchstick again.

The dark confuses her and she rubs the wrong end of the matchstick. The matchstick breaks; she takes out another one, strikes it but this one also breaks. She succeeds in her third attempt and lights the half-smoked bidi from last night. She also lights the earthen lamp and the room is flooded with light, thus one matchstick serves two purposes at the same time.

While trying to rise from the bed, she discovers that the cats have stuck their nails in her salwar or kurta. Irritated, she picks up the cats and flings them to the ground. Even when she flings them with considerable force, the cats touch the ground on their feet. Amma believes that God has blessed the cats that way. They never fall on their backs ... a couple of more curses and that's all,

"Witches, dare again to touch my bed! I'll drain the life out of you two, I will! Rats and rodents play all the night in the room, you two just keep snoring in the soft, warm bed! Now you see what I do to you two!"

And the cats quietly hide themselves in the darkness.

The two cats are mother and daughter, one white and the other black. No one, not even Amma can ever tell as to which of the two is younger. One is called Kali and the other Nikki. They know their names because when called so, they respond immediately.

Many a times Amma pushes them on to the loft above the veranda and shuts the trapdoor, where they remain for long, mewing and growling ceaselessly. But Amma remains unmoved and doesn't open the door. The loft also serves as Amma's granary where she stores the harvested corn-ears and grains. Amma thinks this has two advantages—they dry up easily and secondly there is no fear of the corn-ears rotting. Amma could have left them to dry in the courtyard but then who knows when the gates of heaven would open and the rain-gods send water pouring down? And then there is always the fear of the dust-storms. Alone, how would she gather the corn-ears and bring them in? When she needed grains for grinding, she would take out a few corn-ears, put them in a bag and lash the bag with a thick stick until the grains were completely separated from the cobs. Further ahead in the loft, Amma stores the healthier corn-ears to be used for sowing the new crop.

Amma would never go to the loft in the dark. She is afraid. Even though the movements and smell of the cats keep away reptiles and other harmful insects but who could allay Amma's misapprehensions? Once bitten twice shy. Even today Amma remembers that a black snake had sneaked into the loft through the mud-tiles of the roof. The moment Amma stepped on to the loft it raised its hood and hissed. Amma was back on the veranda in a flash and could hardly breathe for a while. The snake was driven away with great difficulty.

Apart from the corn-ears, Amma keeps many things up there–at the back she has old wool, some bundles, two or three broken lanterns, a few broken umbrellas, empty bottles, old plastic and rubber shoes. On the other side there are eight or ten coils of beul tree fibre and a dowel for twisting it into twine. Neck ropes, halters and muzzles for the cattle are also kept here. She also keeps the bare dried shoots of the beul on the loft. Amma never lights the hearth without these during the winters and monsoons. That is why in the summer itself she ties the green shoots and after they have dried she immerses them in water. When they are ready, with the help of a few women she beats them till the fibre separates from the shoot. This serves two purposes; she gets the shoots for kindling and the fibre for rope.

***

The cow mooes as soon as Amma begins to mutter. Even though the cowshed is at some distance from where Amma sleeps, the closeness between the two can be known from their conversations. Amma knows what the cow says or wants from her and reasons with her while lying in bed. Sometimes she also scolds her, 'Don't make so much noise, Chambi. Let me get up at least, I'll attend to you before doing anything else'.

The cow has just calved and knows that Amma would milk her first thing in the morning. Early in the morning, Amma goes into the kitchen to prepare wheat bran for the cow. If bran is not available at the grocer's, Amma has to make do with whatever is left after sieving the flour. Sometimes left-over food from the night before is given to the cow blended with buttermilk and a sprinkling of salt. Amma also carries a leftover roti or two for other animals. She knows that once one of them has started eating, the others would not have the patience to wait.

In Amma's cattle-shed there are other animals also—a pair of bullocks, one baby cow, and two lambs. The cow is tethered to the right side of the door and the baby cow close to its mother. The lambs have their pegs slightly to the other side of the door and some distance away are tethered the bullocks. The bamboo-ladder stands by the wall. Amma uses this ladder to climb to the hayloft. She stores quite a few bundles of dry grass there so that when she falls ill or when the weather turns bad, the cattle do not have to go hungry. She also keeps big conical and round bamboo baskets there.

After milking the cow, Amma comes straight to the kitchen and it's here that Amma's first tiff with the cats begins. Crouching at the door the two cats wait while Amma is milking the cow. The moment Amma steps out into the courtyard with the milk-bucket, the two cats start following her, often getting between her legs and thereby causing her enormous irritation. Amma curses them but the cats simply ignore her words and become even more impatient. They know that they will be the first to taste the milk. Their continuous mewing fills the house. Once in the kitchen, the first thing Amma does is to pour milk in the cats' saucers.

Now Amma lights the fire. When the weather is fine during the summer, Amma makes the fire with a handful of dry grass but during winters or rains she puts the dry beul shoots or cow-dung upley in the earthen fire-pot and covers them with ash to preserve it from going out. If the upley are insufficient or she feels the fire would not last till the morning, then she presses a few more in the heap of ash. Hardly, if ever, has it happened that Amma's hearth has gone cold. Amma says that in a household the fire should always be alive or it bodes ill for the family.

Amma stokes the fire with the tongs and adds grass or wood to kindle it. She doesn't like to blow into it because it makes her cough. The result is that the whole house is filled with smoke which blackens the walls. Apart from the thick layers of smoke, cobwebs are everywhere on the walls. There's hardly any difference between the blackened and cobweb-filled walls and Amma's face. Amma has also become like the smoke. If one peers long at her face, one would have a feeling that this smoke is not that of the fire-wood or upley but has its source in something smouldering inside her.

Amma knows how to tell time without a clock. There's neither a clock nor a cock around to tell her whether it is evening or morning but it seems that she can hear the changing footsteps of time. She understands fully well when the moon or the stars knock at the doors of the sky. It's child's play for her to tell the time of the day or night. It has become a habit with her to rise at the exact same time in the morning. Sometimes the birds are puzzled as to whether it is they who rise first in the morning or Amma. Birds are chums with Amma and their morning sun descends only in Amma's courtyard. After finishing her morning chores in the cattle-shed and the kitchen, she does not forget to scatter a handful of grains in the courtyard. She keeps a separate store of millets and coarse rice meal from her own share of rations. On the low branches of the trees on both sides of the gate, birds have made their nests and Amma always keeps water-filled pots under these trees for them. This she does especially during the hot weather so that the birds have their full supply of water and do not go thirsty. For this purpose, Amma gets fresh earthen pots every year.

The whole village can hear Amma calling the birds any time of the day. Even when the birds are hovering over her head, she shouts for them to pick up their food once she has thrown the grains in the courtyard: 'Come birdies, come, your food is waiting for you!'

To keep the birds safe from the cats needs special care. Sitting at the door and puffing at her bidi, Amma watches over the birds while they peck at the grains and sees to it that the cats do not scare or pounce on them. Sometimes, to keep the cats busy elsewhere, she goes inside the house and pours milk in the saucers for them.

***

Strange is Amma's lonely world. She is always busy with someone somewhere. She has invented quite a few things to while away her free, lonely time. Hardly is there any child in the village who has not eaten a piece of jaggery or butter-smeared roti from her hands. Hardly is there a woman who while going to fetch water or collect fire-wood has not stopped in Amma's courtyard for a puff of her bidi. There's not a dog in the village that has not tasted a few crumbs of roti with its quota of swearwords while passing by Amma's door or any bird that has not pecked the grains in her courtyard. Even stray animals would not forget to have a casual peep into her courtyard while passing by her house.

If Amma ever falls ill, then a woman or a girl from the village takes charge of her household chores, fetches water for her, feeds her pets. Even cows and cats do not bother her when she is unwell. The birds take care not to make any noise and let her take full rest. This is also a period of complete cease-fire between Amma and those with whom she has regular tiffs. Quite often Amma catches a cold which causes headaches. Then it's the cow that comes to her help by softly licking her hair and forehead. As for the cats, they either quietly crouch around her or just lick her feet, legs or hands. As for the bird-party, it keeps flying around her as soon as the early morning sun-rays touch the earth. They chirp and sing around her as usual for they also wish to be near her when she is sick or unwell. Only the fear of the cats keeps them from drawing too close to her. Perhaps, it is the collective good wishes of her pets that Amma soon gets well.

It has been four years since her children's father died. Like everyone else, Amma also called him Pita. They had a daughter whom they married off when she was quite young. The son was provided with a good education. Pita insisted that their son must become an officer, or there was no fun in having an only son. So, no effort was spared to have him highly educated. Debts accumulated, a few acres of family land were mortgaged. As soon he completed his college education, he got a job. But the old couple had not foreseen that once their son was exposed to the glamour of city life, he would become a stranger to them. His contact with his soil gradually began to diminish. The gap between the parents and the son kept on widening and one day the couple got the news that he had married a city girl. Now they could not face the people of their village.

After many days the son visited the village with his bride and after spending a few days with them he left. The daughter-in-law did not know the ways and customs of the village and while she was there she felt as if she was in prison. She could not stand the smell of raw earth or the stench of cow-dung. The couple had dreamt that when their daughter-in-law would come, she would take charge of the household and Amma would be relieved of her daily grind. Crops would grow aplenty, the number of cattle would increase, their prestige in the village would rise, the daughter-in-law would look after the old couple, Amma would spend her time playing with her grandchildren, and the whole house would be abuzz with activity and reverberate with children's laughter. In fact, while the son was in college, his father had contacted many people of his community who had eligible daughters. He had very grand plans for his son's wedding. Wasn't he the only son, he would ask himself. The ceremony would be on such a grand scale that relatives would talk about it for weeks. And did people talk about it for weeks!

Amma recovers very quickly. And with that begins the old routine: the household chores keep her busy as always. Often it happens that people from the village warn her:

"Devru kaki, why do you strain yourself so much? Your son sends five hundred rupees every month and that should be sufficient for you. Now you should take rest."

And Amma readily replies, "Have you ever heard anyone dying of household work? So long as one breathes, one has to move about. And then so much land, so many animals, so many cows and bullocks, how can I leave them to themselves?"

Sometimes the village pradhan or thakur says to her, tauntingly, "Devru, why don't you sell the land? Give away your cows and bullocks because your son and daughter-in-law are not going to come here. What will you achieve by holding on to them? Now you have grown weak and can't even move about easily."

Amma understands their intentions. They have their eyes on her land and house. She replies sharply, "Pradhan ji, I can manage not only these cows and bullocks but even twice as many. The job is a temporary affair. My son has to come back here. And moreover, this is my problem, why should you lose sleep over it? You tend to your own work"

Amma knows fully well that once she is gone, all her property would be grabbed by these greedy people of the village. They would quarrel over it like vultures. Her son is oblivious of these things but the village is, after all, my village, my very own. A job doesn't last forever. One's prestige or social status depends on what one has in one's ancestral village.

When the postman comes to deliver her son's money order, he often sits with her and tells her stories about city life. After Pita's death, the son regularly sends five hundred rupees every month to Amma but she alone knows how useless that amount is in mitigating her loneliness. She doesn't want any monetary help from anybody but accepts it only to keep up her son's honour among the village people. The land and the cows are enough to meet her requirements.

Amma often recalls incidents from the postman's anecdotes about city life that make her worry about her son and daughter-in-law. How restless city life has become! Everyday something nasty takes place there. Riots break out followed by police baton charge and bullets. How must her son and daughter-in-law be managing their lives under these conditions? And then, there's the little one going to school! This is why Amma loves her village where peace prevails all the year round, no riots, no baton charge or police firing here. But the peace of the village cannot allay Amma's perpetual fear and restlessness that weigh so oppressively on her heart. It's a mother's heart after all. Even if the son has become a complete city man and the daughter-in-law hates to visit her, how can she forget them and their wellbeing!

***

Amma is nearing sixty. During all these years she had never paid any attention to her body. She would not discard old, torn clothes until they were total rags. Her hair, unwashed, uncombed, would always be tied with a torn dupatta. She often thinks of washing and drying her hair but can never find time for it. When her daughter visits, she washes Amma's hair or occasionally a woman of the village washes it for her. Then Amma remains relaxed for days.

Harvest is Amma's busiest time. Amma's agricultural work is taken care of by the village custom of farmers helping out in each other's fields by turn. The whole village comes readily to help Amma. The people of the village know that she spares no efforts in feeding or looking after those who help her in these times. Sometimes the youngsters of the village tell her, teasingly of course, that they would help her in tilling or sowing only if she offered them a few pouches of country liquor.

Amma then picks up her broom and pointing it at them she scolds them, "You rogues, you should be ashamed to say such things to your grandmother. Your mouths still smell of mother's milk and you have the cheek to ask for liquor! No, you will not get any."

Everybody knows that ghee has become very scarce these days, but Amma is very generous with it and keeps up the tradition of feeding those who help her with plenty of ghee and raw sugar.

Amma knows that a new round of tilling is needed when maize saplings start to grow. When Pita was alive, he would do the entire tilling himself with some help from his grownup son. Her married daughter also came home those days. But it needed quite a few helpers to complete the tilling on time, so there would be about thirty to forty neighbours in addition to the family members. Amma saw to it that the tilling began in style with drums and shehnai playing soulful music. Pita was an accomplished shehnai artist and he led the other musicians. Marriages, jatars–religious fairs and processions, and tilling always began with his shehnai recitals. Amma was always by his side at these times. She was specially invited on such occasions. She was an accomplished jhuri singer and no one could match her in singing these love songs.

And when it was the people's turn to work in her own fields, her joy knew no bounds. Pita played on his shehnai, his partner beat the drum, and Amma's jhuries and julfies filled the air with joy.

Amma's lilting voice would waft through the maize-fields and resound across the entire valley, making the young maize plants dance and wave with ecstasy. The rain-filled clouds would frisk and frolic through the sky as if intoxicated with Amma's voice. The whole atmosphere would seem to be charged with joy and people would be filled with hope and enthusiasm. The moment Amma's voice came to a silky stop, Pita would cry out in appreciation 'Bravo! Sha..ba..shayyy!'

Even now sometimes the village women cajole Amma to sing a song or two on ceremonial occasions and Amma obliges but it is obvious that the old fervour is now a thing of the past. The strain becomes too much as she says to the women, 'Now look, even breathing has become difficult for me and you ask me to sing'.

How could Amma breathe easy? She alone knows how silently but relentlessly something has been nibbling at her soul over the years. But she does not want to disappoint her companions. She starts to sing but her voice chokes and the words that do manage to come out seem to be those of a novice and not that of an accomplished singer as Amma is known to be. Her voice breaks down and she starts to cough, her eyes become red, and it appears as if Amma is fighting for breath. Old wounds, so long asleep, seem to wake up and become fresh. In between the bouts of coughing, old memories well up in her mind and float in her eyes. She turns her eyes to the blankness as if someone is calling her. She could see Pita from far away point his shehnai towards her and say, "Wife, let's hear one more jhuri!"

But where is he now…? Four years have gone by since he left this world but it appears as if it happened only yesterday. Amma simply cannot believe that Pita is no longer around. She is often overpowered by his memories and sobs and cries for hours. He was her only support and now he was gone.

During the nights Amma often imagines that he is lying on the cot next to hers. Amma sleeps in the same room which she shared with Pita and his cot is still there because Amma did not allow it to be moved away. To her the cot was an assurance of his presence in the room and this mitigates her loneliness. When he was alive, Amma would get up many times in the night to fill his hookah. The hookah still stands by the cot. Every two or three days, Amma scours it with ash and changes its water. When any village elder comes to visit her, she prepares the hookah as she did before. Its bell metal shines like a piece of silver on the sand.

Sometimes, Amma suddenly wakes up in the night and is overtaken by an illusion. Pita would often fling aside his quilt while sleeping. Amma still hears his deep breaths in the night and notices some movement on the cot. She sits up in the dark and gropes the bed but discovers the cats sleeping there. Amma does not disturb them and quietly slips back into her own bed. Cats do this often, when they do not lie in her bed, they jump on to Pita's bed to sleep.

Amma is firm in her belief that Pita died prematurely. He had stopped breathing all of a sudden. He often comes to her in her dreams and says, "Wife, perform the post death rituals for me in Haridwar-Pehowa; my spirit has not been liberated till now."

But what can Amma do to have the rites performed? So far away from home, Haridwar is another country for her. Sometimes she thinks that if the manes are angry and are not immediately propitiated, there would be neither peace nor prosperity. And this thought keeps nibbling at her heart, driving away the peace of her mind. The son would be held guilty of not discharging his obligations to his ancestors. Once Amma had met a shaman, who told her that he was capable of calling back the departed souls of seven generations.

When requested by Amma to call back Pita's spirit, the man obliged and Amma still exclaims with wonder, "The same voice, the same way of talking, only this time he spoke through the shaman beneath a black sheet of cloth. He told her 'Wife, I have no complaints against you but my heart longs for my son, send him here the next time!'"

But how could she send her son? He has become a city man and no longer cares what happens to her. He will face the consequences one day when things will have gone too far.

***

The bullocks tethered in the courtyard often pull out the stakes. One day when this happened, Amma was sleeping in the sun and heard the lambs bleating furiously. The lambs are Amma's informers. Their bleating tells her that something unusual is happening in the shed, like one of the cattle drawing out the peg and roaming about in the open.

Amma's two bullocks are very gentle but over the last few days they have taken to fighting. They have become jealous of each other. When she heard the bleating, Amma rose and glanced at the lamb. It was circling round its peg. In the process, the rope tightened around its neck and it collapsed on the ground just as Amma reached it. Now she did not know whether to first rescue the lamb or to manage the rogue bullock. When she shouted at the bullock it advanced towards her furiously. If Amma had not found a thick stick it would have flung her into the field. The bullock's behaviour was unexpected and ominous. It means, Amma thought, somebody has cast an evil eye, otherwise it is unthinkable that her cattle would ever disobey her or become disorderly in her presence. She somehow managed to push the bullock back into the shed. Amma then cut off the lamb's rope with her sickle. It was only when she poured some water over it that the lamb opened its eyes, to Amma's relief.

Stakes have always been Amma's worry. She cannot fix them hard into the ground. She has to sit at the edge of the yard of the cowshed to wait for a man or boy passing by to ask for help in fixing the uprooted stake firmly into the ground. This time, she saw the temple priest coming her way. Amma called out loudly to him and when he came close, she bowed to his feet in obeisance and enquired about the wellbeing of his family. When he sat down Amma offered him a bidi but before he could light it and have a few puffs, she went inside the house and brought out the hammer to fix the stakes.

"Pandit ji, first please fix the stakes quite deep into the ground. The bullock almost killed me today."

The pandit removed his big woollen shawl from his shoulders and began to fix the stakes. When he finished, Amma was relieved. The pandit checked the other pegs and assured Amma that those were all right.

Now Amma thought this was an appropriate time to broach the subject that was weighing on her mind. "Panditji, such a thing has never happened," she said, "Tell me what has gone amiss with me or my family." Saying this Amma went inside the house and quickly came back with some wheat grains in a bell metal plate which she handed to the pandit. The pandit sat cross-legged on the wooden seat and upturned the plate on the ground. He placed the grains in a little heap on one side of the plate and then picked up a few grains in his hand. He asked Amma to blow on them. Amma did as asked. The pandit held the grains in his hand for some time; took his hand to his mouth and recited some mantras. He recited the names of devi-devtas and then dropped the grains on the back of the plate. He counted the grains one by one. Amma squatted before him and watched his actions intently. She also recited the name of the devta silently.

Meanwhile, the pandit's face was reddening as if the devta was descending on him. He picked up some grains in his hand once again and handed them to Amma in three instalments, careful that each time the number of grains was only five and not six because while five is an auspicious number, six is ominous. Handing the grains to Amma, the pandit said, "Look, Devru, something is the matter, no doubt. Tomorrow is the first day of the New Year. You must come to the temple tomorrow and the devta will help you. Today, after washing your hands and feet offer some incense dhoop to your family deity and sprinkle gaunch-cow urine, and holy Ganga water. Then throw some grains round your house and feed the remaining with wheat dough to the recalcitrant bullock." After giving these instructions, the pandit left and went home.

Amma did as the pandit had directed her. Now she had to wait for the next day. She was convinced that some evil spirit was playing mischief with her. She would go to the temple and hold a special puja. She would ask the deity about the welfare of her son and daughter-in-law and also ask who had made them turn their backs on her. Only the deity could tell her which enemy had let loose an evil spirit into her house.

***

Next day Amma finished the household chores quickly to go to the temple. The temple is hardly a furlong away. It is situated right in front of her house and every time she steps out her eyes fall on the devta. This is why Amma never leaves any left-over food in her courtyard and sprinkles it with gaumutra or Gangajal in the morning. If the house is clean your mind is also at peace, she believes. But Amma and peace, they have hardly, if ever, been together!

At about three in the morning, Amma reached the temple with dhoop and thick sweet rotis, called roat, for the devta. She took off her sandals near the wall of the temple and sat down quietly in the outer place meant for women. First, she bowed to the deity and then handed the basket of roat and dhoop to one of the kardars, the temple keepers. He took the offerings and emptied them near Bhairava's small temple. He then took out a few pieces and offered them to the deity on Amma's behalf by flinging them in all four directions. He then sprinkled a few drops of gaunch. He put a few grains of rice and a flower in the basket and returned it to Amma as the deity's prasad. Amma accepted it with folded hands.

As she sat there quietly Amma's eyes were on the temple compound where the temple kardars had begun to assemble and the devta's musical instruments had been brought out. The musicians had picked up their instruments: The drummers had the dhol, nagara, and chambi; the horn players had the narsinga, and karnal. Only the shehnai was missing because there was no one who could play it. The absence of the shehnai player struck Amma deeply because the absent shehnai player was none other than her own long dead husband. She was assailed terribly by his memory. He was the one from his family who performed every ritual of the devta as his kardar. He was also the devta's shehnai player. He was present on every important occasion, be it sakranti—the first day of the month, a jatar, or any other work. Amma imagined that he would appear suddenly from nowhere, bow to the deity before taking his position among the musicians, and then take out his shehnai from his bag, set it carefully before breathing into it to produce that soul-touching raga which only he could produce. In the beginning, the sound would be a little scratchy but soon it would change into its usual accomplished tune.

Now that her husband is no more, the devta would be deprived of that musical homage. This thought touched her so deeply that her eyes filled with tears.

The time had now arrived for the panchi, the ritual worship of the devtas. Amma moved a little forward from where she was sitting. When the priest came out from the temple he looked around before taking his seat in the compound. Amma bowed to him from afar. The priest sat on the eastern side of the temple. To his right and left sat the kardars as the panchs. In front there sat the oracles and kardars of three different devtas. On a plate nearby, the panchs had kept dhoop, pieces of jaggery, rice, and vermilion sindur to be used during the worship.

The musical invocation started and various musical instruments began to make a rousing sound. Amma knows that these musical sounds denote the descent of the gods on their human devotees. When the music rose to a crescendo, a strange excitement seemed to charge the air. Every once in a while, a kardar flung pinches of flour and sprinkled gaumutra in the four directions.

The priest had been chosen by the devta as his chief vehicle and he started to lapse into a state of convulsion as a result of the devta entering into him. The music rose to a higher pitch and the effect of it was a greater frenzy among the assembly of devotees. The god had finally arrived. The devotees folded their hands and bowed their heads.

When the devta entered into the priest, he began to thump the ground violently and shout in a frenzied voice, "Protect us".

The assembly repeated the same. A panch poured a handful of rice or grain into the priest's hands and he threw it in the air to suggest that protection had been granted. Now the panchi had begun, Amma was in a state of terror and excitement, her hands jerked involuntarily. The Devta himself called out to her and she stood up startled, "Come forward Devru".

One kardar quickly helped Amma to come forward. The devta moved vigorously; he screamed and beat himself with the heavy link-chains in his hands. Amma remained motionless but a huge storm raged within her. Today she will reveal everything in the presence of the devta, she will seek answers to all her questions that have been building up within her. She can no longer carry the weight of those questions and then there can be no secrets from the divine presence. If she had only one question, she would have asked it quickly but there is a whole crowd of questions, a whole bunch of sorrows welling up within her and she did not know what to ask and how she should go about it. What she did not know, however, was that all those questions and all those sorrows were floating in her eyes. The devta must have seen them all. Isn't it true that he knows everything that goes on in our minds? What can she hide from him?

"Are your bullocks alright?"

"Yes, by your grace, Deva."

"Take these grains of rice as protection. Throw them in your courtyard. From today onwards, no harm will come to you, no sorrow will cross your path".

Amma bowed her head in reverence and gratitude but said nothing. The thousands of questions floating in her eyes had fallen down as two tear drops. ... She thought the devta had taken care of those questions. The priest through whom the devta had spoken those reassuring words looked at her. She appeared to him a picture of infinite grace and composure, a goddess almost. Dumb cattle and gods her only support. When she came out of the temple premises, she saw some women sitting near the boundary wall. One of them stopped her and said, "Devru, Maal, the cattle festival is near and you must come to join the singing every day."

Amma didn't answer and went home quietly.

When she reached home she remembered what the woman had said. She also remembered how in the past she celebrated this festival with enthusiasm and gaiety.

But now she doesn't like to sing or celebrate; whereas in the past such occasions had drawn Amma to themselves as if by force and the womenfolk of the village would anxiously wait for her. The cattle festival was something very special for which the singing would start weeks in advance. The women would assemble at the temple and for hours the place would reverberate with song and dance. The bright moonlight would add to the beauty of the occasion and the valley nearby seemed to respond to the mood of gaiety and joy. Amma was always cajoled to be the lead singer and her songs would waft across the valley and fill it with melody. The village women would joke and laugh with gay abandon. On the eighth day Amma would deck her cattle with colourful ribbons and bells and be the first to take them to water. She would carry a bagful of puffed corn and walnuts and distribute them to all those she happened to come across.

And now the Maal is on the next day and Amma's festival will be as it has always been for the last so many years, all by herself, without her son or daughter-in-law. Only the cats, a lone cow, the two bullocks and the two lambs would be there. These dumb animals will be her fellow revellers. She knows full well that now when she sings, her voice hardly crosses the threshold of her own thoughts. It would hit its head against the boundary-wall of the house and come back to her.

But it's an auspicious festival involving the wellbeing of her life's companions and therefore it has to be celebrated with care and piety. Had it been some other festival, she would have ignored it but this festival of the cattle comes only once in a year and how could she ignore a festival dedicated to her companions in her lonely life? Amma had forgotten to pick the white bungadi and golden sartwaj flowers for making garlands. Sartwajs grow abundantly around the house but for bungadis she would have to go far to the pastures. But they are a must for decking the cattle.

Amma rose early to go to collect the flowers even though it was still very dark. No doubt she had to go a long distance but picking the flowers doesn't take much time and therefore she returned soon. She took out a skein of beul strings from the loft and strung the flowers into four or five garlands in the dim light of the earthen lamp.

It was the day of the Maal but Amma's morning routine today was the same as any other day. She got up and finished the household chores as usual. Then she untied the young heifer and fed it with plenty of green grass. She plastered the courtyard with cow-dung and drew a small sacred diagram in the middle of it with turmeric paste and wheat flour. She placed flowers on this mandap and brought the holy durva grass. She had prepared the pinni balls of wheat dough for the animals quite early in the morning. She now took out live embers in a ladle and poured ghee and dhoop over them. She stood the heifer near the mandap, washed its horns with clean water and performed rituals before it as part of the puja.

Then she went to the cattle shed, garlanded the cow and the bullocks and made marks on their backs with turmeric and rice paste. Bedecked thus the cattle looked beautiful and in a festive mood. The lambs looked sideways at the cow and bullocks while they were being thus decked. Perhaps they were jealous of their friends for the attention they were getting from Amma. Amma had made a lot of pinnis and fed them to the lambs also. While doing all this, the words of the festival song suddenly burst through her lips, 'Maal lagi gaieye...ho maalo'.

Amma could hear the Maal songs wafting to her from the many corners of the village.

And a whole flood of memories gushed through her mind of the times when the family was full and together. Pita would start the day with the worship of the cows. He would go to the cow-shed and wash the cows' hooves one by one and feed them pinnis. He would also offer pinnis to the other cows of the village. Feastings would start in the evening. Varieties of food were cooked in every household. This day used to be very special for Amma but today there is no one by her side, neither husband nor son. As for the daughter-in-law, the Maal is just incomprehensible mumbo-jumbo to her. As always, these memories bring tears to Amma's eyes. Her eyes are usually moist with tears whether she is busy with work or just sitting quietly.

***

Amma heard the postman calling at the gate, "Kaki, here's a letter for you".

Amma ran out of the house. Whose letter could it be? Her son never writes. As for her daughter, she just enquires from passers-by about her old mother. So, taken aback by the postman's call, she asked him once again, "Is it really for me or are you making a mistake?"

"No mistake, Kaki, it is for you. Look here, your name is written on it."

Amma couldn't read, therefore she asked the postman to read it for her.

The postman read and told her that her son was coming home. Surprised, Amma exclaimed, "My son is coming home? Really!"

She couldn't believe the postman's words. The open letter in Amma's hands appeared to her as if it had come to her from heaven. She wanted to stop the postman to ask him if the daughter-in-law was also coming but by the time the question formed itself in her mind he was gone and the question remained stuck in her throat.

She was overcome with sadness. Why should the daughter-in-law come? Who am I to her? Isn't she a city-born girl? How can she like the village, its foul smell, cow dung lying everywhere, smoke filling the village air? She has no taste for village food nor can she collect green grass for the cattle. There are no chairs in the house for her to sit on, no market place or park for her evening stroll. And there is no covered, flush-fitted toilet in the house. And my son could find no suitable girl from a well-bred family in this area. I don't care whether my daughter-in-law comes or not. Most of my life is already past and what little of it still remains will also pass somehow. After all, I haven't drunk nectar that I will live forever. Even if the two of them do come, let them do what they want. How do I care whether they sell off the land and the house or retain it? I am prepared for any eventuality and I shall bear it all.

***

The son arrived late on Saturday night.

The village was considerably far away from the road, about seven miles. Amma had been waiting impatiently for him. After years the two would sit together for a meal.

He came. But went straight to his room. Amma keeps one room locked for her son and his wife. She never opens it for herself. He took quite some time to come out after changing his clothes. Amma lit the lamp and brightened the flame. She wanted to see how strong and healthy he had grown; how he looked, and whether he was still as handsome as he was when he left the village.

Memories of his childhood flooded Amma's mind. He was very young then. After coming home from school, he would fling aside his school bag and jump onto her back. He would be so impatient for his food that he did not even bother to wash his hands. Amma knew his habits and therefore she would keep half a roti and butter ready for him. He would eat and fall asleep in her lap.

But now he has grown older and is an officer. He touched her feet and quietly sat near the hearth. Amma wanted to hold him close and ask tearfully if he had not missed her in the least all this while.... But nothing happened, the two remained sitting without speaking to each other. Amma tried unsuccessfully to control her tears but did not let him see that she was crying silently.

Amma prepared tea and handed him the cup. Then she asked him to wash and have his meal but he told her that he had brought his dinner from his city-home and had already eaten it after alighting from the bus.

He said it in a matter-of-fact manner, unaware of the devastating effect his words had on Amma. She swallowed her pain without showing any emotions. She felt as if lightning had struck her or a huge boulder from the nearby mountain had fallen upon her. A fierce storm was raging within her but Amma was quite used to these things; such storms had made their home inside her.

The son finally broke the silence, "Amma, I have to leave early in the morning. There is so much work to do. Nanhe has to be put in an English-medium school. I tapped all my connections but nothing came of it. The school is demanding thirty thousand as donation for admission".

Amma didn't understand the meaning of his words but somehow gathered that he was in need of money and that is what has brought him to the village.

He said again, "Amma, I won't be able to send any money this month."

Amma told him reassuringly, "Son, why should you worry about sending money every month? After all, God has given me whatever I need. You just focus on your problems and you need not send money anymore. I don't have much to spend money on."

Amma said all this out of genuine concern for his problems but the son felt hurt by her words although he said nothing and remained quiet. Amma too fell silent for long and poked the fire with her tongs abstractedly. But in this silence, there clamoured many questions of several kinds. The difference between Amma and her son was that while she had answers to all the questions, her son was completely in the dark about them. Amma read his face and said, "You must be sleepy. Go to sleep, I'll make your bed."

He still remained sitting. Amma rose and went to his room. She shook out his bedding, spread a new sheet and then took out the quilt from the big trunk and put it on the bed. She looked around the room for long. She was surprised. This room in her house looked so unfamiliar and strange as if she had come to some other house.

He also rose. He was tired. How rundown he looks! Innumerable worries seemed to weigh on his mind. Heart-broken and tired he entered the room. He didn't know how to speak his innermost thoughts to Amma. Though so near, he was so far from her. His mind was reeling with various thoughts and worries. It crossed his mind that he might have to return empty-handed and if that happened, how would his wife take it! How will you manage to pay the admission fees and donation? Your mother, that old hag, is very cunning, she would say, tauntingly. His wife knows that his mother would have saved a good amount from the money that he has sent her every month for four or five years now. There was no harm if she gave it back to them.

He sat in the room for a long time. Restless. Silent.

Amma too did not eat; how could she when her only son had not eaten. He had come back after so long and brought his food from the city! The food cooked by her with so much love lay uneaten. She didn't even smoke her bidi. The cats guessed Amma's dilemma.

Kali was warming herself near the hearth and presently she began to mew. Nikki jumped into Amma's arms and began to lick her neck. Amma knows that when the cats fail to find a prey they shower their love on her like this. Amma held Nikki in her arms and poured a good quantity of milk in her bowl. The two cats immediately let go of Amma and began to slurp the milk. Amma poured some more milk in the bowl.

A strange silence prevailed in the house. Amma holds no grudge against anybody. The cats again come to her. They jump into her lap. The warmth of the hearth and Amma's love gives them unparalleled joy. Amma's love for her cats cannot be measured. She touches and fondles them as one does a small child. Today, she heaped her love on them. She pressed them to her bosom as if they were small babies. She prattled out her heart to them. The cats understand Amma's words and their love for her is by no means less than hers for them. They begin to talk to her meow, meow, ghurrr, ghurrr....

As for the son, he found it unbearable to remain sitting in his room. He came out and went to the kitchen. The kitchen door was shut from inside. It is Amma's habit to keep the door closed when she is there. He heard Amma talking to someone. Who could it be and that too so late in the evening, he wondered. He stepped forward a little and peeped through the crack of the door to find out. And the thought that he had come home to ask Amma for money vanished abruptly from his mind. He felt that he had never left his village home; that Amma was not playing with the cats but with him. Amma was playing with him, cajoling and teasing him and kissing him, running her fingers through his thick hair. His entire childhood rose and stood before him. He wanted to relive those days once again, to sit close to Amma and lean his head on her arms. He wanted that Amma should scold him for his mischief as she used to do in earlier days. In those days Amma's pets were his rivals who shared with him her warmth and affection.

He was about to knock at the door but checked himself and stepped back. A question crossed his mind: Do I really have any claims on her love and warmth? Am I really worthy of it?

While he was debating these questions in his mind, Amma called out to him, "Go to sleep Son, you have to leave early in the morning."

Amma had recognised his step. How had she made him out in this absolute darkness? He had come stealthily. He was amazed. Before he could say anything, Amma continued, "I have put money under your pillow, Son. Take it with you. It will be of some use to you."

"Money...? How did Amma know that I have come to ask for money? How did she read my thoughts?"

But at this moment the thought of money was far from his mind.

He felt like crying aloud, "Amma, I want your love, not the money." But the words were stuck in his throat. He could neither say nor hear anything. He felt as if he were completely enveloped in the thick folds of the darkness, his feet stuck deeply in the ground. He did not know whether he was standing on the soil or below it, whether he stood on solid earth or was suspended in the air, whether he was sitting or standing.

Amma's animated conversation with the cats could be heard easily. She was completely oblivious of everything around her, even of the storm raging in her son's mind, her son who was standing just at the threshold of her room.

He retraced his steps. He looked at the pillow where wrapped in a piece of cloth there lay a bundle of all the currency notes that he had sent to her over the past few years. Tears filled his eyes. Amma seemed to have finally settled the accounts.

Amma's conversation with the cats continued uninterrupted.

Translated by R. K. Shukla & Manjari Tiwari

THE TWENTY-FOOT BAPU JI

BEES FOOT KE BAPU JI

Chachu reached the outhouse and tethered his horse. He pulled out his cap stuffed into the pocket of his sleeveless woollen sadri jacket and flung it into the chulha. The embers of the clay stove were cold and the wrinkles on the cap writhed open languidly as if they were in the last throes of death. He picked up the lantern, opened it, and poured the kerosene over the cap. Then he struck a match and set it afire. The horse whinnied softly as though the burst of flames had scorched him.

Chachu sat near the chulha still wearing his shoes. His eyes were transfixed on the burning cap. The gloomy room lit up for a while and things became visible through the ruddy light and grey smoke. A lantern hung on the wall to the left of the chulha. To its right, a long wooden board was placed on two thick logs. On it lay some bare utensils for his simple tea-roti meals. Chachu's bedding lay rolled up at the back on a spread-out goat-hair kharcha. Five or six nails were fixed right above the mat and from them hung an old umbrella, a cloth bag, one or two shabby kameezes, a churidar with a baggy seat and another sadri.

His horse was tied to the other side of the door and his things were kept in a couple of sacks a little distance away. Next to the sacks was a big wooden chest with a large iron lock on it. Chachu kept all his earnings in this chest.

An awful silence engulfed the room. The fire had died down and the black shreds of the burnt cap stood out on the white ash. They cut Chachu to the quick. He picked up the tongs and drove them deep into the ash. The stench of kerosene still permeated the light darkness. Chachu shuffled back on his haunches till his back touched the rolled-up bedding. He lay down without unrolling it. He raised his arms and wove his fingers together to rest his naked head. He crossed his right leg over the raised left knee and closed his eyes with his face to the ceiling. The horse bent his neck towards Chachu, baffled at being brought home so early from the Ridge. Never before had they returned so soon. They left home in the morning and hardly ever came back before nine or ten at night.

Chachu's heart is laden by several tonnes of trouble. How can one read his face? His eyes are closed and somewhat moist. His brow is creased with wrinkles. There's no knowing how many years have come and gone through these lines, weaving a myriad tales and stories. Those bygone years begin to rise to Chachu's deep-set closed eyes. The events of that day, however, were unprecedented. Chachu had returned bare-headed. He felt as if not merely his cap but all his clothes had been ripped off his body. Everyone around him also seemed to be disrobed. The entire world appeared to have been unclothed. But Chachu's stripped state was different from that of the others. He thought that outer nakedness is far more dangerous than the one inside. Its scorching heat consumed him slowly and painfully. He was stripped even to his mind. His legs felt alien and arms wooden. His whole body had turned into lumber. He walked but his heart was elsewhere. He did not even know how he had reached and entered the door of the outhouse. Had his inner strength helped him crawl home, or was it his horse that had pulled him there? He did not wish to recall what had taken place; or when ... but again and again his bare head galled him. In his seventy-five years he had hardly ever been without his cap. It was so old that Chachu had even forgotten when he had had it stitched. Its white colour had long dissolved into an indistinct shade. It was torn in a hundred places but Chachu had mended it every time with the greatest care .... It was a Gandhi cap. Chachu had loved the cap and Bapu Gandhi ji right from his young days.

Deep in reverie, Chachu turned over to his right and rested his head on the pillow of his arm. The horse bent to the ground and began to chomp the hay.

*****

It was the 2nd of October. Mahatma Gandhi's birth anniversary. Chachu brought his horse early to the Ridge in anticipation of the function. He stood the horse in place and sat by his left foreleg. Unlike earlier times, now there isn't any open space for the horses. Only a little place is earmarked for eight or ten horses on the northern corner of the Ridge, but it is not enough for them. The Municipal Corporation has placed a garbage dumper next to their stand and ambulances are also parked there. The distance between this place and Bapu ji's statue is barely eight or ten hands. Chachu thinks of the statue all through the day as he makes the rounds with his horse up and down the Ridge. He does not remember the date when the statue was erected but Chachu derives inexplicable strength from it. It is to Chachu like a cane is to a blind man, his relationship with it is like that of a head and a cap.

Chachu calmly watched the excitement on the Ridge. Bapu's statue was adorned beautifully. Every year it was decorated only on this one day. The statue was cleaned and polished to a shine. Steps were made to reach up to it. The railings were decorated with leaves. Durries were spread before it for people to sit. Chachu noticed that the durries at the back were unoccupied. Up front, two coloured carpets were covered with white sheets and three or four shining velvet bolsters were positioned upon them. These were reserved for the chief guest and dignitaries. The schoolchildren from the convents and other schools appeared charming in their uniforms. Policemen were stationed on the sides and in the middle of the rows. A few government officials stood with their eyes on the cars and persons arriving from the right. In between, they also kept an eye on the arrangements for the programme. In front, the troupe from the Department of Public Relations sat with their accompaniments, ready to sing hymns to the music of the dholak and harmonium. Behind them sat the party workers. Their white apparel, boat-shaped caps and red ribbon badges proclaimed them followers of Gandhi. Chachu had seen many such programmes over the years. There was a time when the Ridge would overflow with people. Nowadays no one bothers. Only a few young unemployed boys who hang around on the Mall and porters with no work join the function now. Some retired officers and senior citizens do show some courtesy and join in singing the hymns. School children are ordered to be present, to ensure a crowd.

The sun shone gently. As always, this warmth gave inimitable joy amid the wafting cold air on the Ridge. The sound of the siren was heard in the distance. The policemen and officers on duty became alert. The seated children and the few people present there stirred. A few more pony ride pliers had arrived by now but these ghodewalas were only looking to secure customers. Chachu would not take anyone on a ride before the function ended. The Chief Guest arrived. Everyone stood up, except Chachu. If the special secretary had not cautioned the Chief Guest he would have walked all over the white sheet with his shoes.

The customary formalities were performed. The Chief Guest garlanded Bapu and, while returning to his seat, he threw a quick backward glance to see how many people were present. Other ministers and officials also offered their garlands. Bapu's neck was laden with flowers. In his heart, Chachu also offered his quiet respects to Bapu. After the formalities, devotional songs were sung ... "Raghupati Raghav Raja Ram" ... Chachu hummed along to Bapu's favourite hymn and slowly drifted into sleep in the gentle sunshine.

The Sub-Divisional Magistrate stood at the back keeping watch on the goings on. All of a sudden, his eye fell on the flower-laden statue of Bapu and his blood ran cold. His body shivered as though he had stepped out without woollens in the January snows. He wrung his hands inside his pockets with fear and fury .... Someone had taken Chachu's dirty cap and placed it on the statue!

The S.D.M.'s eyes darted to the Chief Guest with a hurried sideways glance. Then he threw a quick look around him, almost everyone was singing the hymns with closed eyes. He tried to muster courage to move forward but his legs shook to a tune of their own. The S.D.M. was flustered but soon the thought of his high office restored his confidence. A Kashmiri porter was standing near him. He whispered something into the khan's ears. When the khan caught sight of Bapu's statue, he could barely suppress his laughter. The S.D.M. looked at the Chief Guest again. He still sat with eyes closed. As the S.D.M. turned back, his eyes fell on Chachu's head. His cap was gone. For a moment, he wanted to tear out the wretched old man's hair. But he had to swallow his rage. When he looked at the statue again the cap had been removed. The khan came with the cap clutched in his hand and quietly handed it to him. The S.D.M. took it gingerly, as though it were a wad of tobacco, and pocketed it hastily. Then, he let out his breath in relief and wiped off the perspiration with his handkerchief.

***

The function ended and everyone left. However, the S.D.M. still stood glowering at Chachu's bare head. The police station in-charge and head constable, who stood on duty behind the S.D.M., had witnessed the scene. Besides the thanedar and the havaldar, an official of the Municipal Corporation and a journalist had also been privy to it. They now stepped forward and congratulated the S.D.M. on how smartly he had handled the situation. He would have lost his job that day if the chief guest, or a minister, or even a senior official had seen Chachu's filthy cap on Bapu's head.

Chachu stirred. His hand went to his head. The cap was missing. He leapt up startled, as though a wasp had stung him. Before he could grasp the situation, the S.D.M. and thanedar were upon him. The S.D.M. took out the cap from his pocket and yelled, "Wretched old man! Can't you even look after your own cap? God damnit, he almost ruined me!" Chachu had never imagined that the S.D.M., who always spoke so respectfully to him and asked after his health while passing by, could be so rude and abusive.

Chachu folded his hands and said, "Sahab I don't understand ... what happened?"

"Why would he know anything, sir ...? Bastard! ... He must have set his cap on the statue and coolly gone off to sleep," the thanedar deduced while tightening the grip on his cane.

Chachu was alarmed and bewildered by this unexpected battering. He entreated abjectly, "Do be fair, Sa'ab. Would I ever dare place my cap on Bapu ji's head ...? No, no Sa'ab ... God forbid, Ram-Ram."

The official from the Municipal Corporation advanced, "Sir, the old man is very clever. The bastard is not as innocent as he pretends to be. He is shrewd and a troublemaker to boot. He goes around complaining that the place allotted to the horses is overcrowded. He gives applications straightway to our superiors. He thinks he's a leader. He must have thought, since all my troubles have come to nothing let me use this opportunity to fix the rascals."

Before Chachu could say a word, the bearded journalist turned and spat the paan spittle right there on the Ridge. Adjusting his bag on his shoulder he expounded, "Don't you know this is an insult to the Father of the Nation. Thank God, nothing untoward happened. Otherwise the opposition would have raised hell. There could have been rioting ... and if the chief guest had noticed, the sahab would have lost his job."

The S.D.M. killed two birds with one stone, for the matter was delicate and involved a mediaperson, "You are absolutely right. And fortunately, you are one of us. Another journalist would have set the cap in the headlines of newspapers."

The journalist gave a faint smile.

All this time, Chachu stood silently with folded hands. He had barely managed to part his lips when the S.D.M. threw the wrinkled cap at him and left muttering under his breath. The thanedar, the official and the journalist, all followed him.

Chachu stood stumped. A crowd had gathered round him but he still could not gather fully what had just transpired. Chachu shrank with shame. The air on the Ridge was stupefied. Sunshine bore down like fire on his bare head. Chachu was drenched in sweat. Drops of perspiration stood suspended in the deep lines of his wrinkles like frozen water in the furrows of a ploughed field. A few drops had also risen in his spare grey beard. Chachu stood humiliated, just like his horse stood guiltily when Chachu took him to task for shying or playing up and scolded him or struck him on his legs or flank with a reed.

The khan who had retrieved the cap stood by taking in the whole scene. There were three or four other khans with him. The khans are often seen on the Ridge. They carry the loads for tourists and the locals from morning to evening. The khan came to Chachu and added fuel to the fire, "Well Chachu, say what you want, pal, but the cap finally reached its right place." The other khans burst out laughing. Chachu was mortified. He wanted to slap the khan across his face but held his peace. Dogs can't digest ghee, he thought to himself.

***

Although only his head was bare, Chachu felt as if he did not have a stitch on him. As if all his clothes had been ripped away. He looked down and saw the cap lying at his feet. His own cap seemed to him like a scorpion. Disconsolately, he swooped up the cap and thrust it into his sadri pocket. It seemed to weigh five kilos to Chachu. He looked round. People were busy with their own selves but he felt as though they were all mocking him. His eyes welled up. He turned to his horse who stood dumbfounded beside him. His eyes were wet too. The horse was Chachu's mainstay, like a cane to a blind man. The two stood lost in each other. If anyone could have read the horse's eyes they would have known who had played the disgusting trick on them.

At that moment, a few tourists approached Chachu and asked for a ride on his horse. But Chachu had turned deaf. He took hold of the horse's bridle and walked on. His eyes were on the ground. His horse walked quietly behind him. All the ghodewalas were half his age. They watched everything quietly, unwilling to invite trouble. Their day's income was dearer to them than Chachu's woe, so they pretended to be unaware of what had befallen him. They did not have even a few words of sympathy for him. The same Chachu who struggled for their welfare, who stumbled breathless from place to place to petition and appeal for their wellbeing, and who was always with them in their sorrows and joys. One or two of them were actually happy that Chachu's customers would now pass to them. They would earn more than they did every day.

Usually, when Chachu returned at night with his pockets full, he loved to hear the sound of the horseshoes. The clip-clop of the horse's footfall was sweet music to his ears. Now and then, he stroked his full pockets and blessed his horse; may he live long, may he eat well, may he always be with me, and be dearly loved by me! Not so today. His pocket was empty.

So was his heart. The shoes nailed into the horse's hoofs pierced Chachu's heart. Their thak-thak was as sharp as the point of the thanedar's cane. It seemed to Chachu that all the people he passed by on the way were repeating what the S.D.M. and the others had said to him. If he walked past a khan, he struck him as his biggest enemy. Once again, the mocking laughter of the khans on the Ridge assailed his ears.

Today's incident was not the first of its kind. But it was the most humiliating and distinct. Chachu had weathered much in his long life. A great deal had taken place in all these years. Several storms had risen and snuffed out the lighted lamps in his heart and eyes. Once put out they never lit up again. He could hardly bring to mind even a few happy moments in such a long life ... his entire life was only as big as the horse's back. No more, no less.

***

The horse neighed. God knows why. Chachu awoke with a start but he did not turn over and remained lost in thought for long. The horse also rested. The door was open and the sunbeams had come half way into the room, brightening it. Chachu was seeing the afternoon sun in his stable-like room in the outhouse after years. He watched the sunshine. It would gradually come further into the room before receding. But, for the moment, bits of its light entered Chachu's soul. He got up. His hand went to his head ... and once more he lived over the painful incident. An old cotton kerchief hung on the nail beneath the sadri. He pulled the parna out. Shook it. A couple of spiders fell to the ground and scurried away. Chachu wound the parna on his head ... as though gathering the splinters of the morning's events ... and tying them up in the cloth.

Chachu went to his horse. He caressed his forehead tenderly. The horse became a child. His eyes dripped love. Only Chachu or the horse knew how this affection steeped into his whole body. Chachu gave the horse some water. He put gram in his feeding bag and gave it to him. The horse began to munch the gram.

Chachu went out and removed his shoes. He took water and washed his feet. He wasn't hungry so he did not cook, nor did he make tea. He removed the small box of snuff from his sadri and taking a sesame seed's measure of it pushed it up his nostrils. He inhaled deeply and water spilled from his eyes. His head cleared after several sneezes. He brought the palm leaf manjari from within and lay down on the mat. The sun was hot now.

As he lay, Chachu looked at the hills ahead. He was astounded. He couldn't believe these were hills of one of Shimla's suburbs. Chachu remembered how there used to be only a scattering of old houses and bungalows with red tin roofs on them. The forests were so thick that everything appeared green and verdant, veiled as they were by deodar trees. Now they are all gone, the red-roofed houses, the dense jungles. A thousand buildings have mushroomed haphazardly. They do not appeal to the eye, rather they seem frightening. Their open windows appear like the wide-open mouths of jackals. Five and eight storeyed houses look like crocodiles advancing towards the sky from among the deodars. The red roofs have almost disappeared now, so has the old-world charm. To Chachu, the scene seemed akin to his son's childish drawings made in class three.

Not even a trace remained of the felled trees. Chachu began to count the remaining trees on the backs of the slopes. Soon he was nodding again .... In his mind he wandered far into the distance ... or travelled back in time, from his seventy-five years ... now he was about sixty. Now forty-five, and then, twenty-two. Then, he crossed the threshold of his adolescence and reached the years between ten and thirteen.

***

Chachu must have been thirteen when he first came to Shimla. How much the town has changed since then! It would take months if Chachu were to describe all the changes .... Chachu's mother had told him that his father had passed away in a road accident. He was their only son. Their fields were fertile but far too small. Chachu came to Shimla from his village to seek work with a distant relative. The kinsman taught him how to look after his horse. One day he died of an illness and Chachu was left alone. But he had made a few acquaintances and he now took charge of the horse. Chachu was illiterate but intelligent and understood things well. An Englishman hired Chachu's horse and his days turned for the better. He quickly learned the trade and also how to behave with the English. He began to earn well and sent money to his mother through someone or the other going to his village.

There were many things about the British, however, that Chachu did not like. The freedom struggle was on in those days. Chachu heard about it from people and began to understand the situation. He learnt that Mahatma Gandhi was fighting to get rid of the British. Many a times, Chachu wished to leave his work with the Englishman but the thought of his mother restrained him. His poverty became an obstacle in the way of his patriotism. Chachu reconciled his heart to his situation and went to work. Meanwhile, his mother arranged a match for him and he was wedded at the age of twenty-two. Chachu fathered three daughters and one boy. The girls were soon married off and the son was admitted to a good school so that he would have a life better than his father's. Not be a slave like him. Become a big man. Chachu worked day and night for his family and his son's education. Time went by. Chachu remained loyal to the one Englishman till Independence. Later, he bought a new horse and began work afresh. In those days, there were hardly any vehicles on Shimla roads. There were only horses and rickshaws.

After passing out from school Chachu's son went on to become an officer in the army. Chachu's wife had passed away. His daughters were content in their own homes. Chachu wanted that his son should not forget his village, no matter where he served. He wished that his son would build a big house in the village, marry and bring up his children there. Instead, his son kept asking Chachu to quit the lowly occupation of a ghodewala. But Chachu paid no heed. He did not leave his work; so, his son left him. He went away and never came back to the village or even to Shimla to look up his father. Chachu went back to the village a couple of times. The old house was in ruins. The cousins who lived in the village had staked claim to his land. Chachu returned to Shimla thinking what should he fight for, and for whom? His son had left never to return.

The ghodewalas did brisk business after the British left. But they were shortly asked to vacate the stables allotted to them. New government buildings were to come up there. They had no option but to leave and to hire rooms on rent elsewhere. Some were so broken that they gave up the trade. Chachu rented this outhouse of a bungalow in a suburb of the town.

There was a time when there was open space on the Ridge for horses and ponies. There were more than a hundred horses then. Later, the number came down to half and slowly dwindled to a mere eight or ten. The then Municipal Committee moved them from their old stand. Now the horses, the garbage dumper, and the ambulances stand in one place. Formerly, the ghodewalas were respected. The Municipal Corporation at that time only granted licences to horses with good lineage and also provided many facilities to them. Now there is no discernment and no amenity. A line has been painted on one side of the Ridge, and the round trips of horse rides are limited within it. At one time, tourists used to hire horses for the steep climb to Jakhu temple. Mud trails were left on both sides of the road for the horses. Now the whole road is tarred. The horses struggle while going up and down the slope. Their shoes slip on the hard surface and the danger of falling is ever present. It has happened to Chachu many times and he was saved from grave harm only by the will of God.

Chachu's earnings have fallen. Ever since taxi cabs and cars have started plying to Jakhu and other places, the demand for horses and ponies has gone down. Still, Chachu is better off than other ghodewalas. The old residents of Shimla prefer to hire Chachu's horse to reach and fetch their children. There's hardly any wedding in the town where Chachu's horse is not engaged for the bridegroom. In the wedding procession his caparisoned horse appears splendid like the one that had pulled Lord Ram's chariot. Chachu has escorted many officers on the back of his horse to their wedding. So many children that Chachu took to school also went on to ride his horse as bridegrooms. Chachu was very happy on such occasions. How Chachu wished to have a similar wedding for his son! He did not want him to sit in the bridegroom's palanquin, as was the custom in the hills. Chachu wished his son to ride his horse. But this was not to be. The son decided to have his wedding in the city. It's been years since Chachu has seen him. He has never set eyes on his daughter-in-law. He has heard that they have a small child.

All of last year, Chachu ran from one office to another to have stables built for the few horses that are left. He also wanted a good-sized shelter to be built on the Ridge where they could stand their horses comfortably and be protected from the rain. But no one listens. When it rains, the horses stand drenched with their heads pushed against the wall of the library building. Chachu and the other ghodewalas take shelter under the horses' bellies. No one pays any heed to Chachu's pleas ... occasionally, a newsman who needs information on times past for an article, offers him a samosa or a gulab jamun at a tea shop. Sometimes, a photographer captures his image for journals and magazines abroad. They manage to earn a few words of praise in the name of heritage but Chachu never gets to see his picture or the articles.

Chachu got up in the midst of his reminiscences. The sun had travelled far. The shadow of the eaves had crept up from his feet to his waist. Chachu pulled the manjari forward where the sunrays would stay till sunset. Chachu wanted to rest to his heart's content that day. But the memories just would not leave him alone. Chachu went in and filled the horse's feeding bag with handfuls of gram. He longed for some tea. Chachu did not smoke bidi or tobacco. He went and sat near the chulha. The cap seemed to grip his eyes. Chachu was maddened. There was no cap now, there was only Gandhi ... his statue .... He came out and once again sat down on the manjari with his back against the wall. The cap laid siege to his eyes and mind. It was everywhere. Bapu was everywhere. Chachu dozed off again ... as if in an opium-induced daze ....

***

Shimla's long story dwells in Chachu's little heart. It is a long past. It can be said that Chachu has inherited the town's history as well as its entire tradition .... Although, he has always been close to Bapu, he feels even closer to him now that he and his horse have been shifted to the side of Mahatma Gandhi's statue. Chachu had once heard long ago that Bapu had won them freedom. Bapu has been part of his heart since then.

Even before they were moved to the new spot close to Bapu's statue, Chachu took his horse to it every morning before making his way to the old stand on the other side. Chachu never forgot to bow to Bapu in reverence. Whenever he found time he cleaned the base of the statue and fashioning a broom out of some leaves he swept the area around it. He removed his shoes respectfully before cleaning the statue. Foreign tourists often prefer to ride Chachu's horse. But Chachu has two principles: one, he never allows English tourists to mount his horse in front of Bapu's statue. Second, he does not take them to Jakhu from the road that winds above the statue. He takes them on the alternative path. If anyone insists on taking the first road, Chachu refuses flatly and passes the customer.

Initially, Bapu's statue was erected at ground level on a low pedestal. A few steps led up to it. Anyone could go up to the statue. It was open to all sides. Chachu's eyes had seen a good deal happening there ... the khans and other porters stopped a while with their loads resting against the pedestal. Honeymooning tourists climbed up with their shoes and clicked photographs as they leaned in from either side of Bapu and kissed each other. The loafing school and college lads draped their western hats on Bapu's head and struck ridiculous poses ... poking fun at Bapu. Sometimes, they pushed a Commander cigarette into his mouth and laughed uproariously. At others, they fixed their dark glasses on his eyes and took pictures as they performed a parody of the Bharatanatyam dance. As if it were not the statue of Gandhi but the skeleton of Michael Jackson.

Even the policemen were not behind in this profanity. When they tired of patrolling their beats, they came and rested below the statue. They placed their canes between Bapu's legs, filled their cigarettes with tobacco and sat puffing at them. Many a times, Chachu had seen a cop hang his heavy woollen overcoat on Bapu's shoulder and urinate towards the back ... His eyes censored the journalists who hung their bags on Bapu's hand which held the Gita while they wrote or read beside the statue. Often, Chachu threw a fit and reprimanded the youngsters and the porters. But, instead of seeing sense, they teased him and called him Gandhi's ghost. Chachu thought of beating up the rogues, of driving them away on horseback. But how many of them could Chachu chase away? All of them were old enough to have hair on their bellies and believed they knew right from wrong. This thought kept him silent. Then again, Chachu loved to see the little children wrap themselves around Bapu's legs, to see them play hide and seek around the statue.

Chachu was present when the statue was erected. At that time, it wore a pair of charming spectacles. But the glasses vanished some years ago and no one took the trouble to replace them. No wonder Chachu thought it mere humbug when people offered garlands to Bapu on official functions. As if the mountain would disappear on closing one's eyes!

One incident, however, silenced Chachu's protests for ever. He did not utter even a single word after that day. He stitched his lips together .... To Chachu it seemed as though the unpleasant episode had happened just yesterday. But Chachu failed to understand why such things happened only to him ....

***

That fateful night Chachu was on his way back from Sanjauli after having escorted a groom to his wedding. It was quite late. It must be past eleven, Chachu had guessed. He walked through Lakkar Bazaar and reached the horse chestnut tree at the border of the Ridge. No sooner had he reached there that he heard whisperings from near the library. Chachu stood still. There were only a few streetlights and it was quite dim. Still, he could make out a few people in white clothes. Chachu did not stir. He looked round the Ridge, no one else was in sight. Only some dogs slept near the rain shelter. Chachu was familiar with them, as he was with the policemen who did duty on the Ridge. But the white-clothed men seemed to be strangers. Just then, one of the boys moved towards Bapu's statue. His beard was black and his head bare. He had pulled up the sleeves of his shirt and sweater to his elbows. One side of his shirt hung out of his jeans. He walked like a cat.

Chachu was dismayed. He stood motionless in the shadows. The boy climbed up the pedestal and stood beside Bapu. He had a small tin in his hand which he upturned over Bapu's head. Then he took a cloth and smeared the black liquid all over the face of the statue before running back. Chachu was shocked to see the top of the statue turn black. The blacking continued to drip downward. The boy rejoined his group. They came out of the shade and swaggered towards Scandal Point. Some of them lighted bidis and walked on smoking. Two policemen, wearing long khaki overcoats, came towards them from the other end. Chachu thought they would catch the vandals. But nothing happened. The police and the ruffians stood together for a while and then all of them walked away. Silence descended on the Ridge. The stillness terrified Chachu.

He looked around. His horse stood by him in the dark. Chachu walked towards the statue. He removed his shoes and climbed up. Bapu's face was horribly blackened. Chachu touched it and a greasy streak stained his finger. He suddenly remembered it was 2nd October the next day. Chachu was alarmed. He snatched the parna from his shoulder and began to briskly rub the face of the statue. The blackness only darkened. The parna turned black but the face of the statue remained pitchy. Chachu did not notice the two policemen come behind him. One of them called out, "Oy, you! What are you doing?"

When the heavy voice reached Chachu's ears the cloth fell from his hand in alarm. They were the same policemen he had seen earlier. Chachu understood their intent. But he hoped fervently that the cops would compliment him for doing a good job. He mustered courage and said:

"Sa'ab! Look Sa'ab. Someone has smeared Bapu's face black."

"Black ...?" A cop repeated in surprise and he spat the bidi from his mouth.

"Yes Sa'ab. I saw Sa'ab. With my eyes. One boy .... There were others with him. They went that way Sa'ab."

The second cop climbed up with his shoes. He removed a flashlight from his pocket and beamed it on the statue. The blackened face stood out at once. He laughed out loud at the discoloured face.

"Now ... I ... know. Aren't you the ghodewala oldie?"

"Yes - yes! Chachu."

"Rascal, are you trying to fool us?" The policeman said in an intimidating voice.

Before Chachu could say anything, the cop standing below said, "The motherf***** must've joined the opposition."

Chachu had never thought they would go this far, "What are you saying Sa'ab? For the sake of God ...."

"Get down scoundrel ... we'll show you." The policeman dragged Chachu down from the statue.

"Bastard! You want to slander the name of the government. You want to get us into trouble."

"Why would I Sa'ab ... why would I do so ..."

Chachu was about to cry. If a car, flashing red light, had not arrived just then they would have beaten him to a pulp. The car stopped right in front of the statue and a policeman alighted from it. Stars shone on his shoulders. He was the Superintendent of Police. The policemen saluted the S. P. with a Jai Hind.

Chachu was petrified now. His tongue froze and legs trembled. He even forgot that his horse was with him. He seemed to have taken cover under the tree on seeing what had befallen Bapu.

"What is the matter ... why are you holding him?" The S. P. asked his men.

"Sir, he has daubed the statue with black ...."

Even before the policeman could complete his words, Chachu pleaded tearfully, "I didn't do anything, Master. I'm telling the truth, Sa'ab. I was cleaning the blacking." Bapu picked up the parna and held it in both his hands to show the S. P.

Chachu's trembling voice distressed the officer deeply. He looked at him keenly and then at the horse who stood as a witness to the truth of the matter.

The S. P. recognized Chachu from before. Chachu's horse had taken his children home from their school or the bazaar many times. But Chachu was unaware of this.

The Superintendent ordered the policemen to run to the control room and make arrangements for cleaning up the statue. Both of them scurried away at once. The S. P. asked Chachu gently, "Chachu, how come you are here so late in the night? Tell me what really happened?"

Chachu sobbed the story out. The S. P. understood the matter immediately. He told Chachu to go home but also said that he could be summoned to his office if the need arose.

Chachu bowed to the S. P.'s feet in gratitude but the officer wouldn't let Chachu touch them.

Chachu took the horse's bridle and walked away. He was still terrified. The horse pulled at the reins and bent his neck towards Chachu. But Chachu walked on silently. Perhaps the horse wanted to talk to him, or to entreat the worn-out Chachu to ride on his back. Chachu, however, never rode his horse. He would not dishonour the back that provided his livelihood by climbing upon it. Chachu now recalled that a few days ago a similar incident had occurred at Chaura Maidan. Someone had blackened the face of Ambedkar's statue causing great ruckus.

***

Chachu became listless after that night. His lips were sewn shut. He did not care whether he found customers or not. Despite everything, though, he still had great faith in God. He thought that the Lord, who had given him life, would also grant him two meals a day. And Chachu did earn as much as before. Now, whatever anyone did to Bapu's statue,

Chachu said not a word. He didn't even look towards it. Still, before leaving for home at night, he cleared away the peanut shells, banana skins, plastic packets, stubs of bidis and cigarettes that people had littered there all day.

Chachu noticed that the trade union leader had not come to Bapu's statue for a long time now. Chachu has watched him come to Bapu for years. He was very fond of the young man. Brown hair. Cat-like white and black eyes. Fair skin. Broad forehead. Wearing trousers and a shirt. At times a cloth bag was slung on his shoulder, at others, he came in sandals carrying nothing. He removed his sandals or shoes, touched Bapu's feet and then turned to make his speech. Nobody and nothing concerned him. Whether anyone listened or not. Whether there were people or not. He just didn't care. But Chachu sat down and listened. Sometimes he spoke on the exploitation of labourers. At others, he exposed the intrigues of the high and mighty. He talked about corruption and warned people of the conspiracies being hatched in the name of religion. His face turned red as he spoke. His eyes became bloodshot as if all those people whom he exposed were standing right in front of him. There were times when the young man came but said nothing. He only sat for hours at Bapu's feet with his eyes closed.

Chachu has heard that someone has murdered him.

Chachu didn't notice when the sun went down. He was lost in his memories the whole day. What else does Chachu have but these? He is a ghodewala. If not for the horse, would his son have forsaken him? Everybody has begun to hate him. How could he expect the daughter-in-law to tolerate a ghodewala father-in-law? It brings dishonour. They are bigwigs with great respect in their high society. How can the father of an officer be a ghodewala? Chachu tries to tell himself that he has neither a son nor a daughter-in-law. Not even a grandson. He is alone. Only the horse is his. They mean the world to each other. They are family. Everything. When he was younger, Chachu could bear all this. But he can bear it no longer. His son comes to his mind again and again. He longs to see him, if only once. But he does not have his son's address and even if he had, Chachu wasn't sure he would recognize the boy .... No-no, why wouldn't he know him? How can parents forget their children? His son's childhood flashes before Chachu's eyes .... Chachu throws himself at the horse's neck and weeps. The horse quietly takes in Chachu's emotional embrace. He feels love suffusing his being; only, he cannot speak.

Chachu rolled up the manjari and propped it in one corner. Shimla sparkled with lights. Chachu lit his lantern. He felt light now, as if nothing had transpired.

Everything returned to normal. Here was Chachu, and here his horse. Tourists all day. Sometimes, children. Occasionally, bridegrooms.

***

The Ridge is being repaired. It is difficult for Chachu and other ghodewalas to sit there. Dust everywhere. Heaps of sand. Truckloads of stone have been offloaded. Chachu has seen such white and grey stones for the first time in his life. A number of labourers sit chiselling them throughout the day and night. Some of them are almost as old as Chachu. Chachu chats with them when he has the time. He wants to ask them about their families but hesitates to do so. He thinks that their sons and daughters-in-law too must have abandoned them.

He has heard that Bapu's statue will be raised ... and sure enough the old pedestal was demolished right before his eyes and a new one was in the making.

Everything happened as he had heard. Bapu's statue went up twenty feet. Now Chachu has to bend his neck backwards to see it. He thinks that if he still wore his cap it would keep falling off every time he looked up. It's good that both are gone, the old cap and the old position of the statue. Chachu approves the change. Now no one will be able to do foolish and shameful things. Mischievous boys will not set their English hats on Bapu's head. No one will stick a bidi in his mouth. There would be no kissing to be photographed. The cops will not position their canes between his legs and the policeman will not hang his overcoat on Bapu to piss. No porter will put down his load there and no one will blacken Bapu's face in the middle of the night. Chachu is free of many worries.

He used to feel that Bapu's statue and he were akin, but now the statue is twenty feet higher. How Chachu wishes he could also be twenty feet tall! These days, people only respect one's stature .... Everyone thinks Chachu is a joke. They make fun of him and no one speaks to him decently. He has no respect. He thinks even the horse is better than him because no one dares touch him ... his one kick is enough! Chachu feels worse than horse dung. Even if he is the story of the Ridge. An old saga. The past. Shimla's tradition .... Nobody cares.

One day, Chachu sat quietly as usual. A voice called out in English, "Hey, old man!"

"Old man ..." Chachu was startled. When he was young, Englishmen of his own age used to call him 'Old Man.' He had heard the voice through his lethargy but recognised that this accent was Indian. Having lived with the British, he knew how to speak English.

He stood up and looked around. There was no English person there. A young woman standing in front called out again in Hindi, "I called you." Chachu looked carefully at the woman. Short hair. Dangling earrings. Gold chain around the neck. Bare arms. White blouse top till the waist. Long, sharp nails. Tight pair of jeans. Face covered with make-up. She was beautiful. Chachu was able to see her innocence behind all the glamour. She held a child of about four years in her arms. Chachu's eyes fell on the boy. Their eyes met. Chachu's face that had been withered for years bloomed into a rose. His face glowed as if oblations of water had been poured over a broken idol.

Chachu couldn't believe that he also knew how to be happy. The horse stepped forward.

The child leaned towards Chachu, but his mother scolded him in English, "No ... no, sweetie ... he's a dirty man."

The spell broke. Chachu was disappointed. He felt cheated, like a child who had tried vainly to grasp the fading moon.

Chachu snapped, "Yes son. I am a dirty old man."

The young woman was startled. She couldn't believe her ears. She had not expected the old man to know English. When Chachu turned to go, she stopped him, "Baba, we want a ride on your horse, please."

Chachu was appeased. So, she had realized her mistake ... must be from a good home, he thought. He stopped and turned. The child still leaned forward excitedly.

Chachu took him from his mother, sat him on the horse and moved forward. Chachu wanted to chat with the boy. To kiss him. To hold him to his bosom .... But all this remained hidden in his heart. The child was chattering away. Chachu supported the little boy's back with his arm. He led the horse for two rounds of the Ridge within the line marked out for the ride by the Municipal Corporation. When the rounds ended, Chachu decided to gift the child a free third trip. After the third round, the horse halted near the woman. Chachu lifted the child and handed him to her.

The woman took out a hundred rupee note from her purse and gave it to Chachu. She didn't even ask the price of the rounds.

Just then, a young man in army uniform came towards them. He must have been in his late thirties. "What are you doing, Niti ... let's go now," he said.

A well-known voice! Ensconced in Chachu's heart since years! Chachu's eyes turned to the young man ... Just then the man too looked towards Chachu. A father's love heaved to life within Chachu. He wanted to clasp his boy in a tight embrace and shower years of affection on him .... Then a voice rose to his mind ... 'dirty man.' Chachu clutched at the horse's bridle. He held on to it tightly. Before turning to leave, he placed the hundred rupee note in the child's hand, who even now was fascinated with the old man.

"Lovely boy! Please take it. Have ice-cream. Eat ...."

The woman was bemused. She understood nothing. But Chachu's tear-soaked voice seeped deep into the young man. He wanted to stop Chachu but he couldn't. Chachu pierced through the crowd with his horse to the farthest corner of the Ridge. The young man's eyes came to settle on Bapu's statue.

Translated by Meenakshi F. Paul and Khem Raj Sharma

THE REDDENING TREE

LAL HOTA DARAKHT

The morning sun comes freely to Munni's door. By this time, she is up and about and has already freshened up. She is used to waking up before the sun, for there is not one lazy bone in her. She has got her energy and hardworking spirit from her mother. Amma finishes eighteen chores before it is light. Her main work is to milk the cattle and to feed them. Whenever Munni wakens she finds her mother churning milk near the clay stove chulha. Sometimes her father also rises early but at other times Bapu sleeps in late. He does not work at daybreak. He only sits on the low wooden patara puffing on his bubbler. Bapu is in the habit of mumbling something or the other along with the sudak-sudak sound of the bubbler. To Munni the rumbling of the bubbler and the mumbling of Bapu are all the same.

Munni is charmed by the morning sun. Sunshine approaches in bits and patches from distant vales. It sojourns briefly at the fields, threshing floors, and granaries; tarries at the new and not so new houses of the villages, and pauses at the footpaths. It comes waking folks, birds, and animals. It fills the air with many different colours ... and its golden rays make their home in Munni's heart. Munni's home is situated on the sloping fields. It faces the hills that overlap each other and the sun peeps into her threshold from behind the straggling branches of the pine trees standing tall on them .... These moments are treasured by Munni ... she comes out into the aangan to greet the Sun God devoutly. She respectfully covers her head with a dupatta and folds her hands in devotion.

Then she scours the small bell-metal pot with ash from the kitchen fire. After washing this lota she fills it with water and does not forget to add a few grains of rice to it. She is careful not to hold the lota from the top with her fingertips for she knows that a vessel is held thus only for ablutions. Instead, she places the lota on the palm of her left hand and covers it with her right. Her first pursuit in the morning is to offer water to Pipal Bhagvan.

Pipal God ... the holy fig-tree, now grown young. Munniya's Bapu, Mathru, has raised it like a son. Pipal within the bounds of one's land brings good fortune. Mathru often repeats this at home and also in the village homesteads. Munni has heard him say so many times.

"Pipal has taken root in our land because of some auspicious act or virtue of a previous life. Now, if we had been from the family of weavers or leatherworkers we could have turned a blind eye to it but Pipal's birth in a brahman home must be rewarded."

One of the village elders would endorse his view, "Yes Mathru, you're right. You are very fortunate and will never want for anything, you'll see. Only, don't give up your dharma, follow your faithful duty to the tree. Water Pipal religiously and see that you never forget." Then another village elder would refer to the wedding of the holy Tulsi plant and Mathru would be in seventh heaven.

"We agree, bhai Pandit, you arranged Tulsi's wedding just like a daughter's. To tell you the truth friend, only fools are taking birth in our community now. They are merely interested in earning more and more money. But Mathru, you saved not only your honour, but ours as well. You can say that you are the father of three daughters, not just two."

Mathru had celebrated Tulsi's ritual wedding with Narsimha Devta with great pomp and ceremony. But this was long ago, before Munni was born. She has only heard about it from her mother but she has seen the lush green Tulsi growing in a clay pot at her husband's house. On many afternoons Munni looks in on Tulsi. First, she goes inside the temple to worship Narsimha Devta and then returns outside to bow her head to Tulsi. A few other pots of Tulsi are also placed nearby. All these plants are married to the deity. But to Munni the dearest Tulsi is the one given in marriage from their home. She is like a sister. Munni sits on the temple steps and lovingly caresses her leaves and waters them. Often, the temple priest sees her sitting there and comes up to her, coughing. As he does now. Pujari Kaka echoes the words of the village elders, "Munniya take a look at your Tulsi ... you were not even born then. What a wedding Mathruey arranged! Not only the village but people from the entire area were invited. Two full feasts were held! Lots of money was spent. It must be said, Munni, your Bapu is a man of great piety."

Munni is delighted at the praise heaped upon her father. Pujari Kaka, in his turn, is charmed by her innocent smile. He comes to her and plants many kisses on her cheeks. Munni revels in this affection. Pujari Kaka is much older than her father and is affectionately called Kaka by everybody. Munni does not get this kind of affection at home. Her Amma and Bapu never display their love for her like the pujari does. For as long as she can remember, her parents only impressed upon her to be responsible and hardworking "... a daughter is another's treasure, she should be

accomplished at making a home." No wonder Munni is adept at every
household chore even at her tender age. She churns milk, makes maize and
wheat rotis, fetches water and forage, milks the cattle, works the millstone,
and even takes grain to be ground at the watermill .... Munni, however,
still longs to go to school. But, Bapu doesn't let her. He believes there is
no use of schooling a girl. He allowed her to attend school till class three.
Then he withdrew her name. Ma used to remonstrate with Mathru for
spoiling Munni by sending her to school at all, "There are children from
all kinds of families in the school. Now our Munni will sit with low-
castes. Even eat with them ...." Bapu also fell in tune with her and finally,
Munni was made to stop going to school altogether. Munni still
remembers when she had stood first in class. How much love and
appreciation the teachers had given her. How many 'well dones' had come
her way! ...

Her silence was broken by Pujari Kaka, "Your Pipal has also grown
young now, Munniya. Your Bapu says he will arrange its wedding next
year. You too are grown ... old enough to be married." Pujari Kaka
lovingly patted her cheek.

Pipal's wedding—and her own .... Perhaps, they would be arranged
just like Tulsi's wedding. Munni returned home with these thoughts.

***

Mathru has two daughters. The elder daughter was married just before
the Tulsi. Munni was born much later. Mathru is still burdened with debt
for his borrowings at the time of the two weddings. When Munni goes
with Amma to work in the fields or to bring green forage, her mother often
points out to her, "That field is ours. The other one too ... that meadow is
also ours." But when Amma does not cut any grass or leaf in them Munni
becomes curious. With a deep sigh Amma tells her that those fields and
meadows are mortgaged to the moneylender. Her father had borrowed
money for the weddings of Kamli and Tulsi.

There was a time when Mathru had been a prosperous landlord. His
forefathers had left him rich fields that yielded such bountiful harvests that
they never had to buy provisions from the shops. This prosperity was a
cause of envy among his kinsfolk and distant relatives in the community.
They could not stand the sight of the swaying ripe crops in his fields.
Some of his relatives had their own homesteads and fields in the village. A
couple of them also had flourishing moneylending businesses spread
throughout the province. Apart from their houses the village also
comprised three houses of weavers and two of leatherworkers. A few

blacksmiths lived a little away from the village. The moneylenders also held these people's lands in mortgage on one pretext or the other. Now they were stripped of both work and land. Times are tough. Everything is so expensive and the income from a daily wage so meagre that it is difficult to buy even bare necessities. Mathru is similarly placed at subsistence level. He has only one remaining field that yields just enough grain to last them a year. It is a piece of four bighas and seven biswas. He also has two small meadows.

In bygone days, Mathru earned his living by performing rituals and ceremonies that require a pandit. He had many clients to whose custom he had a claim in the village and its surrounding areas. But gradually his own relatives weaned his patrons away from him. They took over as their family pandits instead and began to recite sacred legends and perform religious ceremonies, including weddings, for them. Mathru often quarrels with them for snatching away his clients. But no one pays heed to him. His wife counsels him to keep the faith and not get into futile fights, "Have faith in God. What's the use of this needless fight. Let the scoundrels go to hell. In God's house there may be delay but there's no injustice. Ours is a small family. We still have to arrange the daughter's wedding. Just stay calm." But how could Mathru be at peace? The family has to be looked after. The mortgaged fields have to be paid for. The daughter is coming of age. Pipal has to be wed. There are ever mounting expenses. Sometimes Mathru works on daily wages, making or mending roads. Occasionally, he is also hired for work in the forest. Every now and then he is dismissed from work because he does not know any influential person who would put in a word for him. He has heard that such an 'approach' or recommendation was now necessary to be hired by the departments of public works and forests. Also, being a pandit, he could not take up any and every job. Not like the low castes who made do by working for the landlords in and around the village. But he is a pundit. He has his honour to protect and cannot take on all kinds of work. Considering all this, he remains at home for days on end without earning anything at all.

***

Once or twice a month Mathru visits the Narsimha temple to look up his Tulsi. He worships the deity and carefully waters the plant. The Tulsi appears luxuriant today. It seems the deity has embraced this 'bride' with all his heart and loves her much. Other pandits of the village have also married their Tulsis to the Devta but they do not strike one as being in the bloom of youth. Many of them have shrivelled. Mathru knows that it is a bad omen for Tulsi to become weak or to die. There could have been some lapse at the wedding he reasoned or, perhaps, the Devta regarded them with less benevolence. But when he thinks of how grandly he has arranged Tulsi's wedding he is filled with pride. He holds his head even higher in the community. As he sat on the steps with these thoughts, Mathru's eyes alighted on Pujari Kaka. He touched Kaka's feet respectfully.

"How're you Mathru?"

"Very well, by your grace, Dinva ji."

"Come sit down. Let me bring a patara. You've always been fond of tobacco, I'll fill and fetch the hookah too."

Pujari Kaka went into his room behind the temple. He has lived there for years in the service of the Devta. At one time, Mathru was also part of the temple committee that managed the temple affairs. But he is no longer on it. Still, he duly participates in the proceedings of the panchayat at the temple. He gave up his position in the committee only because of the indifference of his people. Mathru cannot but think of the past glory of the temple. It was believed that the Devta had himself appeared at the spot where the temple stands. His elders tell of a cow that belonged to a leatherworker in the village. She would come to graze at that spot for hours and not wander far like other cattle. In the evening, when her mistress tried to milk her she would be dry, as if someone had pressed out and drunk all her milk. The lady would reprimand the cowherd for drinking all the milk of the cow that had just calved. But the boy would sincerely claim that he knew nothing of the matter.

One day the mistress and master trailed the cowherd quietly and hid themselves behind a bush. As the cow grazed she came and stood at one particular place in the pasture. They saw milk flow from her teats on its own, as if something from within the earth was milking her. There was no end to their surprise. Both of them ran back to the village and called the people from the brahman and weaver households. After they too had viewed the spectacle with their own eyes it was decided that the pasture be dug up. At first, they were all afraid. Then an elderly man from pujari Kaka's family picked up a hoe and began to break up the soil. He went on digging till, three or four feet below the surface, the hoe touched something solid. Instantly the tool fell from his hands and he lost consciousness. The others present heard a moaning sound emanating from the earth. They drew near and saw a pindi in the pit. The sacred round stone was bleeding profusely. No one knew how to react. Then the owner of the cow removed his turban and wrapped it round the pindi. The moaning stopped immediately. But the very next instant the Devta manifested himself in both the digger and the owner. They were frenzied by the channelling of the Devta for a long time before the deity declared to the villagers that he was Narsimha Devta. He said that he wanted to settle there and a temple should be built for him. The Devta also said that he would choose the site for the temple the following day.

Next day when the villagers returned to the spot they saw that ants had made a circle around the pindi. This meant that the temple was to be made right there ... and the temple was built. Mathru remembers that in the beginning other castes, especially leatherworkers, were given equal honour in the temple. But now things have changed. Harijans are not allowed into the temple anymore. These rules must have been made later by the pandits and the thakurs. However, there is still a dinva from a leatherworker's family. During panchayats he is even now chosen by the Devta for manifesting himself.

Pujari Kaka returned. He held a patara in one hand and a bell-metal hookah in the other. Mathru has enjoyed smoking tobacco in this hookah many times. Nowadays, where can one find bamboo bongs or bell-metal hookahs? Gone are the days of such delights! Mathru often thinks of buying a hookah again. He did have an old one once but when do wants and necessities spare things of the house? He had to sell it for Tulsi's wedding together with many other old things.

"Here Mathru, sit and have a smoke."

They both sat down. The pujari began the conversation, "Munni had also come yesterday. She is old enough to be married now. Look Mathru, times are bad. You should marry her off at the earliest. In fact, I think you should get both of them married at one and the same time. Pipal has also grown and he too must be wed." "Gurar ... gurar ..." Mathru pulled silently at the hookah for long. Pujari Kaka broke the silence, "Have any marriage proposals for Munni come your way or not? If you wish I will broker the alliance. I know of one or two places where things might work out."

Mathru did not utter a word. He only nodded his assent. He knew both tasks had to be done, but how? He didn't even have a broken cowrie in his pocket. Yet, how could he let the villagers know of his distress? He moved the hookah aside and walked away.

***

The pride he had felt on seeing Tulsi a few moments ago seemed broken. His legs were giving way and he acutely felt Pujari Kaka's eyes following him. He was afraid Kaka may have divined his desperate situation. After all, he is a brahman and unlike the low castes he cannot lay his poverty open to all and sundry. Lost in his thoughts, Mathru reached home before he realized it.

The weddings of Munni and Pipal ... these were two huge responsibilities on Mathru's shoulders. Pujari Kaka had almost roused him from slumber. Not that he did not worry before but now he became very anxious. He felt the crushing burden of his daughter and Pipal on him.

On seeing him sitting morosely by the chulha, Munni's mother asked, "What's wrong ji, aren't you well?" "I'm okay ... okay. You do your own work ..." Mathru replied irritably. Munni's mother knew her husband's routine. She pushed the burning wood further into the hearth of the chulha and touched her finger to the water heating upon it. "The water is hot ji. Freshen up and offer incense to the gods."

She moved the metal basin towards Mathru and poured hot water into it. Mathru leaned against the alcove stacked with firewood and placed both his feet into the hot water. Munni's mother moved closer to wash his feet but till then Mathru had already begun to rub them. She dried the water off her hands with her dupatta.

This was an everyday affair. The wife wished to wash her husband's feet but Mathru never allowed her to do so.

After washing, Mathru offered incense in prayer and returned to sit by the chulha. Munni was somewhere in the aangan playing with Lali's kids. Lali is their goat. She had just delivered two kids. Munni now had two companions with whom to frolic and play.

Munni's mother gazed at Mathru. Before she could question him again, Mathru himself began to speak:

"Pujari Kaka was speaking of Munni and Pipal, but ...?"

He stopped. He reached for the bubbler and shook out the dry ash in the bowl into the chulha. Munni's mother slid the tobacco box, lying next to her, towards him.

"He is right. Munni is old enough to be married. Proposals are coming for her from many people. Yesterday, Dinva's wife also brought a proposal of a boy from their relations."

"That's fine ... fine ... but Pipal has also grown young. If it were to be married first ...?"

Munni's mother seemed displeased with the idea.

"Ji ... if you ask me, get Munni married first. It is enough that we married Tulsi to the devata ... even if Pipal remains unwed it does not matter much ... we also have to see to our resources. People say all kinds of things. But has anyone helped us in any way till today ...? All the fields were lost on the marriage expenses of the elder girl and Tulsi. Now even the one small field we have will go."

Mathru did not appreciate his wife's advice. He frowned.

"Talk sense, woman! What do you know about the scriptures? Is there anyone else in the village, in the entire area, fortunate enough to have Pipal born in their field? ..."

Before she could answer Munni came into the house. They did not want to speak of this matter in Munni's presence. Although she was young, she understood everything. But Mathru's wife was upset at her husband's words. If Munni had not come in when she did, she would have told him a thing or two. Deep in thought, she put the dough into a bowl, placed the griddle on the chulha and began to roll the rotis. Munni sat down to the right of her Bapu to cook and puff them up.

To Munni's mother, her daughter came first. She believed that Tulsi and Pipal had come to her home not to bring good fortune but to make them destitute. If they had to give away only two daughters in marriage they'd be less in debt and their fields and meadows wouldn't be mortgaged either. What mortgage! These were actually sold, for they would never be able to return the loan. Instead, there was more money to be borrowed. She knew her husband had no option but to mortgage the one remaining field.

***

Nowadays, Mathru cannot sleep well at nights. He wakes with a start in the middle of the night. He sits up on the bed and gropes for the matches. When he can't find them, he moves towards the chulha and looks for the tongs in the corner. He uses them to extract a glowing coal from the ashes and blows on it. He coughs and is overcome with wheezing for a while. When his breath eases he blows at the live coal again. As his breath brushes the coal the things in the room become visible in its glow. He picks up the small lamp and touches the ember to its wick. He blows on it and the wick catches the flame. The bubbler lies near the head of his bed. He reaches for it and fills the bowl with tobacco. He gets into bed, supports his back against the wall and begins to smoke.

His eyes fall on Munni as she lies sleeping at a little distance. She is fast asleep. Mathru watches the light of the lamp gathering on her face. A few strands of hair have fallen across her cheek. Mathru has never looked at Munni in this light. Her innocence, her nascent youth, her looks ... are all fit to be married. It seems to him that Munni grows older with every passing moment. As he smokes, all kinds of thoughts come to his mind. What else can he do but think. Times are expensive. If only he were employed things would be better. He is reminded of Gangu from his community who had arranged a grand wedding for his daughter a while ago and had also given substantial dowry. Despite this, her in-laws had turned up their noses with contempt. Perhaps they had also wanted cash. He belonged to the high caste ... he couldn't even grovel and beg. For, above all, he must be mindful of his honour and dignity. But a daughter's responsibility is foremost. The marriage of Pipal is also a great virtuous deed .... Who cares if the remaining land were lost; it is his own field, after all, and he can do whatever he likes with it. Moreover, he would earn all through his life and pay off the mortgage somehow.

His heart begins to swim in the high seas of hope. He snuffs out the lamp. The tobacco still smoulders in its bowl and he smokes the bubbler in the dark. Its rumbling sounds eerie in the unlit room. It seems as if the tuneless pointless noise were emerging from within him. He removes the bowl and blows on it lightly to kindle the tobacco. When his breath meets the glowing leaves, the room is filled again with an uncanny light .... Munni's face is lit up momentarily in the glimmer. Mathru feels a kind of ache inside him. This pain is enormous. Only one who has daughters can understand this piercing pain. To top it all there is the anxiety about his community. A daughter is a duty, a responsibility ... and Pipal is a religious virtue, a sanctifying rite—a samskara. Mathru dives in deep waters between the two. He fears he would lose face in the community if his daughter's wedding were not impressive. And if Pipal remained unmarried then folks would say that Mathru is not a true brahman, for he has behaved like a low-caste.

***

Pujari Kaka had fixed the girl's marriage. Many constraints were now enjoined upon Munni. Dos and don'ts were enforced. Now her mother did not let her go out alone. Amma herself took the cow and goat out to graze. She did not send Munni alone to fetch forage grass. Munni could not play with other children from the neighbourhood anymore. Amma scolded her if she insisted on going out to play. All these developments were beyond Munni. She had a vague idea that she was soon to be married but a wedding meant nothing more to her than hopscotch or the marriage of the potted Tulsi. She sat silently in the aangan or at the window at the back of the room and gazed for long at their only remaining field.

She too did not sleep well. Her Amma and Bapu being the reason. Ever since restraints were placed on her, she had seen them upset and worried. She tried to figure out what worried them by trying to overhear their talk. But the two of them were careful when she was around.

That day Munni had retired to bed quite early. She pretended to be asleep and waited for Amma-Bapu to begin talking. She wanted to find out everything that troubled them. They sat near the chulha with their anxieties and despair. They were in a hurry to discharge their duties and be free of them. When Munni's Amma began to talk Mathru shot a glance at Munni. But she had drawn the rough woollen pattu over her head. He was reassured that she was asleep.

"You had gone to Gardhari's house, did anything work out or not?"

Mathru heaved a deep sigh. His breath failed him as he spoke and his face flushed.

"He will give the money. He asks that the field be mortgaged."

"What choice do we have? We have to do something to raise the money."

The wife's words struck Mathru's male pride like a hammer stroke. He could hear his unworthiness ringing in them. He was not fit for anything. Fields were being sold to arrange weddings. His earnings could simply not be spared from the expenses of daily living. How can weddings be arranged on meagre daily wages? But then, even the Sun and Moon are in debt. He is a mere mortal. A son would have been of great support, he thought; for all said and done, daughters were another's treasure.

Munni's mother knew that her husband was offended by her words. But how could she turn her face away from the truth. She changed the topic to bolster his spirits, "Look here ji, it is our field not someone else's father's. To beg is shameful. We will take money only for what we'll sell. And we are still able to earn a living. After these responsibilities are taken care of, we'll have the rest of our lives to pay back the debt. Also, if we can't get back our fields, so what? We do not have any sons whose marriages we need to save for ... we'll arrange these two weddings boldly and grandly."

Munni's Amma had spoken wisely and Mathru was reassured. She was right. Of what use were lands and fields if honour were lost? Nevertheless, the pain of parting with the fields rose to the fore. His eyes welled up and Mathru took many quick puffs of the bubbler.

"Munni's Amma, I don't want to give the field away. We haven't yet been able to free those we mortgaged earlier .... Only this one small doru is left. How much we have laboured in this doru. No one else in the village owns such a doru ..."

Mathru's voice had become pitiful. Munni's mother was also reduced to tears. She turned her head away towards the corner and wiped her eyes with her dupatta. A deathly stillness had overcome the room. Munni clenched the pattu so tightly that her fingers tore it. She had never before seen Amma and Bapu cry. She wanted to put her head in their laps and also weep bitterly but she could not move. Her eyes rained down tears and her bed was soaked. But no one knew her pain. And, anyway, her pain meant nothing.

Mathru broke the silence, "But the burden on our heads will be removed with Munni's wedding. And Pipal will also be taken care of."

Munni was a heavy load on her parents! Munni's heart rose to her mouth on hearing this. She was beginning to understand the situation now. The field was being sold for her. She wished she had never been born into this home. She was filled with disgust for herself. She was the source of all the problems in the house. She was inauspicious and so was Pipal whom she had watered and cared for every day. She wanted to cut him down to his roots ... to remove the cause of her parents' misery ... for, the flute would not play if the reed itself was broken. But, what would she do about her own self?

***

Next morning–if anyone had watched Munni closely they would have seen how the worries of the household had seeped into her face and sleepy eyes. She had grasped her Amma-Bapu's distress even though she had no idea what marriage really meant. All marriages were the same to her, whether it be Tulsi's, Pipal's, or her own. But she could not accept the selling of the field to get the daughter married .... As usual, the sun was rising from the other side of the hill. It had its customary golden brightness and red lustre ... wonderfully brilliant! The crops were ripe and green, the branches swayed and the birds chirped .... But, when there was darkness within Munni's heart how could she see the shining light outside .... She had not washed her hands and face today. She had also not scrubbed the lota. She just managed to fill it with water and left the house with it. She walked out of the aangan and crossed the fields and footpaths to reach Pipal. She looked towards the east from where the drowsy sun was rising behind the golden clouds. The rays were bright, golden and red. They sat on the leaves of Pipal and filled them with grace and loveliness. As Munni gazed at Pipal she felt his sweet charm spreading through her very being. She looked at Pipal with great desire. Never before had she looked at him so eagerly. She was attracted to his glorious appearance. She felt Pipal smiling back at her. When his leaves touched each other, their rustling awakened a longing within Munni .... She was wide awake now. Her natural playfulness surfaced and she burst out:

"... you are getting married ... you know ... married."

Then she paused to think how Pipal would be made to sit in the bridegroom's palanquin ... she exploded with laughter ... and laughingly poured the water on his body. She turned back ... and told him, "I am also getting married ...." Perhaps she wanted to ask him who would offer him water after she were married and gone to her husband's home? ... She took another long look at Pipal. The rustling leaves made a sweet sound. The streaming breeze poured music into her ears. The tenderness of the glowing red colour and the soft music were giving birth to an incredible joy within her .... She had begun to like Pipal even more than before. As she returned, from some distance, she saw the women of the village entering her aangan. Preparations for her marriage were afoot. She had heard that people from her in-laws' home would come today, which was why the house was being plastered with mud and cowdung and being whitewashed.

She did not go into the house, instead she placed the lota on the stones bordering the veranda and continued behind the house to the very field that was to be sold for Munni's wedding. Bapu had grown mustard in it. The mustard was flowering. To Munni the field seemed like a huge carpet of yellow flowers spread far and wide. She moved to the middle of the field. She was drawn to a ladybird sitting on a flower. She picked up the little tota panchhi and placed it on her palm. Then she shifted it to the tip of her right forefinger. She pointed the finger up to the sky and recited, "fly ... away panchhiya, pass or fail ... fly ... away ..."

And the ladybird actually took wing. Munni was amazed. How did it fly? Why did it fly? She had left school years ago. She remembered when the exam results drew near how she would go with other children into a mustard field. They'd place a ladybird on their fingers and say ... "fly ... away panchhiya, pass or fail ..."

If the panchhi flew away the student would certainly pass and if it kept on sitting quietly the pupil was sure to fail. She didn't go to school any more. She had not taken any exam. How had the panchhi lied ... could it be that everything which was happening was also a test ... but how would she pass it ... a daughter is a docile cow, wherever the parents drive her, she goes ....

***

The wedding dress from Munni's in-laws had arrived. The wedding was fixed. The auspicious hour for both Munni and Pipal had been determined. Pipal would be married one week before Munni. Her father had already chosen a verdant Suni plant to be his bride.

Nowadays Munni did not even wait for sunrise. As soon as she awakened she took water and left the house. But she did not return quickly as before. She sat for a long time with Pipal. She gazed at him and caressed his leaves. She touched his body and tried to embrace it.

***

That evening Munni overheard Bapu saying that he would settle the sale of the field the next day. Gardhari's servant had brought some papers for Bapu on which he had to put his thumb impression. Munni was anxious. There was little time between the night and the morning. She just could not sleep. She had seen Bapu get up several times and smoke his bubbler. Its rumbling made a frightening din, similar to the flooded streams and rivers of the rainy season. Amma-Bapu were miserable at losing their field.

Today, Munni rose before anyone else. She quietly removed the wedding dress from the wooden box and hid it under her dupatta. She quickly filled the lota with water and crept away. In the distance the clouds sleeping on the hills and valleys were being filled with crimson radiance ... the sun was rising.

By the time she reached Pipal the sun's rays had settled on his leaves. He appeared to her like a resplendent bridegroom. She was unable to look straight at him today ... She placed the lota of water at the base of the tree and went behind the bushes. There she donned the new wedding robes. Folded with them were a comb, a mirror, some bangles and a small box of sindoor. She had learnt the ways of married women from her mother .... She wore the bangles and combed her hair. She was charmed by her own reflection in the mirror. Then she wrapped the new dupatta round herself and settled it so it covered her forehead and veiled her face a little. She looked at her new image reflected in the mirror. Munni was overcome with shyness ... but then she thought of her father who was to give the papers to Gardhari today ... the field was to be sold. She panicked. Urgently she bundled the mirror, comb and the box of sindoor into her old clothes and tied them up into a knot in her old dupatta.

... Munni came softly towards Pipal. She looked around ... took stock ... she had a secret to keep ... there were fears ... an urgency ... she removed the box of sindoor from the bundle of clothes and pulled a branch of Pipal towards her. She emptied the sindoor box on to a leaf and pulling it towards her she filled her parting with the vermilion powder.

It seemed to her that the stem and leaf were the hands of her tree. That they were her Pipal ... that he had married her by ceremonially filling the parting in her hair with sindoor .... She picked up the lota. Her heart was not playful like before. Now it was not merely a religious duty to offer water to the tree. Nor was it a matter of simply obeying her Amma-Bapu's injunction .... It was her faith. Belief. Triumph .... She thought of the panchhi ... it seemed to be saying, "You have passed Munni ...." Shyly and modestly, Munni offered water to Pipal with love. Then she put aside the lota and touched her forehead to Pipal's trunk with reverence ... the first greeting of a bride ... her eyes welled up as she bowed her forehead to her husband. She got up and moved away a little. She gazed openly at Pipal now. The crimson light of the golden sunrays had turned the tree vermilion. This rosiness also glowed in Munni's heart.

... Munni turned homewards. Married Munni. Bride Munni. Munni who had staked herself for her father and their field .... To her, marriage meant nothing more than filling sindoor in the parting of her hair. She thought she had removed from Bapu's shoulders the twin burden of herself and Pipal. She wanted to reach home before Bapu left .... She came to a standstill at the low wall of the aangan. Just then Bapu stepped out of the house, coughing. A cloth bag hung from one shoulder wrapped in a pattu. He held a stick in his right hand and a package of papers in his left. As he crossed the threshold Bapu's eyes fell suddenly on Munni. He stopped abruptly. Who was this girl? She had come dressed as a bride–but he could not place her. Amma too had come out the door and she stood behind Bapu. Bapu moved forward. Shyly ... fearfully ... Munni inched towards him. They came face to face. As soon as Bapu recognized her, the ground beneath his feet began to give way. The heavens seemed to break. His breath was stuck somewhere in his throat. Before he could muster words ... question ... scream or shout ... Munni fell at his feet with a new-found poise ... "Bapu, I am married."

The bundle of papers fell from Mathru's hand.

Translated by Meenakshi F. Paul

DAAROSH

DAAROSH
DAAROSH

Kaanam had probably not slept well in a long-long time. Today too, she began to read the newspaper with sleepy eyes. An unexpected news on the first page startled her. She read it all in one go and ran to her papa's room. He was lying on the bed awaiting his morning tea. Kaanam's sudden arrival there with a newspaper in her hand filled him with misgivings. Before he could ask her, Kaanam placed the newspaper before him and said, "Chhote Papa. Chhote Papa. Here, look at the news!

But he looked more carefully and curiously at her than at the news. For the very first time he had felt a kind of completeness and confidence in her voice. There was an intensity and freshness in her eyes, perhaps it was the eagerness of making him read the news quickly. Before Chhote Papa could pick up his spectacles lying close by, Kaanam started reading out the news herself. She didn't even hear Chhoti Amma come in and read on breathlessly.

" ... Two young men of the tehsil, with the help of some accomplices, forcibly kidnapped a girl of the village who was going to see the tournament with her friend to a nearby school. They took her to a cave close by. Then the friend and other youngsters left. Only the one who wanted to marry her stayed on and had sex with her against her will ...."

Kaanam read so far and stopped suddenly. There was utter silence in the room. The morning sun rose gradually and the sunrays entered through the window. The light filled the room with a kind of freshness. Kaanam felt it deep inside her. Her Chhote Papa and Amma, however, were quiet. Kaanam saw fear lodged in their eyes. This fear had occupied their house for years, somewhere in Chhote Papa's mind or in the sleepy eyes of Kaanam. The fear had never allowed her to sleep in peace and this news deepened it even more. Chhoti Amma stood stunned at the threshold with a tray of tea in her hands. Kaanam reached across the fear and silence and asked Amma to draw near. She took the tray from her, placed it on the table and made her sit on the bed. She started to read the news again:

"The parents of the girl had taken the matter to the courts. This was the first occasion when any family had challenged the tradition."

Chhote Papa left his bed on hearing this news and stood beside Kaanam with his eyes fixed on the boxed news item. The silence and fear of a while earlier seemed to be leaving with the sunrays that streamed into the room. A peculiar radiance had spread across it.

Now Kaanam began to read the news as if someone were delivering a speech from the stage:

"... The court, declaring this incident as being against the dignity of the woman and of the law, had ordered punishment to both the young men on the charge of raping the girl. This historical judgement was pronounced after having found them guilty under the Indian Penal Code (IPC) sections 366, 368 and 376. The one who had sexual intercourse with the girl was handed four years imprisonment along with a penalty of three thousand rupees; while his friend was sentenced to three years imprisonment and a penalty of fifteen hundred rupees. In its judgment the court said that the tradition of kidnapping a girl and marrying her forcibly is unfortunate. This tradition, in which girls and women are humiliated and treated like animals, is a blot on society. The court asked the state government to realize the seriousness of this problem and take necessary steps to end this social evil."

After reading out the news, Kaanam hugged the newspaper to her bosom.

It was startling news indeed! Kaanam and her Chhote Papa would never have imagined that a village girl or her parents would move the court in this way. The redness of the morning sun seemed to have dawned on their faces too. But Chhoti Amma was sitting quietly on the bed. It seemed that these two had forgotten that a third person was also in the room. Kaanam noticed the tea in the tray only when Chhote Papa yawned. The tea had already run cold. Kaanam shook Amma and embraced her—

"Amma, let's have some tea now!"

Returning to the present, Chhoti Amma looked at them in turn. Instead of any cheer or excitement, there was rage in her eyes. It seemed she had been completely immersed in the news but now she stood up, picked up the tray from the table, and said "Merely three thousand rupees as punishment for rape ...? Such a villain should have been hanged or shot dead at the crossroads!"

Kaanam remained quiet but Chhote Papa replied, "It's not a matter of rape, Sumi. It is a long tradition ...."

"But, either ways, it's the girl who was dishonoured."

Now Kaanam spoke up, "Amma, I understand your pain. But when all this is being done in the name of tradition, someone has to do something about it .... I think this is a great beginning."

Chhoti Amma went to the kitchen but Kaanam wished to read that news loudly in the alley, in the neighbourhood, and in the street. She wanted everyone to hear it. She had not been so happy even on the day when her MA result was declared and she had received the gold medal for topping the university. To her it seemed that this judgement had come in her own favour.

Chhoti Amma returned to the room with the tea. They all sat down to have it. For quite some time, nobody said anything. Then, Kaanam once again broke the silence—

"I wish Bade Pita would have done the same at that time."

Once again, the past which had dogged Kaanam and her Chhote Papa for long began to weave in and around them. Although they lived in the city, which was far beyond the boundaries of their traditions and where there was no such fear, deep within her Kaanam was always afraid. She did not possess girl-like playfulness and her self-confidence was constantly shaken. Even though, she received abundant love, security and acceptance in this house, but the memory of an incident troubled her at all times. Sometimes, it almost drove her mad and silent tears flowed incessantly from her eyes. They streamed like a ceaseless river, like water flowing mechanically from the eyes of a statue.

***

That past was Kaanam's older sister. Years ago, she had been kidnapped in the same manner by some young men right before Kaanam's eyes. She watched it all standing helplessly. The incident was still alive within her. To her it seemed as if it had occurred just yesterday. Time and again, her sister would come to her mind and ensconce herself as a fear somewhere deep inside her, or flow from her eyes in the form of tears. At times, she dwells in her eyes as though she were still there, and cries, "Sister! Sister! Please save me." Even today, the pain of that incident distresses Kaanam and cuts her to the quick. She does not sleep well or open up to anybody about it. It seems as if she were a zombie and her short life is burdened with a mountain of suffering. She wakes up at night and cries. For hours she stands in the balcony that cuts into the darkness and gazes at the vehicles and people going by. Whenever Chhote Papa hears her stirring, he gets up and holds her in his embrace. He strokes her hair and caresses her lovingly. His very touch reassures her and counsels her to forget the tortuous past. Then he tucks her into bed and quietly pats her like a child. Kaanam does not want that he should have to stay awake till midnight because of her but she has no control over things. She pretends to be asleep so that Chhote Papa can go away. However, Papa well knows and feels Kaanam's sentiments.

She hardly remembers how she had managed to study so far. As if all these years had simply been counted off her fingers. Even after so much has transpired, Kaanam has a spark in her which Chhote Papa recognises. He wants to see her carefree and self-confident, for which he had provided Kaanam the right environment and education. Today, as she read the news, he had undoubtedly seen a glance of that image. He had felt the passion of that energy in her. He was very happy today as if the news were a result of the education he had given her. He had seen the dam of her pent-up feelings burst and although he didn't know where the limits of this dam would end but he was happy with her freedom.

Chhote Papa enfolded Kaanam in his embrace, she clung to his chest and after years she openly wept floods of tears. Several times he removed his spectacles to wipe the tears welling in his eyes. Chhoti Amma also covered her eyes with her dupatta. For how long could she have controlled herself on seeing such a scene. If somebody were to witness the sight they would have known how a dam standing in this home for years had suddenly been breached.

All this continued for long, then there was calm after the storm. Everything settled down naturally. Chhote Papa eased Kaanam away from his chest and stood her before him. He took her face in his hands and thumbed her tears away. He looked at her for long. It was for the first time that he had seen the pain in her eyes up close. Heaps of pain. And many dreams for the future hidden in them. Her own village, and her lonely helpless mother ... and God knows what else. He said, "Bete, society is not going to change because of the court or its judgment. Even though there are many faults in them, the reach of traditions and customs is much higher. In order to eradicate social evils, one must go to the people and win their confidence so that they understand their good or bad results. I believe that we will be able to do this."

Kaanam listened quietly.

***

Kaanam must have been six years old when Ma, in the midst of many pressures from the family, sent her to the city. Because she lost her innocent childhood on the day her sister was kidnapped from her side, she was always afraid and trembled even at the slightest of sounds. She cowered close to Ma at home and didn't eat a thing. She woke up from sleep and screamed, "They have kidnapped my sister. Somebody, save her." Then she would shiver for hours and her whole body would turn feverish. She stopped going out to play in the village. She followed Ma everywhere. At home, apart from Ma there was her Bade Pita, her eldest father on account of being the oldest husband of her mother. Bade Pita had become a frightening figure for her now.

The youngest, Chhote Pita, whom she called Chhote Papa, had run away from the village to the city after his matriculation. Manjhle Pita, her middle father, lived in the doghri located in the distant fields. Kaanam's elder brother also lived in this secondary residence with him. He was responsible for tending to the sheep and goats at the doghri. There were some ten to twelve horses as well. They came home from the doghri every other day. Before the winters, Manjhle Pita and her brother, along with some workers, would take the sheep, goats and horses to the plains or to a place where there was no snow. They then returned only at the beginning of summer.

They were three brothers. Only Kaanam's Bade Pita had performed the marriage rituals. However, Ma was wife to all of them. Perhaps, the youngest brother had not liked this and so he had gone to the city. There he lived at a relative's house. He worked for them and also continued his studies. Thereafter, he found a job there. He also got married in the city. He never came back to the village after that. The middle brother had accepted the situation and tied his life to that of the livestock. Ma and Bade Pita had two daughters and a son. Kaanam was the youngest of them all. Ma gave the name of the middle husband to her son. Both girls were given the name of the eldest. However, Bade Pita had always resented this because he felt that he had the first right over the boy.

Kaanam's father was a well-known figure in the village. At first, he remained the village headman and thereafter he was continuously elected as the Pradhan. At home too, he had the same powerful position. However, Kaanam's mother had not allowed him to completely dominate her.

Kaanam knew very little about her mother at that time, but today she could empathise with her pain. She definitely remembers that Ma was not at all willing to give her sister in marriage to the young man who had abducted her. But the girl was her first concern. Second, it was her eldest husband's will as well, so she ultimately had to give in. Kaanam recalled everything that followed.

One week after the day on which all this happened, some people had come to their house. Kaanam was taken by surprise as two youngsters among them were the same boys who had abducted her sister. There was also a middle-aged man with them. As soon as she saw them, Kaanam began to scream. Bade Pita slapped her into silence. Kaanam can still feel the sting of that slap on her cheek, whose meaning she only understood at this age. The sorrow and fear inside her had deepened further with the slap. Those people spoke with Bade Pita for a long time. Kaanam watched everything from behind the door. The middle-aged man was a 'Majomi', the mediator. He was the maternal uncle of the boy with whom her sister was to be married. He kept touching Bade Pita's beard or his feet while talking. Sometimes he also placed his cap on Bade Pita's feet. All this continued for a long time. Then the Majomi took out a bottle of liquor from his bag. Along with it, he placed five rupees and a canister of butter near Bade Pita. Bade Pita accepted the gifts. If he had not, then it would have been known that he was not ready to marry his daughter into that family. Kaanam's Ma had already asked him once to reject the gifts.

After this, the Majomi got up and embraced him. Both of them were happy. The youngsters touched their feet. They embraced the one who had kidnapped the girl and with whom the marriage had now been fixed.

The Majomi had not only given honour money to Kaanam's Bade Pita but had also offered money to the village deity. The next day, all the people of the village gathered at the devta's temple. Plenty of wine was drunk and there was singing and dancing. The deity had also given his consent to the marriage. Kaanam's Bade Pita knew that even if the bride's side had already taken the bottle of wine, butter and honour money, many a times it is difficult to get the devta's consent in such matters. But he himself was the headman of the village; and in addition, he was also the head of the devta committee. After this, Majomi and the young men returned to their village.

After a few days, Kaanam's Manjhle Pita went to the boy's home and came back with her older sister. These were the happiest moments for Kaanam. Her happiness knew no bounds when she saw her sister. She ran into her arms and embraced her. She laughed and cried at the same time. Her sister, however, remained silent. Kaanam saw her despondency. Her eyes were red, her lips wrinkled. Her chapped lips and swollen eyes revealed that she had stayed awake crying for many nights. Kaanam now understood that she had wanted to tell her all that she had been through but Kaanam's young age had come in her way. Kaanam had been a child then, what could she have told her?

How beautiful and playful her sister had been! There was hardly any girl like her in the village. Fathomless lakes lived in her deep black eyes. Roses bloomed in the smile of her lips. Her laughter was amazingly sweet. The fine swell of her breasts further ornamented her youth. She hummed constantly and the lyrics of the natis were always on her lips. She teased all irrespective of their age. But today, she appears like a statue to her. She neither says anything nor hums. She also doesn't play with her or tease her. Kaanam wonders to herself, I don't know what those goons have done to her. The statue occupied Kaanam's mind.

The wedding rituals started after this. The same young man came with the wedding procession as a bridegroom. Kaanam watched him furtively. For many days it was like a festival in the home. People sang and danced day and night. Intoxicated. Unmindful of the world. It was the same for both men and women. But Kaanam was all alone in this crowd. Occasionally, Ma would look for her and forcibly make her eat something, otherwise there was no one else who cared for her. Her sister departed once again. She went far away from her but this time she did not cry. Kaanam watched the wedding procession leave from the stockade of a field above the house. She would have continued to sit there if Ma had not come looking for her in the evening. She came back home with Ma. Now she neither cried nor felt afraid in the night. Ma looked at her intently sometimes and her eyes brimmed over with tears. Perhaps, Kaanam's silence troubled her. That is why Kaanam was able to leave home and come to the city without Bade Pita's permission. She doesn't know what Ma would have had to bear after she ran away. But today she trembled at the mere thought of it.

***

Kaanam didn't know how so many years had passed by. She continued to study even as she lugged her past along. Probably, there was no girl in the village more educated than Kaanam; not only in the village but in the entire region. Ma thought that she would forget everything in the city. After completing her studies, she would take up a job or marry a man of her choice. She would not return to that past. Kaanam would not have to face all those things that she herself had suffered or which the other girls of the village still underwent. Although, all this was slowly being left behind, yet there were still some families who couldn't free themselves of these traditions. It was the only world they knew. Even though many boys of the area had become officers but they still had to bear the same situation. Those who married according to their own choice could not return to the village. The family would ostracise them. The devta would also take offense. But for Kaanam's Ma, the present was no different from the past. For her, the contemporary was the same as it used to be years ago.

One day Ma was taken by surprise when she received a letter from Kaanam. She wrote, "Amma, I am coming to you." Ma was illiterate, so she had asked a boy to read the letter to her. On hearing this, she felt extremely happy for an instant but the very next moment she trembled. She had probably never thought that Kaanam would return to the same limitations and restrictions from which she had been freed. She pleaded repeatedly with the boy not to mention the letter to anyone, but for how long could it have remained a secret in the village. Ma was in two minds. On the one side, she was very curious to see how her young daughter had turned out; on the other, the traditions and customs of the village frightened her. She was irritated. "Kaanam has gone mad. Is she without her senses? How will she adjust in this deceitful environment? This society will swallow her up. What use have her studies been? If she had someone of her own, she would have asked them to stop that mad girl from coming here. Make her understand. But with whom could Ma have shared the feelings of her heart?

The entire village came to know about Kaanam's coming. Bade Pita got extremely angry when he heard about it. Back home, he had a fierce fight with Kaanam's mother. The whole blame was placed squarely on Ma's head, "You must have called that shameless girl back. She should have died in the city to which she ran away from home. Hasn't she already done enough? What more will she do now? What will the community say? I will not be able to show my face anywhere", he raved. Ma listened quietly. What could she say? Sleep deserted her and it seemed as if her mind had a thousand wounds. Her heart seemed to burn with every breath that she took. She shivered with fear at the very thought of an unexpected or unprecedented happening.

Ma's fixed eyes had now started to look out for her. When and with whom she would come. Whether she would be able to recognize her after so many years or not? She tried several times to conjure up Kaanam's face in her eyes, but the same scared and nervous Kaanam would appear before her eyes. Perturbed, she invoked the household goddess time and again.

***

Kaanam's Chhoti Ma and Chhote Papa saw her off with moist eyes. Kaanam touched their feet and after taking their blessings she boarded the bus. Buses had now started to ply to the village. Kaanam would have to change two buses in order to get there. The city fell behind and retreated from Kaanam's eyes and heart. Now it's only the village–Ma and the memories of the past were there. Kaanam was happy that buses had started plying to the village now. Roads had reached even the distant mountains. She imagined her village as more modern than what it had been earlier.

When Kaanam reached the mountains away from the city limits, she felt a new world inside her where the splendour of nature captivated the mind. In place of the crowd of the city, the sound of the reckless vehicles and the constricted world of two rooms, Kaanam felt a newness in her heart at the sweet sounds of the river and cascades, the rustling of fresh air from the dense forests and an unusual freeness in the environment. But she didn't like the cutting of the mountains to such an extent just for the road. Concrete houses had been built inside the village. The bus stopped for hours at many places due to landslides caused by monsoon rains. Stones fell from the mountains at some points. Kaanam read signboards at several places on which warnings such as "Beware of the Falling Stones" had been written. Among these life-threatening dangers the sincerity and confidence of the mountain workers strengthened Kaanam's self-confidence. She soon realised that all this was happening due to the reckless use of dynamite together with disorganised and clumsy methods of working.

It was dusk when Kaanam's bus reached the village. Some people, who had boarded the bus from nearby stations, looked at that unknown girl with surprise. A few boys had also tried to tease her but Kaanam sat there as if she didn't know anything. The village was close by. As she reached home, the dog barked to inform the family of her coming. Bade Pita himself opened the door. At that time Ma was making rotis on the chulha. As her eyes fell on the door, her happiness knew no bounds. How young my Kaanam has grown! Instantly, that nervous and scared little girl who lived in her eyes for all these years departed. She scolded the dog to make him quiet. For a moment even Bade Papa was surprised, but he soon realised that she was the same girl. He didn't stay there even for a moment as if she was not his daughter but a girl from the neighbourhood who had come to borrow something. Ma stood in front. She looked at her to her heart's content and then embraced her, unaware that her flour smeared hands would soil her new clothes. She clutched her to her bosom. It seemed that Kaanam was enfolded in the arms of her small world. Her parched eyes suddenly began to rain. Kaanam was drenched. Where else had she found this love? For how long she had craved it. Releasing her from her embrace, Ma took her face in her hands and looked deeply at her. With her eyes she conveyed so many things to her. Bade Pita did not come out of his room intentionally. Kaanam's arms, heart, and eyes kept yearning for him. She wanted him also to embrace her and show affection like her mother. She went inside and completed the formality of touching his feet. Manjhle Pita was also there. Although he embraced her, yet Kaanam didn't feel love akin to Ma's in his arms.

Kaanam took off her shoes. She picked up her suitcase and made to enter her room when she noticed the dog watching her intently from where he sat behind the door. It lived with Manjhle Pita. It was so big that it reached up to Kaanam's waist. She looked at it affectionately. Kaanam found strong love reflected in its eyes. She immediately called it close to her. Perhaps, it had wanted the same and within seconds it bounded close to Kaanam circling around her. Ma was surprised because she had scolded it to go away from there. Bade Pita was surprised how within seconds the dog had accepted the stranger Kaanam as its own. Otherwise, even sparrows could not sit in the aangan for fear of it.

***

Now Kaanam's daily routine was very different from before and quite uncommon. She did not bind herself to the limits of the village and its surroundings. She did go, however, to the famous temple of the village on the day following her arrival. It was Chandika Devi's temple, in whose aangan much of her childhood had been spent unawares. Ma accompanied her to the temple. For a long time Kaanam stood sombrely outside the temple wall. The priest looked at her with surprise. Ma explained:

"Don't you recognize her, Pujari ji? She is my Kaanam ... Kaanam."

The surprise left his eyes and Kaanam detected a flitting affection on his face but the priest quickly gathered himself. Before she could touch his feet, he slipped hurriedly inside the temple. Ma did not like this but she noticed a slight smile on Kaanam's lips and she was embarrassed.

Kaanam bowed sincerely to Devi Ma at the threshold of the temple. She offered some money and flowers to the Devi and returned quickly. The problem of the priest was also solved. All this while he had been wondering how he could bless this disgraced girl.

Ma was solemn. Many thoughts came to her mind. At some distance from the temple, Kaanam asked Ma to sit with her in the field.

"Amma, you know, don't you, how old this temple is?"

Nodding, Ma mumbled something. Kaanam did not attempt to decipher it and went on, "She is the richest, cleverest, and also the mightiest Devi of our area. Ma, do you know why she is venerated so much?"

Again, Ma said nothing. She only glanced at her in surprise.

"Amma, it is said that they were eighteen brothers and sisters. Banasura was their father. He had married Hirma forcibly and stayed with her in a cave for many days. When the children grew up then this whole country had to be divided among them. The elder brother was very clever.

He asked for the best portion of the land; but in spite of being the youngest, Chandika did not agree. She revolted and took her favourite area".

Ma still listened quietly.

"—and Ma, a very powerful demon already reigned in this area. Chandika fought a fierce battle with him and killed him. Not only this, she also killed many of his allies. In this way she captured a large region and began to rule here. That is why she is our chief goddess."

With folded hands Ma once again bowed her head towards the temple.

"Amma, I am also the daughter of this Ma."

Ma was startled.

"Forget the Kaanam of years ago who lives in your eyes. I am today's Kaanam. I need your blessings and also of Devi Ma."

Ma relaxed. Her eyes again filled with tears. Kaanam saw faith in them.

"Ma, I did not study to secure a job. I will stay with you and help you in your work. The courage and confidence that I have are given by you."

Ma hugged Kaanam.

With a choked voice, she said, "Live long my daughter, live long."

***

Kaanam got up at dawn, brushed her teeth, had her bath and went for a long run in the village. She then exercised for a while in the aangan. Ma was not afraid for her anymore. She was free from worries about her. Kaanam spent most of her time helping Ma. She knew that Ma has always worked like a machine in this house. No one helped her even a bit. Ma got up around half past three or four in the morning and gave everyone tea before going out to the cowshed to milk the cows and buffaloes. She then fed and milked the goats before getting on with her daily chores. She would bring five or six bundles of grass and leaves from the jungle. Then, she cooked lunch. After finishing all this, she took the animals to graze in the jungle. She returned at dusk and after tending to the animals the household chores began once again. Kaanam was surprised to see that every evening people from other villages came home with Bade Pita. They sat drinking copiously and Ma sat until midnight to attend to them. She would have her dinner only after everybody had eaten. In addition to this, she had to satisfy two husbands. Also, she had to pluck seasonal fruits off the trees, and dry and preserve these for winters. Apricots and apples being chief among them.

It was also Ma's responsibility to take cereals and grains to be ground at the watermill. She also took part in the village festivals and festivities. All night long, she danced and sang the nati with the women of the village. Ma had grown quite frail. It was a marvel that she could do so much work. Kaanam thought that it was surely due to Devi Ma's blessings that Ma could bear so much. Not only this, once or twice in a week Ma had also to make grape wine. But Kaanam had never seen any resentment in her eyes or a frown on her face. She had never felt that Ma was ever tired.

Kaanam had become burdensome for Bade Pita. He hated even her shadow. Kaanam's habits pierced his heart like a needle. That a girl should wander freely, work out, and go to other people's homes to laugh and talk was shameful for him. Many times, after a few drinks, the villagers also brought up the matter. He would vent his anger on Ma when Kaanam was asleep or out of the house.

Kaanam was now quite intimate with the village girls and women. People talked about her in the village but they hesitated to talk openly. Partially because she was the daughter of the Pradhan who had dominated the whole area for years.

Kaanam wore a woollen jacket over her simple salwar-kurta. In the village, she had also started wearing the local cap with the green strip. It became her greatly. Altogether, she had extraordinary talents. Her beauty was unparalleled, unmatched and incomparable. When she walked through the village, everyone was stunned by her beauty. Many boys of the area had their eyes on her.

One morning, without telling anybody she went to the village of the girl and her parents who had filed the case in the court. No one knew Kaanam there. She enquired her way to their house. The family were surprised to see her. When she introduced herself, they welcomed her into the house with affection and talked for long with her. Kaanam was perturbed when she met the girl. She had withered to a bag of bones. She neither talked to anyone nor ate well.

Kaanam asked the father of the girl, "You have honoured us by filing a suit in the court. I have come here to thank all of you for this."

The girl's father heaved a deep sigh as if he were broken inside. He said, "Daughter, today it seems that we made a big mistake. We are paying for it now. So is our daughter."

Kaanam was silent for a moment. She had not expected such an answer. She collected herself and said, "Why do you think like this? It is a matter of pride for us."

"Daughter! You're the first girl who thinks so and have said this. You don't know all that we have had to face after the case. The community has ostracised our family. All the marriage proposals we sent were turned away. How can one fight society all alone? These traditions are deeply rooted among us. We have ruined our daughter's life. See, what she looks like. It seems she has forgotten even to talk. She doesn't go anywhere. She sits near the chulha with her head bowed, crying all the time.

Kaanam understood the whole situation. She called the girl to her lovingly, made her sit near and then asked her name. She comforted her and kept looking at her. She thought to herself how strange these traditions were. If the girl had given in quietly, she would have been a wife. Now she is wasting away with the blot of rape on her. Kaanam was filled with such abhorrence for her society as if all this were happening with her.

"I'll take her with me. Don't worry about her. She'll return to her normal self like she was before."

Kaanam announced her decision without asking for permission. No one could object.

Bade Pita was furious when he saw Kaanam bring the girl home with her. He came to know that she is the same girl who had defied tradition. He said nothing to Kaanam but quarrelled with Ma in front of her. Ma did not say anything. The matter began to be discussed far and wide. Also, the girl belonged to a lower caste community. A storm swirled up in the house. Everyone began to question Kaanam's Bade Pita about it when he ventured out of the house. Till now nobody had ever dared to say anything to him. But now he had lost all respect, and that too on account of his own daughter. He felt like breaking Kaanam's limbs. She was his misfortune. But still, he never dared to look his daughter in the eye and talk it out with her. Kaanam had tried to speak with him several times but she did not succeed.

Kaanam was successful, however, in her efforts to counsel the girl and bring back her lost confidence. She felt as if the girl were her own sister whom she had lost many years ago.

The festival of flowers began after a few days. Kaanam kept busy with Ma in cleaning the house. After finishing the domestic chores, all the girls and women of the village went in groups to the river bank to pluck flowers and make garlands with them. Nowadays, their main work was to fetch the flowers.

***

One day, groups of women and girls were on their way to pluck flowers. Kaanam was trailing quite behind along with some girls. There was a road below the village. As soon as they reached the road, Kaanam saw a white Maruti car at a distance. But nobody else took notice of it. However, within the fraction of a second, three or four young boys surrounded the girls. The other girls slipped away and no one harassed them. It was clear that they had come for Kaanam. She was quick to understand. Perhaps the girl living at Kaanam's house had sensed their intentions. She clung to Kaanam. But one boy pulled her away by her arm. Then one of them took hold of Kaanam's arm and they instantly began to drag her towards the Maruti car. The boy who had grabbed Kaanam's arm was perhaps the one who wanted to abduct her.

No one knew how Kaanam managed to escape their hold. After that, the way Kaanam beat them with blows, kicks and head butts was enough to amaze anybody. On hearing the noise, the girls and women who had gone ahead came running back. Kaanam was fighting with the boys. She held the boy who had first touched her by the scruff of his neck. Nobody knew how she flung him several feet away. Half-dead, he tried to get up many times but fell back again. Kaanam spat towards him from afar. Before the others could be reduced to the same condition, they fled in the Maruti car. Now, he lay there all alone. If the other women had not stopped her, Kaanam might even have killed him.

The women and girls wondered from where Kaanam had got such strength. In this fight, one of her earrings had come off ripping her ear and drawing blood. Her kameez was torn near her chest. The girl who lived with her covered Kaanam with her shawl. Another friend picked up her cap that had fallen a little away and placed it on her head. Kaanam was relaxed and cheerful as usual; as if nothing had happened. But, through the crowd she looked furtively at the young man staggering forward. If she had gotten more time, she would have thrashed him good and proper.

***

No one went to the riverbank to pick flowers. All the women and girls returned to the village with Kaanam. In the evening, the news spread in the wind all over the village, panchayat and neighbouring areas. When Kaanam's Bade Pita came to know what his daughter had done, he almost went crazy. The pent-up anger of many days spewed out of him like poison. At first, he started to fight with Kaanam's Ma. He shouted whatever came to his mind. He was also drunk. Then it was Kaanam's turn. He slapped her face with all his might. Kaanam could have prevented him if she had wanted. She did not. Even though it was a slap, this touch of her father seemed to her no less than an expression of his love. With a confident smile still on her face, she said, "Bade Pita! I am not Sunam that a few goons can come, carry me away on their backs, and tie me to their stake."

His eyes turned red. He began to shake with rage. Ma stood at the door afraid and mute.

"You hussy! Do you know what you have done? I am the Pradhan of the area. How am I to face the people? They'll spit on me. Ill-gotten wretch, why didn't you die the moment you were born?

He then dragged in Kaanam's Ma from the door.

"Do you see your girl, you slut? She has disgraced us. On top of that, you should know that this is election time."

Elections had become more important for Bade Pita than his daughter's dignity. What else could Kaanam have expected of him? She spoke up, "Bade Pita, protecting oneself is not disgraceful. You should be proud that your daughter has saved her honour."

"Honour ...?"

His legs began to tremble.

"Honour ... did you have any that it has been saved today? Still, I did my duty as a father. You would have been married into a good family .... To the son of the MLA. Do you know that?"

Kaanam was petrified. The ground beneath her feet shook, as if someone had poured many pitchers of water over her head. She had never imagined that her own father would arrange something like this! There was no fear on Ma's face now; instead, anger could be seen clearly all over it. She suddenly grabbed hold of his jacket collar and screamed, "So this was your doing! You put your own daughter at stake! Oh, you are such a praiseworthy father! I commend you!"

Had Kaanam not supported her, Ma would have fallen down on the stones in the aangan. Kaanam felt today that she was not his daughter, perhaps she never had been. Had she been, he would never have done what he did. She wondered whether Bade Pita was her real father or was it Chhote Pita ... She was mortified at her thoughts.

Today, Kaanam wept feeling a deep pain. It seemed as if the mother and daughter would flood the aangan with their tears. Bade Pita still ranted. People from neighbouring houses gathered around to see the spectacle. Then Kaanam gathered herself together. When she looked at them with her moist eyes they seemed to be struck by lightning and all of them went back to their homes.

Ma, of course, had cried but she was also happy at having saved her second daughter. A fear that had always resided in a corner of her heart had gone away today.

Kaanam missed her Chhote Pita very much today. In her mind she touched his feet in reverence. And also, of Chhoti Ma. She remembered how they had insisted that she enrol for martial art classes. As if that training were given to her just for this day.

***

The news spread far and wide that Kaanam had beaten the MLA's son half-dead. The older men and women of the area thought this went against their culture and tradition but young boys and girls praised her in their hearts. The people with whom Kaanam was associated began to respect her even more than before. But to her this respect and affection was quite meaningless. She wanted to receive these within her home. Perhaps, from her Bade or Manjhle Pita ... but she would never get these from them .... Ma's deep love was with her, however, and to have Ma's support was to have the support of all women and girls.

The imminent panchayat elections had gained intensity. Everyone was busy discussing the polls. Kaanam was surprised how the deceitful politics of the cities had also entered into the villages. Every day she saw a score or so people gather at her house. Bade Pita had money ... there were bidis and cigarettes ... wine and meat ... parties and feasts. All night, Ma remained busy providing for them. Kaanam also helped Ma but she completely disapproved of these activities. She began to persuade Ma also but when Ma said that she was not only a mother but also a wife, Kaanam had no answer. This was Ma's entire world. But Kaanam's world extended beyond the threshold of the house too.

Nominations were to be filed. Kaanam's father was the first one to file his nomination. He was sure that as always no one would contest against him. And if anyone were to stand, he would not win. For he was also the devta's treasurer ... the panchayat, its people, and even the devta were on his side.

With Kaanam there was only the girl from the outcaste community. Both of them went to Devi Chandika's temple. The girl stopped at a distance from it. She knew that outcaste people could not go inside the devta's aangan. Kaanam understood her thoughts. She took her along to the threshold of the temple and bowed to Devi Ma's feet. Today she had neither money nor flowers. She was empty handed. As she turned to go back, the priest called out to her, "Bitiya, take Devi Ma's rice and flowers with you."

Kaanam was taken aback. As she turned, Pujari came into the aangan and placed some flowers and rice, red with vermilion, in both the girls' hands. Kaanam was unaffected but the girl was astonished. After returning from the temple Kaanam entered the court aangan of the school, much to the surprise of the people standing around there. She went up to the election officer, took the nomination form, filled it and turned to leave. Everyone followed her with her eyes. They were all astounded.

This news reached her home before she did. It also spread all over the village. As she reached the aangan, a group of ten to twelve girls and women surrounded her. Kaanam, however, felt all alone even within the garland of their arms. A girl hummed a nati. An unprecedented joy was reflected on all their faces. Beyond the circle of their arms, Kaanam's eyes fell on Ma's face as she sat near the stove. Ma's face appeared serious in the light of the burning wood. For Kaanam it was not difficult to fathom her expression. Bade Pita sat dejected near her. Kaanam looked at both of them with enigmatic eyes. Bade Pita stirred the embers of burning wood with a tong. Kaanam saw him sitting beside Ma for the first time. Despondent and hapless.

The words of the nati began to sound all around and the girls in the circle began to dance.

Daarosh: Daarosh is a word widely spoken in a tribal area of Himachal Pradesh. It means to use force or power. The tradition of 'coerced marriage' that prevails in that particular area is called "Daarosh dublub", which means to "marry forcibly."

Translated by Khem Raj Sharma

THE SADDLE

JINKATHI

Bhunda: A typical, unique, and fearsome festival of the hill people! In older times this festival was celebrated every twelve years but now there is no definite date or time for this festival. The special feature of this festival is the participation and central role in it of a rare Dalit community of the hills, called beda. One member of a Dalit family of this community is chosen and consecrated with ceremonies and rituals as a brahmin for the purpose of this festival. On the day of the festival, he is worshipped as a deity, an incarnation of divinity. A huge, long rope made of grass is tied from the top of a hill to a huge pole. The beda sits on a saddle fitted on the rope and slides down to the end of the rope. This is nothing short of putting the person's life on the road to death.

Sahajram was no longer a dalit. He bathed in cold water and then underwent all the necessary rituals and ceremonies for his initiation into brahminhood. After these rituals, he was symbolically cleansed of his low caste impurities and transformed into a holy brahmin. People had visions of their deity in him. Otherwise an untouchable, Sahju was now a brahmin. Now he had to observe certain sacred rules of becoming a brahmin for a few days during the Bhunda celebration, which included a onetime meal, no cutting of hair or nails and complete abstinence from sex. His food and clothes were now the responsibility of the temple. Not only this, the temple took upon itself to meet all the requirements of food and clothes of his entire family for the duration of the festival. Now the special rope for the main festival had to be made ready.

One day the people of the area accompanied Sahju with music and dance to gather the special 'moonj' grass on a hillock. The cutting of the grass was a sacred ritual and Sahju had to be the first to touch the grass with a sickle. He was followed by the other people of the village in cutting the grass and gathering it in bundles. When sufficient quantity had been cut and made into bundles, it was brought to the temple and stacked in its compound. Sahju had to spin this into a rope for the festival. When the site of the celebration was inspected, it was found that the rope had to be five hundred feet long. To bear the weight of one person it had to be 25-30 centimetres thick.

Sahju had to leave his bed quite early in the morning in the brahma muhurta, the moments just before sunrise, to have his bath. After the morning ablutions, he would get busy with the spinning of the grass-rope. The spinning of the rope was considered a sacred act. While he was at it, nobody could pass before him nor talk to him. Nobody was allowed to touch the rope. If by oversight or carelessness someone touched the rope it would be considered defiled and unclean. A lamb had to be sacrificed immediately and a new rope would have to be spun. Many kinds of thoughts floated through Sahju's mind as he sat spinning the rope. He recalled one of his ancestors who had died while performing Bhunda. That ancestor had also spun that rope of death straw by straw. Such thoughts came to him the whole day. His wife, sitting at some distance in a corner, watched him silently. Quite often her eyes would fix on Sahju's face and she would try to read the thoughts swirling in his mind. Sometimes she would find a clear trace of death on his face and sometimes signs of joy and prosperity. She would also try to gauge the sense of contentment and happiness arising out of his transformation from dalit to brahmin. But, at times, she would suddenly think that the face she was watching so intently was not of her husband's but that of a crook, a hypocrite, on whom the mask of a brahmin had been forced for the pleasure of the on-lookers, that her husband was nothing more than a mimic playing someone else.

When Sahju stopped spinning the rope, people could come close and talk to him respectfully. If the grass-bundles decreased in number and were likely to be insufficient for the rope, more grass would be cut and brought to replenish the stock.

***

The revival of Bhunda on a grand scale was the brainchild of Pandit Bhagwan Dutt Sharma. He had recently retired from the post of a tehsildar.

Soon after his retirement, he had organized a grand feast in his village to which he had invited a large number of persons from the neighbouring villages in addition to the people of his own. His old and new friends from his old office were of course there but he had not forgotten the local Member of the Legislative Assembly who was specially invited to the feast. The MLA was accompanied with the whole paraphernalia of district officials and administrators. One of the guests was the village deity. When Sharma ji demitted the office of the tehsildar and proceeded to his village, he came in a procession of over fifteen cars and jeeps with the English band playing popular film songs. This was an effort on his part to make people remember that he was a retired high official of the government and that they should not think he had lost the earlier glamour and authority, at the same time, he also wanted to project his image as a pious and religious person.

A whole variety of food was prepared for the feast, wines of different taste and labels were kept ready. Five goats were butchered. The people of the village could not recall any such feast in their living memory. The feast remained a talking point for a long time. Sharma ji had planned the feast to succeed on many fronts but these were all his personal secrets and he did not want anybody to smell them out even faintly. He knew in the core of his heart that his official position and authority and the glamour it carried was a matter of the past. And people pay obeisance only to the chair and position. Once these are gone, even a dog will ignore you. You may be a man of millions but without position and authority, you are as good as nobody in the eyes of the public. Of course, Sharma ji had retired but when in office he had amassed huge wealth. People respected and feared him and he was a person you could not overlook. He had obliged many. He was certainly not a person of integrity but conducted his affairs intelligently and cunningly without his image being sullied in the public eye.

Even though he had retired at the age of fifty-eight, he hardly looked forty. Red cheeks, unwrinkled face, a few silver streaks in the hair cleverly coloured in henna-paste, broad forehead, sharp chin, all gave him an air of youthful exuberance and energy. A thin line of moustache added to the glamour of his personality. The big sandal and kumkum mark on his broad forehead distinguished him in a crowd. Before he retired, his dress was never complete without a tight-fitting coat and a tie of matching colour. His clean rose-coloured handkerchief always peeped out of his coat pocket. His immaculate dress and his upright gait were a matter of envy among his superiors in office but they kept it to themselves and never dropped even a casual hint about it. But after retirement, he changed his sartorial style. Now he dressed himself in a kurta-pyjama and a Nehru cut jacket decorated with a coloured handkerchief peeking from its pocket. Even now he looked distinct and different from others.

Sharma ji's family was the wealthiest in the village. They were three brothers, and all three were the most important persons in the villages of the entire area. They could be called big landlords. Sharma ji's own family consisted of his wife, two sons, two daughters-in-law and three grandchildren. His two daughters were married and happy in their families. His elder son was in the catechu business, the younger was a Block Development Officer and he also looked after the family estate. The land holdings were well-irrigated and fertile. Apart from grains, vegetables were also grown and thus the family income was very good. The family owned two Qualis jeeps and two trucks. Nepalese labourers worked in the fields all the year round.

The first thing that Sharma ji did post-retirement, was to get into the village temple committee. Before doing so, he attended quite a few ritual activities of the village. When it came to selecting the chief of the committee, people found there was no one who deserved this position more than Sharma ji. The result was his unanimous selection. This was the beginning of Sharma ji's new life as a religious person. He now wanted to use this position as a stepping-stone to become the village pradhan. And he began to plan for it in advance. He wanted to do something spectacular which would spread his reputation far beyond the narrow confines of his own village so that he could reach not only the local MLA but also the state Chief Minister. The village deity could be used as a dice in his game, he calculated.

His was a predominantly brahmin village where the brahmins of all the five gotras lived. The village was considered an ancient sacred place. For a long time, the Bhunda festival was regularly observed here after every twelve years. There still stood the remains of many ancient temples which were also of archaeological importance, apart from being sacred sites. There used to be four or five dalit families also in the village. One of these families was of the beda caste who always donated one male member of the family to play the chief role in the Bhunda festival. But many years ago, an ancestor of the family had died because the sacred rope had broken midway. Sharma ji had heard about this festival from his elders and the talk of the accident was fresh in his memory. When the beda was seated on the saddle on the rope and asked to slide down, the saddle got stuck at a point and would not move by any means. The beda was suspended midway on the rope. All attempts to make the saddle move downwards failed. People began to hit the rope with sticks and the rope broke into two. The beda fell hundreds of feet down onto the rocks and died instantly. This was a very inauspicious happening for the entire area. This incident was followed by a mysterious epidemic and nearly half of the village population perished in it. In view of this calamity, the brahmins of the village expelled the beda family and other dalit families from the village, holding them responsible for the inauspicious episode that had swallowed so many persons.

Sharma ji found a readymade occasion to show off his dominance and stature. He knew that no Bhunda was celebrated in the village after that accident, but this was celebrated in the neighbouring villages, even though very rarely. During his days as the tehsildar, Sharma ji himself had organised this festival but care was taken that a huge net was kept ready to keep the beda safe in the event of the rope giving way. At many places where no beda caste was to be found, a male goat was used as a substitute.

One day Sharma ji expressed his long-suppressed desire before the members of the temple committee. The members were in full agreement with him. The deity's fury had not subsided and an evil shadow was still looming over the village. The only cure for this was to hold the Bhunda. This would restore the village to its earlier prosperity and happiness. But the question was how to collect lakhs of rupees needed for the purpose. It was difficult to hold such an expensive festival at a time when prices were so high and essential things so scarce. But Sharma ji had the solution ready. He immediately made a donation of one lakh rupees to the temple committee. This gesture boosted the morale of other members. Another source of money suggested by Sharma ji was to sell off the gold and silver ornaments offered to the deity in all these years. After all, the deity's wealth is to be spent on the deity himself. There is nothing wrong in it. The committee agreed.

Now the question was to find the bedas. No one in the village could recall where the people expelled from the village so long back had gone and settled. But Sharma ji was not one to give in easily. He took upon himself the responsibility to locate them. Sharma ji's active involvement in the matter proved reassuring to the members and they all approved of it. The news got around quickly and people were deeply touched by Sharma ji's concern for the welfare of the village. People from far and near would come to him to seek his advice and suggestions in difficult matters, whether religious or otherwise. The satisfaction of being in the centre of the area's affairs far exceeded the attention and respect he had enjoyed during his job as a tehsildar.

Sharma ji was delighted. He had silently visualized the elaborate plans and activities for the occasion. He had also made up his mind about inviting the state Chief Minister as the chief guest on the occasion. When the news of the imminent event spread through the village, the villagers refused to believe it. They were initially unwilling to participate in the festival. But Sharma ji and other members of the committee finally succeeded in persuading them to participate. After all, who would like to be deprived of the spiritual merit it would bring them!

Sharma ji's biggest problem was to search for the village of the bedas. There was no trace of them in the region. The most compelling thing was that the person to be chosen for the ceremony should be from the same family whose member had died earlier when the sacred rope had broken and the whole village had to suffer the fury of the deity. The elders and priests of the village were of the opinion that the beda family's curse still haunted the village. After all the beda who had fallen to death was blameless. And so, if another member could be found to perform the ceremonial sliding from the rope the curse would be lifted and the village would be blessed for holding the long-discontinued sacred festival.

Sharma ji took a few elderly persons with him and approached the local MLA. He said to the MLA, "See Vidhayak ji, our village is going to hold Bhunda after about one hundred and fifty years. You must secure the presence of the Chief Minister as chief guest. This will help you as well as the people of the village." Sharma ji was politeness embodied when placing the proposal before the MLA.

The MLA was confused and could not respond immediately. He had also heard from his elders about the accident in which the beda had died while performing the rope ceremony. He himself came from the dalit community and had contested from a 'reserved' seat. He puffed at his cigarette and thought for long. His mind went back to what had happened many years ago. He calculated his own possible gains and feared losses. He thought of his Dalit voters who had not supported him wholeheartedly in the last election. Another thing that occurred to him was how to connect to the traditional values and beliefs in this electronic age. And the third thing that occurred to him was to restore the honour and prestige of those dalit families who were expelled from the village. The occasion offered itself before him as an all-in-one kind of thing.

The MLA was delighted but did not allow his emotion to come into the open. A mock smile rose to his face and he said, "Sharma ji, you are great! You have not forgotten your traditions even though you were in government service. People usually go senile after retirement. There are many who could not survive the shock of retirement even by two years. And here you are! You've taken such a huge responsibility on your head. It will be a great service to society. I am with you. Whatever you ask me to do, I will."

Sharma ji was mighty pleased. He secretly bowed to the family deity. Everything is fine by his grace. But no sooner had this consoling thought crossed his mind than certain other worries raised their heads and he became serious. Noticing this, the MLA asked, "You look slightly worried, Sharma ji?"

"No, no, Vidhayak ji, I am ok."

"Well, I've committed myself to you. If you have something weighing on your mind, tell me, please."

There was another person who had accompanied Sharma ji. He first looked at the MLA's face and then turned to Sharma ji. He divulged Sharma ji's worry:

"Sharma ji is worried about finding the beda family whose member had died during the last festival."

When the MLA heard this remark, his eyes turned red and a deep sense of insult and humiliation surged into his heart, as if it was he himself who had been expelled from the village. But he regained his composure soon enough. "Why should it weigh on your conscience, Sharma ji? Just give me a piece of paper, I'll write down his address. That family is settled at a great distance from here but now that you have decided to hold such an elaborate ceremony, the distance should be no obstacle. Of course, it will need a good deal of persuasion and cajoling. Even though the accident took place so very long ago, the wounds of humiliation take time to heal."

Sharma ji and his companion squirmed with embarrassment but Sharma ji was elated that he had finally succeeded in extracting the desired information about the long-ago disgraced beda family. He took out his pocket diary and handed it to the MLA. The MLA took out his pen from his jacket and wrote down the address.

Sharma ji took back the diary and fixed his eyes on the address. He was taken aback when he saw "telephone" as part of the address: "Telephone!"

The MLA almost lost his cool, "Yes, why not, Sharma ji? Shouldn't they have telephones and other facilities?"

"Oh no! What are you saying, Vidhayak ji? That wasn't what I meant. In fact, I am happy the search has become so easy".

"But, no Sharma ji. You shouldn't contact them on telephone; otherwise, the whole plan will fall through. You have to approach them with grace and dignity. The task is difficult. Now, your experience as a tehsildar is on the test. Let's see what happens."

Sharma ji knew the MLA was taunting him but at stake was his own interest. He got up, bowed to the MLA and left.

When long ago, the dalit families were forced to leave the village, they wandered about for many days, looking for food and shelter. Many of them died. With much difficulty, they approached a family which helped them with a piece of land on which the expelled families raised their huts and thus a small hamlet of poor dalit families came into existence far away from their ancestral homes. Sharma ji had never heard of that village, much less its name.

When Sharma ji came back to his village and told the temple committee about his success, everybody was very happy. Sharma ji took two more persons with him and set out to invite the beda family. They went by car but left it at the end of the road. From there it was seven kilometres of a steep hilly track to the place where the beda families lived. Sharma ji could not walk for long. During his tehsildar days, a pony was always at hand on such occasions. But now he had to depend on his own two feet. Somehow the party managed to reach the beda village a little before sunset.

What Sharma ji saw with his eyes on reaching there could not be really called a village. There were just about four or five huts on the slope near the ravine. The roofs of these houses were made of unshapely stone slabs. Only a couple of houses had two storeys but all the houses were clean. Barley and wheat crops thrived in small fields on either side. One wide pathway from the yards of those huts disappeared at some distance on the other side. When they neared one particular house, they were greeted by two or three barking dogs but right at that very moment a woman came out of the house and the barking stopped. She said something in her local hill dialect but Sharma ji could not make any sense of it. A moment later a grownup man also came out of the house and Sharma ji started talking to him. That man could, with considerable effort, follow Sharma ji's chaste Hindi. And when Sharma ji mentioned about the beda family, he pointed him down the pathway. Sharma ji and his companions followed the path.

When he had gone some distance, he saw a two-storeyed house. Following the pathway, he walked ahead and found himself in the courtyard of a house.

An old man was sitting there puffing at his hookah. He was dressed in a gray woollen kurta-pyjama and a red round cap on his head in the style of the local hill populace. To his right two kittens were playing with each other under a kilta basket. A lamb would come running from the house, knock the kilta with its head, under which the kittens played, and run back inside. When the kilta tumbled towards the old man he would push it back. In a basket before him, there lay fawn coloured wads of wool which the old man   span on his spindle in between his puffs. Sharma ji's eyes followed the spinning movement of the old man's spindle for some time. There was a scythe lying close by. Then his eyes fell on the old man's ears, the big circular earrings dangling from them astonished Sharma ji.

Before Sharma ji could say anything, another man came out of the house. He appeared to be in his mid-forties. Seeing strangers in the courtyard, he stopped dead. Sharma ji lost no time in introducing himself. On hearing the name of their village, the old man coughed loudly and continued coughing for some time. When the coughing stopped, he quickly set the kilta right and pushed the kittens inside. Sounds coming from inside the house indicated things being set right there too. The spindle dropped from the old man's hand and he grabbed the scythe lying nearby with his right hand. He bent his neck slightly and had a thorough look at the newcomers. Blood appeared to float in his eyes as his contempt rose higher and higher. He trembled with anger. Sharma ji surveyed his face but couldn't dare to look into his eyes. He felt as if the old man would throw his hookah and chillum at him or attack them with his daraat. The old man took several quick puffs at his hookah. Sharma ji felt as if he were trapped in its gurgling sound.

Sharma ji mentioned the Bhunda very cautiously and the old man stood up panting. He appeared to be possessed by some supernatural power. The moment he tried to strike Sharma ji with his daraat, the man who had come out of the house caught hold of his hand. He somehow managed to control him and dragged him inside. Even then the old man looked back at Sharma ji with his neck bent. The ground beneath Sharma ji and his companions' feet seemed to have slipped and they quickly moved from the front of the house to the back of it.

Inside, the two men were talking and their raised voices entered Sharma ji's ears like boiling oil. He was in a mental fix and not able to decide whether to stay put or to go back. Sharma ji had never imagined the helplessness in which he found himself that day. All his grand plans for holding the Bhunda seemed to be vanishing in thin air. The thought came to him that they should leave the place at once. But the layers of selfishness in his mind were so deep that his feet automatically began to move back to the yard.

The younger man came out and shouted at them, "Go away from here, all of you. Do you think we do not know how our ancestors had been thrown out from the village, insulted and disgraced? Should we go there to go through the same humiliation all over again? How could you think so? We are no fools. Rest assured if it had happened today, we would have given you a fitting reply."

For a moment, Sharma ji was stunned and stricken with fear but when he noticed that the man was unarmed, he went near him. His interest was at stake; he folded his hands, "Look, brother, we had no role in whatever happened to you. I am prepared to seek your forgiveness for that. In fact, we came here precisely for this purpose and we are prepared for any punishment you choose. We are willing to take on our heads all the shame of our ancestors' actions. And not just we who are standing at your door-step, but the entire village is ashamed of that incident. We want that you perform the ceremony and share with us the merit that would accrue from it." "But your ancestors treated us shabbily and destroyed whatever we had. With what face have you come here today? Grandfather is unwell, you should thank God for it, otherwise, you cannot imagine what he would have done to you." Having said this, he held his head with both hands as if some terrible calamity had been prevented.

Sharma ji stepped forward and held that man's hands in his own intimately. He said very softly and politely, "Brother, do not think that we have come here on our own. The devta's will has brought us here. Who are we, of what worth? It's all the wish of the devta. We can only plead before you with folded hands. We are prepared to fall at your grandfather's feet."

Sharma ji found truth in the saying that if it suits your interest you should not hesitate even to call an ass your uncle.

At the mention of the devta the man relented a little but did not say anything. He withdrew inside the house. At the door a boy handed him a container of water, which he poured down his throat in one go. Sharma ji was at his wit's end. He thought that all his plans had gone waste. Inside the house, the old man cursed loudly in his own tongue. When at last the man came out, he brought three plastic chairs with him. When Sharma ji saw this, he regained his composure. The man practically threw the chairs down in the courtyard.

By now many men and women had gathered in the yard. All of them were amazed to see these brahmins pleading and bowing before outcastes like them.

The tense and suffocating atmosphere relaxed a little. All three brahmins sat down in the chairs. They were silent. Then the man lifted the kilta and the two kittens ran out. Setting aside the wool basket and the hookah, the man introduced himself to the newcomers: "I am Sahaj Ram, Sahju for my family. That old man is my father, now above hundred years."

"Above hundred years...?"

Sharma ji and his two companions were amazed. Above hundred years! But the old man didn't look his years.

The way Sahaj Ram spoke clearly suggested that he was not illiterate. Sharma ji did not want to prolong the matter. He came straight to the point and once again expressed regrets over the old unfortunate incident. He even apologised on behalf of the village and the deity. Sahju thought about the whole thing for a few moments, then went inside the house again. The persons standing in the yard also went inside. For a long time, they whispered among themselves. When at last they came out, Sahju agreed to participate in the Bhunda. Sharma ji and his companions stood up with folded hands. They thanked them and slipped away. Although their faces shone with satisfaction but the wounds on their minds were so deep that no one spoke till they reached the road.

It was quite late in the evening when Sharma ji and his companions reached the village. When in the morning Sharma ji told the members of the temple committee about having found the beda, they were overjoyed. Talk of the Bhunda festival entered every home of the village. Preparations for the festival started in full swing. It was clear that the people of the village were brimming with optimism for regaining their long-lost opportunity of earning merit. They almost forgot their daily chores of looking after their crops and cattle.

People also began to talk about the Bhunda festival. First of all, a meeting of the entire village was called, which was held in the compound of the village temple. There is a platform about a metre high at the main gate of the compound. The village panchayat members and the temple committee have their meetings here. There are special stone seats on the platform for the panchayat and temple committee members. Sharma ji was head of the panchayat and had his seat in the centre. The temple committee and other panchayat members sat in a semicircle around Sharma ji. The rest of the villagers sat lower around the platform. The temple priests finalised the auspicious hour and date of the festival after long consultations with the devta's oracle. Sahju was appointed unanimously as the 'beda' for the festival.

When Sharma ji informed Sahju about the auspicious hour and date of the festival the latter put forward two conditions: one, that the rope would be of the same length as the one made by his ancestor in the last Bhunda; and second, that no safety net would be spread below the rope. The second condition struck Sharma ji like a rod. He did not think it proper to say anything on the spot but it was certainly a worry. Suppose, there was no net and the same mishap happened again, all his plans would come to nought, he thought. He found no solution even after pondering over it for long. He then left everything to the grace of the devta. There was no alternative but to accept the beda's conditions.

Now the whole village became busy with preparations for Bhunda. The temple committee members entrusted the village people with many tasks and responsibilities associated with the ceremony. Apart from this, each family was asked to donate five hundred rupees in cash and one maund of grains to meet the various expenses of the festival. The people agreed to the set contribution and began to sweep and clean their houses. Each family relieved one member to help the temple committee with the arrangements. Roads and pathways leading to the village began to be repaired and readied. Some collected big vessels and utensils, others brought leaves from the jungle and made plates with them, still others collected donations from door to door. A truckload of things was brought from the town almost every day and people carried the material to the temple together.

When the news of the Bhunda ceremony spread abroad the district administration also took notice. Even though formal invitations had not yet been sent by the temple committee, government officers and officials began to come there. Apart from them, people from the police department and cronies of the local MLA also began to visit the village. Sharma ji was at the centre of this whole hullabaloo. His views were sought in every matter and everything was being done in his supervision. Dreams of a bright future filled his eyes. The sluggishness that had set in after a few days of his retirement was driven away by the glow on his face. He began to feel young and energetic as if he had just taken over as a tehsildar.

As per the programme, a few chosen people went to fetch Sahju from his village. He was brought to their village with great fanfare. He was accompanied by his wife and child. The Bhunda ceremony was to take place six months from the day Sahju arrived in the village. Sahju beda and his family were lodged in a room in the chief devta's temple. It was a particularly pleasant surprise for them that they now lived inside the mukhya devta's temple whose compound was still out of bounds for dalits.

The rope grew longer with every passing day. When the spinning finally ended, Sahju and his wife looked at the rope intently, as if it was not the rope which had been completed, but his own life which had now run its full length. Both were in deep pain and anguish because Sahju was preparing the means of his own death. But there was also in both of them the sense of joy and contentment of a dalit becoming a deity in this ancient tradition of Bhunda. This sense of joy was enough to overpower the fear of death. But perhaps the most overwhelming source of joy was the applause and respect they were experiencing after long years of exile and ostracism. The unforgettable joy of sitting to eat in the line of brahmins and enjoying the proximity of the deity, even temporarily, could not be overlooked.

When the temple committee members were informed that the rope was ready, they uncovered the hawan-kund for the sacrificial fire, which had been dug out at a consecrated spot and kept covered. The ceremony of bringing fire was to be performed according to the injunctions of the sacred scriptures. The fire must be brought from the hearth of a Kraushtu brahmin of the lineage of Sri Krishna. Shastri ji's family was the only one which belonged to this gotra. A few members of the temple committee, along with some goldsmiths, went to his house at midnight in a procession. They carried with them a brass plate and a ram. After performing many rituals, the twigs of a deodar tree were used to light a fire on the brass plate. The plate was placed on the head of the ram, which was then brought to the sacred spot in the temple compound.

The poor ram! Surrounded by drums, kettledrums and other traditional instruments it became the fire carrier for a time! Everyone was in attendance of the ram. Perhaps at that moment the ram, like Sahju, had felt more honoured than the brahmins. As soon as the procession reached the hawan-kund, the plate was taken off the ram's head and placed in it. Then the ram was swiftly sacrificed.

The fire was lit. An image of Yagyeshwari Devi was made on the hawan-kund. Its consecration happened with the slaughter of the ram ... Now this fire offering would continue till the last day of Bhunda.

The idol of the mukhya devta was to be taken out from the sanctum as the main part of the rituals. This idol of the chief deity was usually kept in a cave-like portion of the temple and it was brought out only on special occasions like the Bhunda. With it were brought out many small idols and their belongings. On normal days a small replica of the mukhya devta was kept in the lower floor of the temple for daily worship, other rituals and processions. People knew that the doors of the temple had been locked after the last Bhunda. Naturally, people were more than eager to have a glimpse of the chief deity. Everybody was not permitted to remove the devta's idol from the sanctum. Tradition said that this could be done by a brahmin of the village with three persons of the goldsmith community. All the three were tonsured and panchratna, small pieces of five gems, were placed in their mouths. A shroud was wrapped round them in the name of a dress. They entered the sanctum in the dark and they brought out the idol and whatever accessories they could find in the darkness.

The moment the chief priest had a glimpse of the devta's idol, he was taken aback. The idol was made of a cheap metal made to look like the original. Only the chief priest could guess the metal of which the idol was made; nobody else had any inkling about it. People, over-taken by faith and frenzy, hailed the deity with gusto .... The actual idol had been stolen from the temple some years ago. The stolen idol was made of precious metal and a diamond was embedded in its forehead. When exposed to the sun, the idol would emit a liquid as if it was sweating and the drops would collect in a small saucer placed at its feet. The drops were considered sacred as the wash of the devta's feet and people would scramble to receive just a drop of it. The idol was said to be worth crores of rupees but nobody realised that the idol now present before them was a fake.

The chief priest stood transfixed. He sent the brahmin and the goldsmiths back into the temple but they returned empty-handed. The chief priest immediately went into a trance as if the spirit of the devta had entered into him. His condition was worth watching. His whole body trembled; his face had turned black and frightening. His eyes were blood-shot. The members of the village panchayat had never seen such fury. This foretold a calamity. But, the saying that God resides in the mouths of the panchs began to come true. All the panchs, members of the temple committee and those present there, prayed with folded hands that somehow, by the grace of the devta, the ceremony could be completed without any obstacle. Later, whatever the deity wished would be complied with. It took a long time before the deity's divine power left the chief priest. When normalcy returned, the chief priest spoke only to Sharma ji, the head of the panchs. When Sharma ji heard what had happened, he was deeply perturbed. But both of them decided to keep this secret to themselves. If the secret became public, the momentous occasion would be ruined.

On the day of the festival, people came out of the temple compound with the usual fanfare of music and dance. They went around to all big and small temples. Each one of them lighted a sacred earthen lamp there and ceremonially invited all the major and minor devtas to the festival. Deities from other places were also invited whose processions began to arrive one after another.

Next day, all the devtas were assembled at one place. Sacred pitchers were placed in a circular formation. In the middle was the sacred pitcher of the chief goddess of the village. Now the Kraushtu brahmins began chanting sacred verses from the scriptures. The chief priest had an old handwritten parchment from which he was reading the verses addressed to various gods and goddesses. On the second floor of the temple, someone had drawn the portrait of a devadar tree with vermilion and the sacred pitchers were now placed near the portrait.

The third day was devoted to the water process, the day of worshipping Varun. The village women, dressed in their traditional apparels, arrived in the temple compound early in the morning. Their procession started from the place where Sahju and his family had been lodged. All of them bowed to him with reverence. It was a pleasant surprise for Sahju's wife. She knew that even an eighty-year-old woman of her caste had to bow before a ten-year-old brahmin girl. But today this was reversed. Sometimes she would laugh secretly at this reversal but as soon as she glanced at the rope, she trembled with fear. She imagined that a messenger of death had taken the form of the rope and he could swallow up her husband any moment. Sometimes, she imagined that the rope was actually a pack of wolves waiting to pounce upon and eat up her husband.

When she looked at the multicoloured clothes of the women, she was temporarily transported into a spectacle of colours. While she was thus alternating between fear and joy, the procession of brahmins came out from the temple accompanied by the music of many instruments. It was a procession of priests, temple committee members, temple helpers and dancers. There were also nine brahmin girls decked in colourful clothes and ornaments. They were carrying red pitchers on their heads. The procession trudged to the eastern side towards a well. On reaching there the pitchers were filled with fresh water. Ceremonies were performed then the pitchers were placed on the girls' heads again and the procession moved back to from where it had started.

A day before the Bhunda the temple and the village had to be secured from evil spirits so that the main ceremony would pass off smoothly without any obstacle. All the priests together performed all the necessary rituals for this purpose. Each priest stood half-clad before his devta with a special vessel in his hands. They took some time to finish the rituals and chanting of sacred verses. Now the divine energy entered into them. The various musical instruments were played to please the deities. Then the people lifted the chief priest of the mukhya devta on their shoulders. The chief priest was instructing the performance of the various rituals. Other priests and people began to follow the procession. The procession went around the village. There were many in the procession who fired shots in sheer joy. At many places, goats were sacrificed and the pathway was practically drenched in blood. After the circumambulation of the village, the procession once again reached the temple compound and the fire sacrifice started. This hawan was a tantric ritual. The priest went to the roof of the temple and moved around in all the four directions. A goat was sacrificed in every direction. When the priest came down, the priests of other deities came back to their own normal selves.

This ceremony was known as 'Shikhapher', Sahju explained to his wife. It means that all the evil spirits have been driven out and they could no longer create any obstructions in the Bhunda. His wife hardly listened to Sahju explaining the intricacies of the ceremony. She only watched her husband's face. Many questions were swirling in her mind to which she wanted to seek explanations from him . She wanted to ask why he would not be allowed to remain a brahmin after the Bhunda. Why do they have to revert to their old untouchable status? Why is it that an untouchable is worshipped as a brahmin only for the duration of the ceremonies? And suppose an accident happened and her husband died, then which of the devtas, in whose honour numerous goats and lambs have been slaughtered, would bring him back to life? There were many more such questions which she wanted to ask but she managed to suppress them somehow and sat there speechless. She was trembling secretly as if all the evil spirits, ritually exorcised just then, had taken residence in her mind.

Sahju guessed what was going on in his wife's mind, but he had no answers to her questions. He only felt a huge load weighing on his mind. This was probably the burden of such unanswerable questions. And there was no one around to answer them. No member of the temple committee, no priest, not even the devta could answer the questions. The rituals being performed before his very eyes appeared to be empty and meaningless.

Sahju and his wife could not sleep that night nor did they talk to each other. Each was entangled in his or her questions. There was fear in Sahju's mind but his joy was no less. His mind went back again and again to his ancestors. God knows in which places they would have been established as manes. For Sahju, becoming the beda in Bhunda after such a long gap was a way of regaining the long-lost honour of his dead ancestors.

Morning came. It was the last and most important day of Bhunda and also the last day of Sahju's brahminhood.

The couple rose early in the morning. The rope was worshipped at the hour determined by the astrologers. Sahju handed the rope to the rajputs of the Khash caste. They lifted the bundled rope carefully and put it on their shoulders so that no part of it touched the ground. They took the bundle to the well where it was given several ritual baths. Then they again lifted it to their shoulders as before. The rope's weight had doubled. It was not easy to carry such a heavy bundle of the rope to the temple compound but they did it quite effortlessly. A huge pole was fixed there and one end of the rope was tied tightly to it. The hillock where the pole was fixed was very high. It was really frightening to look below from the pole. Now the other end of the rope was thrown down to the foot of a lower hillock where also a pole was fixed and people standing there grabbed it in their hands and tied it to the pole. Sahju's condition of not having the protective net had been accepted. However, to avert an accident a large number of policemen, home-guards and village people were standing there, alert and ready for any eventuality.

As beda, Sahju was given a new ritual bath on behalf of the mukhya devta and after the investiture ceremony with the sacred thread he was now a full-fledged brahmin. He was dressed in a long flowing kurta with a pagadi on his head. Now he was worshipped ritually as befitted a devta. For the duration of the ceremony he was no longer a human being but the incarnation of the deity. The hour had come for the main ceremony. One person went inside his chamber and came out carrying Sahju on his back.

Sahju's wife had now to part from her husband. The moment of parting was heartrending. She had been provided with new clothes on behalf of the temple which were snow-white, like the clothes of a widow. She was quite unwilling to put on the widow's clothes but she had to give in to the tradition of the ritual. She was surrounded by many village women and in no position to refuse or protest. From a married woman she had to become a widow and it was a really painful moment. She watched helplessly as one by one the various markers of her wedded state were removed. The women undid her hair and removed the bangles from her wrists. She felt as if she were being sawed alive. When it was all over, she took her child and began to walk with the procession to the spot where the rope had been suspended from the pole on the top of the hillock. The child was watching the whole spectacle uncomprehendingly. He could not understand why his mother had been denuded of her marriage symbols or why his father was being carried on someone's back.

The priests now began to chant sacred verses for the occasion. The verses were similar to the ones chanted at the sacrifice of a lamb or goat. The musical instruments also played funeral music. The air seemed heavy and a deep sadness prevailed. People all around looked sad and pensive. It seemed as if death had suddenly snatched a loved one from them. While he was being carried to the appointed spot, Sahju was wrapped in a piece of shroud and five gems were placed in his mouth, which signified imminent death.

The Chief Minister had already arrived to add glamour and grace to the ceremony. He was surrounded by the local MLA and a number of district officials. For their convenience a raised platform had been erected on one side of the hillock so that the dignitaries could watch the whole show. Sharma ji had seen to it that nothing went wrong in the welcome of the coveted guests.

In the midst of this, Sharma ji spotted a palanquin. The palanquin was accompanied by some persons. Initially, he couldn't understand what was happening. The palanquin reached them. An old man was sitting inside and puffing at his hookah. Sharma ji didn't take long to recognize him. He was Sahju's father whom he had met in the yard at his visit to Sahju's village. He was accompanied by a number of persons from his village. Sharma ji was stunned. He had never thought that people of Sahju's village too would come to watch the ceremony with so much pomp and pride. Many questions flashed before his eyes but he couldn't think of any answers. He could only watch things unfolding themselves now. Sharma ji went to receive the old man with some members of the temple committee, and with a fake smile of welcome he took the party to the spot and seated them near the platform where the Chief Minister was sitting. Neither Sharma ji nor the village people could reconcile to the fact that a dalit had arrived with such fanfare. They thought that the privilege of travelling in a palanquin was only their birthright. Sharma ji quickly went away from there and stood near the pole where Sahju was to slide down the rope of the Bhunda.

Sahju's fear-stricken wife was sitting on the ground where Sahju had to land after sliding down the rope. She prayed quietly to all the gods and goddesses for her husband's safety. She knew that it was these gods and goddesses who last evening had ordered the evil spirits to leave the village. She was shaking within and could not feel at ease. Sometimes she felt that she should burn the clothes she had been forced to wear and go to her husband and persuade him that he should kick away the whole paraphernalia and refuse to become a god. We are quite okay the way we are. We're happy in our small family without this temporary honour and esteem. God forbid, but if the rope cracks and breaks! She almost collapsed when this thought occurred to her. Had the women standing beside her not come to her rescue, her head would have struck against the nearby rock. Sharma ji became nervous when he saw her condition. He began to sprinkle water on her. She regained consciousness after a few minutes and Sharma ji was relieved. A happily married woman was undergoing the agony of being a widow even though her husband was alive and present.

When Sahju reached near the pole, his eyes travelled across the frightening gorge down to where his wife was sitting near the pole to which the last end of the rope was tied. In his bones he could feel all those fears and miseries which his 'widowed' wife was going through. Tears filled his eyes. A sharp pain shot inside and pierced his whole being like a knife. It became unbearable. For the fraction of a second, the feeling came over Sahju that his breath would stop before he sat on the grass-seat fitted to the rope. Somehow, he gathered himself and became aware of the countless eyes in the crowd watching him. These eyes seemed to plead with him with a kind of greed in them. There were prayers for his safety but the prayers were accompanied by selfishness. The prayers were for themselves. Those eyes wished that he remains alive so that their selfishness could be satisfied, their families remain healthy and happy, their lands and crops undamaged, their cattle unharmed, no evil shadow should ever cast its malevolent eyes on them and their children. All eyes were fixed on Sahju who was to slide down the rope. Nobody could guess what his wife was going through, nobody bothered to console her. It was a great event for fulfilling the personal wishes and self-interests of a whole mass of people.

For a moment Sahju was also overwhelmed by the feeling that he was at that time the greatest and most honourable person. Not merely the upper caste brahmins and rajputs but gods themselves were bowing to him and begging for spiritual merit.

Sharma ji considered himself the most respected and busy person in the world today. Everybody seemed to be talking only about him. He was standing right by the side of Sahju's wife. He joined in the prayers and aspirations of the crowd but his motives were different from the others. He prayed for the cleansing of the village from the old stigma attached to it and for his own name and fame which would help him to enter the public life in future. Other thoughts were also crowding his mind. He wanted that as soon as the beda touched the ground safe and unharmed he should be the first to lift and take him to his kitchen so that any evil shadows which might still be present in his house might be exorcised and driven out forever. He wanted his family to be the first to receive the beda's blessings. He knew that today the beda is God himself and his entering Sharma ji's house would be absolutely auspicious. He did not want to let go of this opportunity to earn merit. The other upper caste people of the village also harboured similar desires.

Sahju offered prayers to God, respectfully evoked his family deity and bowed to his father. He remembered that ancestor who years ago had fallen from the rope into the jaws of death. Then he shook the rope slightly, lifted the grass-saddle and fitted it to the rope. The rope and the saddle had been prepared by Sahju himself. Two bags of sand were tied to either side of the saddle to maintain the balance. For Sahju it was the horse which he had to ride to travel the long distance to the mouth of death. This was necessary to wash off the stigma from the village and also to partake of the merit thus accruing. But not as an untouchable but as a brahmin and divine spirit. Many kinds of feelings were stirring in his mind. He thought that his 'rare' beda community is also a grass-saddle which has been used by Sharma and other upper caste people for centuries to earn merit and fulfil their self-interests. What will the untouchables gain as compensation? A momentary brahminhood or divinity! He laughed loudly and began sliding down the rope, waving a white piece of cloth. He felt as if he was descending to earth from the skies. Half way down the rope he became nervous, the balance had tilted slightly but he managed to hold on.

Had he fallen from that height, he would have smashed to pieces. The drums of the deities beat furiously and the atmosphere was thoroughly charged. Sahju's wife's heart missed quite a few beats in the commotion.

When Sahju reached the pole at the other end of the rope, he stopped and balanced himself on the rope. He had slid down at great speed and the saddle could not be halted easily. But it was astonishing to see the way he checked his speed and now sat dangling on the rope. Everything came to a standstill for a short time. The heartbeats of the crowd practically stopped. Drums and music stopped and a deep stunning silence spread all around. The fear of something ominous happening gripped Sharma ji's and the crowd's hearts. My God, is it going to be a repeat of the old catastrophe! Sahju was safe but his saddle was stuck. The temple workers, priests, and Sharma ji collected near the pole. Sharma ji cried out suddenly, "Sahju, you've reached your destination. Now get down to the ground."

Others joined Sharma ji in his cry.

But Sahju remained unmoved as if he hadn't heard the shout. Something in him was trying to burst out, break out. He was feeling the hurts and wounds inside him. Sharma ji folded his hands and begged Sahju in a trembling voice to come down. All temple workers and brahmins folded their hands but this had no effect on Sahju. A storm was gathering in his mind. He felt that he was not Sahju but a circus dancer dancing to someone else's tunes and as soon as the show gets over, he will be forgotten and abandoned. Those who are shouting his praise today will tomorrow shy away even from his shadow. All the honour and hospitality being showed him today will soon become a thing of the past. He looked at Sharma ji, the temple priests and all other brahmins in the crowd as a flock of evil monsters and infernal creatures who had taken hold of him and made him a plaything in their hands. What actually belonged to him was only the point of the rope where he sat. This small portion of the rope alone was his honour, his prestige, his sacredness, and all. The moment he touched the ground, all this would vanish, leaving him behind a dalit as ever, empty-handed, hungry and rejected. His anger surfaced. He glanced at the crowd. He saw his father slowly come towards him in his palanquin with upraised hands as if he had been finally rewarded fully. He saw in his father's eyes the sparkle of his victory but also read the script of pain and humiliation behind it.

Now Sahju's eyes turned towards the dalits standing in one corner of the ground. The maximum voices of exaltation were coming from that direction. Their hearts were clean and unblemished. Their voices were untainted by any selfishness. Their clothes were tattered. There were women whose breasts showed through their torn and ragged kurtas. Their hair was uncombed. Instead of coloured ribbons, there were pieces of grass and dried leaves entangled in their hair. Their children were also with them who had naked legs and bodies or were dressed only in tattered shirts. There were blisters on their feet and unfathomable pain in their eyes. Sahju felt ashamed of his forced brahminhood.

Voices echoed in his ears once again, "Well done, Sahju, well done. Come down. You are the most precious deity of Bhunda today.

Sahju burst out laughing, "What deity? Which deity? I am an untouchable, merely a plaything. All the merit is for you. What frauds you upper caste people perpetrate! Do you know, Sharma ji, I am the greatest pandit at this moment, the most precious deity, everybody's object of reverence. But as soon as I come down, I will be the same old untouchable and you will all become upper caste brahmins and thakurs again. The priests and brahmins who today are standing before me with folded hands and beseeching eyes will tomorrow run away from my shadow for fear of being polluted!"

Sharma ji was stunned and speechless. He could never imagine that such wild thoughts would enter into Sahju's mind on a sacred day like this when he was the object of reverence of the whole area. His words cut through his heart like a knife and he wanted to overcome this situation quickly. He regained his composure and pleaded with Sahju, "No, Sahju, don't think such things. How could such a grand occasion have happened without you? You are everything to us today."

Sahju roared with laughter again, "But only today, Sharma ji. What about tomorrow?"

Sharma ji couldn't think of anything. His mind had gone numb but he did not take long to steady his thoughts. He came straight to the point, "Don't say such things, Sahju, for God's sake. Now tell me what you want. You touch anything today and it will be yours."

"Take your time and think again, Sharma ji, before you commit yourself."

"Sahju, there can be no two opinions about what I've said. On this day you are our God. Just say it, please."

"Then return our lands, Sharma ji. We want to settle here, in this very village from where your ancestors had chased us away."

This was an unexpected blow. Sharma ji wasn't prepared for it. He felt as if he was going to faint. A passing thought came to him that he should teach an appropriate lesson to this low-caste scum of the earth right now and tell him how he should talk to his superiors. But the occasion demanded that he swallow this bitterness. He was sweating and wiped the sweat drops off his forehead repeatedly. That Sahju would turn the tables on him and that too on an occasion like this, had never occurred to him even in his wildest imagination. But today this beda can say and do anything without any let or hindrance. He could ask for anything. Sharma ji turned to the temple committee members and the priest as if seeking their advice. They all agreed that nothing could be refused to Sahju today. Sharma ji had to say yes and he said it. Sahju knew that any gift, whether in cash or kind, given to him today could not be taken back. He gently pushed the grass-saddle on the rope and slid down to the ground. The crowd burst out with joy and gave shouts of jubilation. Sacred music was sounded all around and it filled the air. The atmosphere was now charged with devotion and holiness.

The people gathered there to witness the Bhunda thanked their family deities for the opportunity of earning spiritual merit in such full measure but Sharma ji, the priests and other upper-caste people of the village felt cheated and insulted. They had never wanted that dalit families should again come and settle in the upper-caste village. But now Sahju had been given back the lands and other properties on the occasion of the Bhunda and the gods were witness to it. They knew that they could not turn away from their promise as that would invite calamity to the whole village but despite this fact, they could not reconcile to the situation of bending before the dalits. Their dream of inviting Sahju to their homes had now fallen flat. They seemed to have been bitten by a poisonous snake.

The celebration was at its peak. Joy overflowed everywhere but Sharma ji, oblivious of the bustle around him was fighting the numbness that had overtaken his body and soul. People were streaming towards him, congratulating him for reviving the long-discontinued festival but he was lost in his own dark dreams. His condition was strange. He had lost his poise and control. He welcomed visitors with a faint smile and behaved crazily when alone. He broke into a song without any reason. He felt as if people were celebrating his defeat and public disgrace. He behaved like an abnormal person as if the evil spirits exorcised by the priests and the beda had converged on him and were dancing before him in a frenzy. The priest, the temple committee members and the people of the village became worried. They all surrounded Sharma ji.

At that very moment, the Chief Minister and the MLA came to meet him. They congratulated Sharma ji and patted him on the back. The CM said, "Bhai Sharma ji, now we understand your charisma. Only you could have organised such a huge function. You have killed two birds with one stone. You have removed a big obstacle from our path. What was the name of the beda, by the way? Oh, yes, Sahju, right Vidhayak ji? He created a miracle to be sure because we were hard put to finding a dalit candidate for the coming parliament elections. Wah, Sharma ji, you have proved to be the miracle man for us, really."

Having said this much, the Chief Minister and the MLA left, but Sharma ji looked frozen and dumb and did not even acknowledge the CM's thanks and congratulations. All the blood in his body seemed to have dried up. He felt as if he had received a severe blow on his cheeks. Whatever hope there had still remained was now completely wiped away by the Chief Minister's words.

People lifted Sahju on their shoulders. He, his wife, and other members of his family now began to collect the gifts of money, ornaments, and clothes offered with gratitude and reverence by the inhabitants of the village.

Translated by R. K. Shukla

M.COM

EM DOT COM

Ma did no work this morning. She neither lit the hearth nor mixed wheat flour and pounded corn in water to make cow feed. She did not pour buttermilk into the cat's bowl nor put water in the birdbath hanging from the tree in the aangan. She simply picked up the torchlight and lit her biri as she stepped out of the house. Ma never forgets to take along her sickle. She locked the door and went over to the cattleshed.

Morning times are very busy for Ma. The moment she wakes, birds begin to chirp in the aangan. The cat becomes excited for milk and buttermilk. The cattle moo in the shed and Ma talks with them from the kitchen. But nothing of this sort happened today. The train of silence began from the threshold itself. Nowadays, Ma listens to the new bhajan album 'Kabir Amritvani' on the tape recorder, but it too was silent today. The cat did not trouble Ma either and crouched quietly in the corner. There wasn't a single bird in the aangan. They all sat in a hush round the birdbath.

***

Ma felt a chill as she opened the door of the shed. It seemed as if there were nothing but darkness inside. She looked around in the beam of the torchlight. The animals stood gloomy and quiet. Their eyes were wet. When Ma turned the light on the dead buffalo lying in the corner, her heart heaved into her mouth. It had died in labour. Tears welled up in her eyes. She wiped them with the corner of her dupatta and closed the door.

She looked towards the east from her aangan. Pale light was only just beginning to infuse the dawn. Mornings come later in winter anyway. Ma guessed that it would be about seven o'clock. She didn't feel the need for the torchlight now and placed it on the empty space above the door.

The news of the buffalo's death had not reached the village or the women would have come by now to mourn its passing. Ma had not told anyone. Had she so wanted, she could have asked a village boy to go and hail the leatherworker but at this time she thought it best to go herself. She

knew that if she sent anyone else, the chamar would curse her amply in his
heart, though he may not say anything aloud to the messenger. Times have
changed. There's hardly any courtesy or sense of right or wrong left in the
village. Whatever little civility still exists is merely to keep up
appearances. The boys of the new generation are rude to your face. They
have no respect for elders. How many old people are left anyhow? Ma
looked at her own home ... for so many years she has run her household all
alone. It is a large setup. Untilled land does not look good. Moreover, the
kinsfolk in the village would pass judgement if she left it barren. Even
though she only manages to cultivate the land through buari, the practice
of villagers working by turn in each other's fields, but no one could point a
finger at her for not looking after her land. She also has enough cattleheads
in the shed. No one could say that this widow's household was going to
ruin.

      She has two sons. She gave them both good schooling. Then they left
the village to work in far-off places. They married there and have children.
The daughters-in-law are not interested at all in the village or the
homestead. In any case, what would they do in the village? They find the
smell of mud and dung offensive. Her sons do come around once in a
while to look her up. And they have provided Ma with all amenities.
Telephone. Colour television. Gas stove. Milk churner. Tape recorder ....
Wrapped in her thoughts, Ma had reached the bus station. Thankfully, she
had not met anyone on the way, or they would have asked her where she
was off to so early in the morning. The bus was already idling, ready to
depart, but Ma paid no attention to it. She was astonished to see how much
change had come over the place in such a short time. Ma remembers that
there used to be a big pond at the spot where the bus station stands now.
Ma and all the people of the village used to bring their cattle to water here
after grazing. Schoolchildren sat around it washing their wooden writing-
boards. Bits of fuller's clay with which they plastered the boards lay
scattered about. Inkpots and pens were strewn here and there. Forgotten
books and notebooks could be seen. Pens with blue ink were half-buried in
the mud. Anyone who did not know where the village school was situated
could have easily guessed that it was close by. Up ahead, there was a stone
wall on the west bank of the pond. On it grew small five-leaved chaste
trees. Among these bana trees was a niche in which stone images of the
manes were ensconced. How many times Ma had come to pray there and
had moulded and installed figures of her forefathers. But today, all that has
vanished. It seems that time has swallowed each and everything.

      Now there's a biggish ground here with tread marks of innumerable
tyres. There's neither water nor the merry bustle of children. No animal

wanders over anymore. The many truckloads of sand, grit, iron rods, and cement have reduced it to a heap of dust.

Ma passed by the bus at first but then she stopped short. The way to Parsa chamar's house could also be reached via the road. She thought to herself ... what will people say ... won't they say that she is foolish to walk when the bus was available right there .... Or, that her sons did not give her money. Moreover, she would save time if she took the bus. Till the dead buffalo is removed from the shed, Ma cannot eat nor feed the animals. The sooner the chamar takes care of the buffalo's carcass the better. At this thought Ma turned back towards the bus. Then paused and rummaged in the pocket of her kurta. She found a few coins in there and came and sat on the bus.

The bus moved in a few minutes and soon arrived at the place where Ma had to alight. She walked down the fields and saw the chamar's house. She thought of hailing him from where she was ... but not sure whether someone would hear her or not, she climbed further down. Many years ago, when Ma's ox had died then too Ma had herself come here to call Parsa. Ma cannot remember when Parsa chamar had last come to her house to collect his chhamahi, his once-in-six-months cropshare in lieu of his services through the year. When her husband was alive, Parsa would come around at least once a month with mended or handmade shoes for Ma and Pa. He would stay over and they would chat about all kinds of things late into the night. But now it has been years since Ma had shoes made. There was no need. It's the age of plastic. Shoes can be bought cheaply for twenty or thirty rupees. Simple. These mechanical times have created distances between people. Ma had now reached Parsa's aangan. She was surprised to see his house. It used to be a mud house. The walls were made of packed mud and rough clay shingles covered the roof. The stink of raw hide permeated the fields and the barn. But today there was nothing of the sort. Had she come to the wrong house? As she stood there wondering, a little girl came out of the house. She hesitated on seeing Ma standing there. Ma asked, "Munni! Is this Parsa's house?"

The girl did not reply but darted shyly back inside.

A while later, an old man craned his neck to peer out from the door. The hump on his back was visible under his rough woollen shawl. His deeply wrinkled face appeared like a parched field that had been ploughed. He recognised Ma as soon as he saw her, "Arey bhabhi, is it you?"

He greeted her with warmth and respect. Ma was calmed. Her heart melted.

They promptly asked about each other's wellbeing from where they stood, then Parsa said, "Come on in, it's very cold today. We don't get the sun before twelve o'clock."

He turned inwards but Ma stopped him, "I won't sit Parsa. My buffalo has died in labour. It was her first calving." Ma's voice choked. Her eyes welled over. Parsa stood still for a moment. Then he went in. Ma was reassured that now Parsa would fetch his knife and basket and go with her. When he returned, however, he had a low wooden stool and a mud-plastered brazier in his hands. He gave Ma the patara to sit on and placed the angithi before her. He also sat down close by. He took out a packet of biri from his pocket and gave one to Ma. He lit his biri with the fires of the angithi. Ma lit hers likewise. Taking deep puffs, they sat smoking together. Ma broke the silence, "Did you also not come to the village in all these years?"

"I can't walk much now, bhabhi. Climbing up the slope makes me out of breath. And now even my legs are giving up."

"But you didn't even come at harvest time. I alone owe you your share of so many chhamahis."

Parsa drew a deep breath. He coughed. Pain covered his face.

"Let bygones be, bhabhi. You may have held on to this courtesy but others treat me with contempt. Everyone is not like you. It is a village of high caste brahmins and yeomen kanaits ... I went there many years ago. At the time of your husband's death. I thought I'd also collect my chhamahi while I was there, but the brahmins refused outright. They said, 'Parsa, who gets shoes made or mended these days. One can buy them in shops now.' As you know bhabhi, you are valued only till you're needed. Otherwise, no one cares whether you live or die!"

Parsa adjusted the fire as he said this. Ma's restlessness grew. She only wanted Parsa to finish what he was saying and then go with her. But he went on, "In the old days, there were no shops. No roads. At that time Parsa mattered. No wedding took place without me. I carried the trunk filled with things required for the ceremonies and it was I who provided the leaf-plates. And shoes, of course, were mine. Now people don't need carriers or shoemakers. Times have changed bhabhi".

His face was suffused with resentful annoyance. Ma watched him silently. She wanted to ask him who disposed of the brahmins and kanaits' dead animals now but could not bring herself to do so. She was about to request him once again to accompany her but Parsa continued, "Forgive me bhabhi, you are one of us. If it were a brahmin or kanait, I wouldn't have allowed them to so much as stand in my aangan ... Now no one in my house makes shoes or disposes of dead cattle. My children don't want any one of us to continue doing this work. The elder son has become an officer in Shimla. The younger one has a shop at the bus station. How don't you know this bhabhi? As for myself, I don't go anywhere now."

Ma was confounded and dismayed on hearing this. She remembered that Parsa's stone workstation used to be at one side of the yard. As she glanced towards the end where the thiya should have been, Parsa told her, "See, my things used to be there. I tried to tell my sons to at least let the thiya remain there. But they wouldn't hear of it. They hate our traditional work as much as the brahmins hate us. They broke the thiya and also threw away all the tools. Now they have built a latrine over there."

As he said this, Parsa picked up the angithi and shook it. The embers began to glow. He got up to go inside. Ma had seen that his eyes were wet. Perhaps, he was sad to see his heritage torn down like this. He wiped the corners of his eyes with his shawl.

At the threshold he seemed to remember something and said to her, "Talk to my son, he will help you out."

Ma was a sight to see. She could neither sit there nor go away. Anyone who could have seen her would have been moved to pity. Her eyes travelled again towards the thiya corner. She recollected how in days past, she would go into the house to sit there. So many other people from the village too sat around Parsa. There would be brahmins, kanaits, kolis, chamars–all kinds. There was no caste pollution or untouchability. At that time Parsa was not a chamar but a great craftsman. A skilful master. The little girl came out of the house again and ran to the latrine. She shut the door quickly. The stench of faeces entered Ma's nose. She covered her mouth and nose with her dupatta and walked away. She wondered what to do, where to go. There was only one hope now, that Parsa's son would do something for her.

***

The sun had climbed quite high in the sky. There was no one in the house. The animals must be hungry and thirsty. Ma walked with long strides. She reached the bus station. The shops had opened by now. Ma looked around ... tea shop, provisions store, cloth shop, cigarette-biri stall, and a barber's shop. Her eyes fell on one more shop. There were a couple of small machines in it. Ma didn't know the boy sitting inside. The rest belonged to her area.

As she stood looking at the shop, she heard a voice calling to her respectfully, "Tai, where have you been so early in the morning?" She turned to see Budhram, the barber. He was sweeping his shop. He said again, "Tai! Come sit, have some tea."

Ma did not want to sit but then thought maybe Budhram would persuade Parsa's son to carry away the buffalo. She went in and sat down. She told him the whole story in one breath. Ma's face was very anxious. Budhram smiled slightly when he had heard everything, as if there was no problem at all. He pointed to the shop next door and told her it was Parsa's son's shop. He flung the broom under the bench and went out. Ma followed him. They reached the shop. Parsa's son was called Mahendra. Ma felt a little relieved. She tried to tell him that she had just come from his house, but he paid no attention to her. Budhram gestured to her to sit. Then he told Mahendra that her buffalo had died. Mahendra asked Ma's name and then began to search for something in his computer. Ma stretched upward on her chair to see better. Letters ran across the screen. She subsided when he turned on his revolving chair. He began to tell her, "Mata ji, we do not have your name with us. Nor a list of your animals. Brahmins and kanaits have already registered with us. You can also register."

Ma couldn't comprehend a thing. She looked at Budhram with surprise. He explained to her, "Tai, see here, the names of all the villagers are written here, along with the list of their livestock. Look, here is my name (he pointed it out). Whenever an animal is born or dies, it is entered here for a fee. If your name had been registered then Mahendra would have sent an email in a minute to call a few men from the town; and by evening your buffalo would have been removed from the shed."

Ma's worry grew. She asked in consternation, "But Budhram, how will they dispose of the buffalo?"

"Tai! They will come in their vehicle. Pick up your buffalo from the shed and take it away. They will cut it but not throw it away like our chamars. They will carry the flesh, bones, skin, everything with them. There will be no filth in the fields, no vultures, no rioting dogs."

Ma's head was in a spin. Nonplussed, she got up to leave. Her eyes went from Budhram to Mahendra and then to his machine. She was simply at her wit's end now.

Out on the street, Ma turned to look at the shop again. The name of the shop was blazoned in big bold letters–**m.com**.

Translated by Meenakshi F. Paul

MA READS

MA PADHTI HAI

I have come back to the village after months. Ma lives here alone. The front door of the house has been left open today. On most days Ma is up early and out of the house, the door shut behind her, doing outside chores. Her mornings are spent in the cowshed, feeding and watering the animals, milking the cows, heaping dung.

Even today Ma's not in. I have walked into her room. Its flooded with light from the morning sun. Today I am here with the rays. Intimate as her room seems, it also looks a little forlorn. It's crammed with all sorts of things–in the same way as it gets crammed with the morning light. The wooden ceiling above has cobwebs hanging from it–a few flies caught dead in them. The walls are in similar state–layers of cobwebs and dead insects pressed against them.

Things are scattered everywhere. Nothing is in its right place. On the right side of the door, as you walk in, there is a clay pot for churning milk, covered with a rag. Ma must bring it here after she's done with the churning next to the hearth. To the left is a basket stuffed with unspun sheep wool. A few wads of wool sit on top of its pressed layers. A spindle is lying on the side. Date leaves are strewn in one corner and amongst them lie a few mats made from plaited date leaves. An old, small table, with a TV on top, is placed in another corner. Right next to the pillow is a canister covered with a shabby cloth, on top of which sits the telephone. The electric bulb looks discoloured; it has been completely taken over by insects.

From the wall, above the bed, hangs a strip of wood holding an oil lamp. A long line of soot travels all the way up to the ceiling. Ma probably uses it in the event of a power-cut. The smell of bidi lingers in the air. I look under the cot and find bits and pieces scattered there as well–half smoked bidi butts and burnt matchsticks. There's dried anardana on a date board. A few gooseberries. Some walnuts. Five ripe, unpeeled cobs of corn tied together–the first corn from the harvest, perhaps saved for the deity. Several bundles carrying a variety of dahls … All these things live with Ma, her intimate friends and companions, while I sit amongst them like a stranger. They look at me as if they are trying to place me. I wonder if they are mocking me. Ma … home … courtyard … gate … fields … granary … land … property … they are all mine but how far I have come from them! The sun has drifted beyond the edge of the terrace. The rays have gathered and edged into the courtyard, drawing away the light from the room … I can sense darkness at this hour of the morning. It's much darker within me though, than it is without. I might be in Ma's room, sitting on her bed, soaking in the fragrance of her love, but the sense of living away from home for years keeps that love from reaching me!

I forget that I am carrying a parcel of books in my hands. I have brought these for Ma. To this day I have never given her a single book of mine. Nor have I been able to invite her to any of the book launches. Whenever a new book arrived, I had it launched by the Governor or the Chief Minister of the State, knowing fully well these people had nothing to do with literature. Exactly the way those who shout from platforms slogans about abolishing poverty have nothing to do with the poor. Or those writers, for that matter, whose pages exude the sweet scent of rural life but who have little to do with the dung and earth of the village itself. That is, an apparition, a false display. Or shall we say, it's like setting one's house on fire in order to watch the spectacle?

It is not that I didn't want to invite Ma. Or that her memory wasn't constantly with me. But several fears had lodged themselves in my heart. I felt that the times had changed. How would Ma 'adjust' amongst these big people!

To begin with, even getting her on to a bus is inviting trouble. She'll start feeling sick right away. Will start vomiting. When she finds some relief from that, she'll pull out a bidi and matchbox from her pocket, light it deftly under cover of her shawl and begin to smoke. A few puffs, and she'll start coughing so badly you'd think she was drawing her last breath.

If somehow or other she manages to reach the ceremony she'll be under constant scrutiny from the other guests. Her crumpled clothes, her plastic shoes will draw sneering looks. And the whole time there will be the smell of bidi on her breath. Her hair would be in a mess. Even though she'll keep her head covered with a shawl, strands of gray hair will hang untidily down, blades of grass and dry leaves caught in them. As soon as people find out my 'mother' has come they'll approach her to offer their congratulations. They would want to talk to her. Some may ask her questions. Writers and journalist friends will, of course, seek information. I can't imagine what Ma would say to them. She might utter something quite foolish. And everything will be ruined if she gets a coughing fit in the middle of the conversation. And then if she feels the urge to smoke, she'll promptly light a bidi and start to smoke then and there. When tea and refreshments are served she obviously won't know how to use the cutlery. Everyone's attention will be drawn to her hands. Cutting grass, heaping dung, churning milk, chopping wood, making rotis, her hands will be full of cracks ... and they will smell of cow-dung and mud ... people may not say anything to my face but they are bound to gossip ... this is the mother of the great writer–utterly ill-bred ... and if I somehow get through that, I'd still have to deal with harsh words from my children.

Lost in these thoughts, I lie down on Ma's bed. I feel my childhood returning. As if I am resting in Ma's lap ... She is cradling me to sleep ... it has been years since I felt such love and comfort. My heart says I should lie still ... never to rise.

I marvel at myself that I have a village in my works, the whole gamut of village life, poor people, fields, and granaries. And Ma. Her love ... but I have come a long way from those certitudes ... a long, long way ... Lying on Ma's bed, I start to search for the writer within me ... but he's not to be found. He has many faces. And perhaps those faces are hidden behind a string of masks. To enhance my status in 'elite' society ... to make a name for myself ... to earn kudos from people ... But that achievement, honestly, has no relation to my true self. Unconsciously, my hand reaches for the books lying on the side. The touch conveys me once again to the peak of my success ... So what if I didn't invite Ma ... It's okay. Everything's okay. We are living in the twenty-first century. Why, then, should we go on shouldering the burden of past traditions? Hills and villages, cow-dung and earth, fields and granaries look good on the printed page. In real life they are hell, they are ...? ... And all said and done, I have come here to honour Ma! There are writers these days who have either split from their parents or handed them over to old age homes ... I'll place these books at Ma's feet and seek her blessings ... I will repent. She'll be happy to see what a great man her son's become? He's a writer ... these books appear to bolster my ego ever further.

I am caught up in these thoughts when my hand falls on Ma's pillow. I sense something hard underneath. Still lying on my back, I stretch my right hand to reach under the pillow. I am startled. I sit up and hurriedly push the pillow to one side. It looks like a book. I pull it out and I am stunned by what I see. My eyes sink deeper into its covers. My breathing becomes laboured. As if all the blood in my body has frozen in the veins ... This is *my* book. I quickly pull away the layers of rags next to the pillow and drag out all the books buried beneath ... they are all mine. For a second, I wonder if these are the books from my parcel, accidentally placed here next to Ma's pillow. But my parcel is still with me, untouched. The copies by the pillow are Ma's own.

I take the first book in my hands. I turn the pages. Pressed between them are blades of grass, butterfly wings.

When Ma goes out to cut grass, she must sit there leafing through its pages.

I pick up the second book. It carries the sweet smell of mustard flowers … I flip through and find yellow flowers stuck in places. There's also an occasional sprig of wheat.

When Ma goes to the fields to pick greens, she must sit there and turn its pages.

Now I pick up the third book. It's a novel I wrote. The fragrance of Raat ki Rani starts to fill the room. My eyes drift across the courtyard and I spot the plant. How tall it's grown! Its branches have spread everywhere. My mind wanders to the past. Summer nights, awash with the light of the moon, often saw Ma haul me on to her lap and tell me stories … Flowers from the Raat ki Rani are preserved between the pages.

Ma must sit under its shade and read this book on moonlit nights.

The fourth book is immersed in the smell of buttermilk and flour. The pages carry the impressions of fingers still sticky from dough. In places, the words have become illegible from butter grease.

Ma must look upon it while cooking rotis or churning milk.

The fifth book is now in my hands. Its pages have the whiff of the dark about them, the smell of bidi seeped inside. I observe the pages, turn them over. The words have dissolved and disappeared in places. In between is the residue of ash from a lit bidi. A dead firefly is stuck in one place.

… perhaps Ma holds it in her hands on a moonless night and reads. Perhaps, remembering me, she cries a little and then sits up, late in the night, smoking.

Now I drag the sixth book from under the pillow. I feel restless. Beads of sweat form on my forehead. This book has several pictures of my father too. There's either Ma or myself in them. Ma must share her writer son's success with his father in her memories.

I put this to one side and start searching the pillow again. In the folds of the bed, I find yet another book. I take it out. This is my seventh book. My surprise knows no bounds. This is the new book that was launched only a week ago. Its pages smell of cow-dung. Impressions of dung-stained hands are left here and there. Strands of white sheep wool are stuck in a few places. Ma must sit in the cowshed, amongst the animals, and look at it.

My eyes are streaming. I can't remember having cried as much in my life before. As if my wealth, status and the arrogance inside me were raining down on Ma's bed. Like a wretched bed-bug I feel I am sinking and drowning in its layers. Every pore of my body is filled with shock and shame. My head is falling between my legs. In spite of my abject state, there is some comfort that I can still draw from shedding tears which prevents me from sinking further. It seems as if all the objects in Ma's room are showering their love on me, helping me regain my composure. I steady myself. Surprisingly, my heart feels lighter. Just as in my childhood, crying for some object, I'd drop off to sleep in Ma's lap and wake up without a trace of grief remaining.

Suddenly a voice breaks the silence.

'Dadi! Dadi! ... Newspaper.'

Ma is gathering cow-dung. On hearing the call, she promptly drops the basket and grabs the newspaper from the hands of the postman. I rise from the bed and look out from behind the door. He is Amru postman. His house is not far from our own. He comes to see Ma regularly.

Everything is becoming clearer. Ma is looking at the newspaper. The postman is pointing something to her in its centrefold. Ma carries the newspaper inside, puts it down somewhere in the cowshed, and starts to pile up dung as before.

I assemble the books spread on the bed and place them beside Ma's pillow. With my parcel of books in hand, I walk out. I feel I am carrying a huge burden on my head. I feel my whole being mocking me. Having finished all her outdoor chores Ma is now about to step inside … I quietly step out.

Translated by Ira Raja

SAVARNA DEVTA, DALIT DEVTA

SAVARNA DEVTA, DALIT DEVTA

It was quite late in the night when I returned home. My return was sudden and unexpected and involved a lot of physical discomforts and mental agony. I didn't have any torch or portable light of my own nor did it occur to me to borrow one from one of my neighbours. I was terribly upset and my mind was reeling under a mixture of pain, anger, and fear. After traversing nearly five kilometres of steep hilly track, I managed to reach the level pathway and looking back, it astonished me how I had walked such an altogether new path and a long distance in complete darkness. I touched my shoulders and my hand slipped into the bag slinging from the left shoulder. Over the bag straps lay the shawl and in the bag was my shehnai. I felt reassured because it had just crossed my mind that in the hurry and nervousness I had left the shehnai behind.

It was completely dark where I stood and I looked across the hills over the far away plains where in the houses dim lights could be spotted with extreme difficulty. In fact, it seemed from the distance that the thickening dark was forcing the light to disappear from the surface of the earth. Tired, I looked at the sky. Exactly above my head appeared the Milky Way with its cluster of stars, reminding me of a number of stories my grandmother had told me about it. But these stories didn't stay with me for long and vanished soon as a flash of lightning. It seemed that the darkness within was much deeper and thicker than it was outside. Fear enveloped me and I couldn't see things around me. Many a time when my glance fell on a rock, hedge or cluster of trees, I felt someone was squatting there and watching me or some animal was stealthily slouching to pounce on me. Then the next moment I would feel a terrible figure slowly taking shape in the dark and moving menacingly towards me, a figure without recognizable limbs. Could it be a ghost or a witch or some other creature even more terrible?

I noticed a slight tremor in the nearby hedge. It was certain now that some animal had noticed my presence and out of panic had jumped down. My teeth jammed and I couldn't open my mouth when I tried. My tongue too seemed to have congealed somewhere in the cavity of my mouth. My limbs went numb as if a whole pitcher of freezing water had been poured on me. Then a strange, strong smell assaulted my nostrils and I suddenly remembered what my father had once told me: if someone walked alone along a path in the dark, then a lion would give him invisible company and one should not panic. He himself had had many such experiences, he told me. But the very thought of a lion walking along with me, even though friendly, chilled my bones but it also seemed to reassure me that I was not alone after all. Then suddenly the name of God broke through my lips and I knew it was fear that had forced His name on me.

My village was very near now. What would father say seeing me return all alone so late in the night! What would mother and grandmother think! I sat down near a rock to reflect on this. The stars shone in the sky in their full glory and their glimmering light from afar to some extent lifted the weight of darkness that had been pressing down on me for quite some time. The cold mountain wind rubbed itself against me and I felt considerably relieved. And when I ran my fingers on my face I felt that the skin there, which a moment ago felt so tense and tight, was now loosening. It was probably the effect of the sweat drying up. I could feel this loosening all over my body. I had walked quite a distance and my body had become warm, now it was relaxing and it felt good. I took out my shawl and wrapped it round my body to ward off the cold.

***

Last evening the devta had come to Leeladas Sharma's home riding on his rath, the tastefully decorated ceremonial palanquin. Two more devtas had also arrived on their raths to his house. Some time ago Leeladas had promised offerings to the devtas in return for the fulfilment of his wish. Thus, it was to be celebrated as the jatra of three deities on the same day, making the occasion trebly auspicious. Father asked me to attend the ceremony as a musician, my first such assignment. His intention was to initiate me on this holy occasion as a future musician to take over from him the family profession of serving the temple deity. He was in no mood to allow me to continue my studies after class VII, whereas I was very keen to acquire education. Father had enlisted himself in the service of the deity while still a child and he wanted the same from me also. He bore with whatever came his way while serving the temple without ever complaining about the kind of treatment meted out to him by the upper caste people nor did he ever say anything about it to his family members. His duty was to play the shehnai on auspicious occasions along with other musicians.

Father was known for his musical talents, specially his soulful shehnai recitals. In the entire dalit community in and around the village, there was no one to match his shehnai skills. Apart from playing the shehnai at the temple, he was also invited on social and festive occasions to give public performances. He never demanded any fixed fees and accepted whatever people gave him. He was free from greed for money and never ran after fancy things. What really warmed his heart and immensely pleased him was his ease with his instrument and in the heart of his hearts, he knew that he was an accomplished shehnai artist. He relished every word when people spoke admiringly about his recitals and was so carried away by the praise that sometimes he forgot even to eat. But he was modest about his talent and attributed it to the grace of Goddess Saraswati and the temple deity.

He wanted me to take over from him the duties of the temple musician and become even more famous. But I had no inclinations towards music and always pleaded with him not to force me to discontinue my school and allow me to pass at least high school. But the village school was only up to class eight and for high school, I would have to go to the town which was quite far from the village. Moreover, poverty did not permit me to stay away from home in the town. My father knew my keenness for education and secretly approved of it but the thought of poverty weighed on him so much that he would not openly admit it even to himself. Therefore, when he dissuaded me from going any further than what the village school offered, he did so against his innermost wish. Another reason might have been the pressure of my own caste people in the village but the reason of poverty was real and I understood it quite well. I was the first ever dalit student to have passed the class eight examination and it was a matter of pride as well as jealousy for the dalits of my village and the surrounding ones. I had also stood first in the whole district while many savarna students had failed.

I wasn't interested in playing the shehnai. It is true that on a few occasions during school festivals, I had tried my hand at this instrument and the flute only to accompany student-musicians of the school but I didn't have any technical knowledge of music, apart from what I had casually heard from my father about the finer points of taal and swara. Nevertheless, I could play the shehnai passably well. When father heard about my performances in the school, he imagined that I was on the right track and that one day I would blossom into a famous shehnai artist. My school prizes for music further boosted his hopes and ambitions about the birth of another and much more accomplished musician in the family.

I was genuinely respectful towards my father but occasional tiffs and arguments between us were quite common. And the main reason for this was his excessive, almost servile deference towards the brahmins and thakurs of the village. Many things had happened during my growing years in the village which only increased my dislike and hostility towards the savarnas of the village. At least one incident often flashed before my eyes and whenever father talked about the brahmins and thakurs, that incident stood like a wall between us.

***

One day, when I was in the fifth standard, I accompanied father to a ceremony in the village temple. It was probably the sankranti day. People of the nearby villages had assembled in the temple on that first day of the month to solve petty village disputes in the panchayat. Most of these people were those who believed that their homes were haunted by inimical spirits which would be exorcised by the deity through their prayers. They also came to collect consecrated akshat rice from the temple for the health and well-being of their cattle. There used to be quite a crowd of people on these occasions who came to seek relief from headaches or stomach-aches.

These temple panchayats started with a special ceremony and would always be held in the afternoon. The bajantaris would start playing all the temple instruments, with father on his shehnai. When the music reached the highest pitch, the chief goor of the temple on whom the shadow of the deity was supposed to descend would start shaking and shivering until his whole body was in a complete convulsion. He would give a sudden jolt to his head, his cap would tumble down and his long hair would fall on his shoulders. Music would continue at its highest pitch. The gathering would watch the goor spellbound and get convinced that the goor is now in complete possession of the deity. His eyes would become red hot and face black. The other goors would also now feel the deity's shadow descending on them and they would also start shaking and shivering like the chief goor. They held small iron chains in their hands, which they shook and struck their backs thrice or five times. It was a sign that the other deities had now entered and possessed the goors. Thus possessed, the goors would bend to the ground, screaming 'hooooooo'. Now the chief goor would bang the ground with his hands and shout 'rakkhe' for 'protection'. The other goors would repeat the chief goor's words. To control and guide the ceremony five panchs huddled around the goors. This was the beginning of the dharmachar which would be followed by the 'petitioners' who would come one by one to reveal their problems and seek the deities' grace. The chief goor would give a patient hearing to each one of them and console them by offering solutions. These solutions were first communicated to the panchs who would pass them on to the aggrieved persons. Among the solutions was often the order for arranging a jatara of the deities or the sacrifice of a goat at the temple. On the day I am talking of, when the people had dispersed, something came over me and half-wittingly, I sat down on the steps of the temple. When the priest noticed me, he was furious. He came running towards me and gave me a hard slap on my cheek. Then he caught hold of me, dragged me to my father and almost threw me on the ground before him. And father, instead of protesting at the priest's behaviour, gave me one more slap. I cried for some time, then came back home but those slaps got stuck in my soul. In no time rumour got around that the low-caste shehnai-player's son was a rascal and had behaved disrespectfully with the priest. This incident dismayed me so much that I began to hate the brahmin students of my school and when safe I would play all kinds of pranks on them to tease and humiliate them. The brahmin boys took revenge by abusing and taunting and calling me by my caste.

The other incident was no less humiliating.

One day the second wife of the priest, who was much younger than him and very pretty, was coming back from the village well with a water-filled pitcher and in the narrow lane, I collided with her without any design. The lane was so narrow that two persons coming from opposite directions could not cross without colliding unless one of the two turned back to allow the other to pass. She had seen me coming from the other end of the lane and warned me to let her pass but I was adamant and asked her to turn and walk back. She paid no attention to my words and continued advancing. Since I was in no mood to oblige her, I also did not turn back and instead managed to cross the lane almost rubbing shoulders with her. No sooner had I crossed the lane than all hell broke out. She threw down the pitcher on the ground and began shouting and abusing. I turned back, went near her and asked, "Panditain, I didn't touch you deliberately. Then why are you abusing me? But when the other day you were lying naked under Jagaru chamar's son, you were not contaminated, were you?" Now that her secret was out, her face turned red. She had been publicly exposed and she could not bear it. She became terribly nervous and desperate. If this became known all over the village, how would she show her face? She had to do something about it. She threw her broken pitcher in the field and went home shouting and swearing. She complained to her priest-husband that the shehnai-player's son had not only touched the pitcher but had a scuffle with her. The complaint reached my father and the thrashing he gave me that day I can never forget in my life. By the time I reached class eight, I had told father several times not to be unduly deferential to the brahmins. But this always worked him up and he detested being counselled by a boy of hardly any consequence, that too his own son. I changed my attitude in order not to hurt his pride but the wound of humiliation on my own psyche simply refused to heal.

***

Father had not been keeping well for quite some time now. Another jatara procession was in the offing. Father had become very weak due to his prolonged illness. He found it difficult to control his breath which was so much needed in the one who played the shehnai. But the thought that this time he would not be able to participate in the celebrations was weighing on him. Over a long time, it had become almost a rule that at least one member of my family would participate in the sacred ceremony of the jatara. His duties were already decided. For the dalits of the village, these sacred ceremonies always entailed lots of duties.

This time I became the scapegoat to perform the duty in the name of the devta. And though unwilling, I had to go.

When I reached the temple, the priest asked me where my father was. I told him about his illness and the priest became a bit worried, but when I told him that I would play the shehnai, he looked at me in surprise. The people of my community assured the priest that I was quite skilled in playing the shehnai and that I would not disappoint the devotees. But he said nothing. I knew full well that he did not like my presence. Perhaps somewhere in his mind, the thought had occurred that it was good if I stopped studying and took up the family profession of playing the shehnai. After sometime his face relaxed and he began to talk to me in normal tones. The head priest and others probably saw in me the future shehnai artiste of the temple. They lauded my devotion to the temple and my regard for the family tradition. They seemed delighted at the idea of my giving up school to play with the temple musicians.

Father had taught me a few tips of the shehnai, for example, which particular tune or song should be played when the deities' chariot came out in a procession, or when the devotees began to dance in praise of the deities, etc. I had learnt these things by watching the rituals and I had the confidence of performing as the occasion demanded.

All these memories flashed before my mind's eyes while I sat in the middle of that stony track in the shivering cold under the open sky. I was completely oblivious of my surroundings and my inconveniences. My first day in the service of the deity had ended in a fiasco and caused so much bad blood. My mind was abuzz with dark thoughts that weighed on my heart. I was prepared to bear the punishment that the temple authorities imposed on me but what was really chafing at my heart was the way my father would react to my action, his disappointment at what his imbecile son had done, how his reputation had been sullied by his own offspring, and so on. With how much assurance and pride he had sent me in the service of the deity, and my insolence and obduracy had turned all his hopes upside down! I knew that when he was told what had happened as a result of my rashness, he would deeply repent his decision of sending me to the temple. He would feel not only deeply hurt but humiliated as well. He would also conclude that his good-for-nothing son was a gone case and past all hopes of reform. The good name and reputation that he had built over the years would vanish in thin air.

***

I just couldn't figure out why I became so upset when the deity's procession reached Leeladas's house. There was no proper arrangement for the musicians to sit and perform although there was plenty of space in the field. There was a small tarp spread on bamboo sticks on one side of the field and the rest of it was open to the sky. The entire attention of the organizers was on making the best possible arrangements for the deity's chariot and priests and the upper caste devotees. For others, especially dalits of the village, dry grass had been laid out without any cloth coverings. The weather was terribly cold but no arrangements for fire were made and people were made to sit in the open in the freezing cold. It was the month of November and we, the poor musicians, had no warm clothes and could fend off the cold only by sitting near the fire. To sit in the open in the freezing night with dew and frost falling from above, the very thought of it made one shiver.

Even when the ritual worship of the deity was over, we continued playing our respective instruments in the hope that someone from among the organisers would take pity on us and give blankets and fire to mitigate our misery but nobody took any notice of us. We had also heard that the brahmins of this village hated the dalits much more than anywhere else and did not allow them to enter even their courtyards. While we waited helplessly and watched the activities of the organizers, the upper caste people who had come to watch the pooja were amply provided with blankets, quilts and even braziers to keep them warm. Meanwhile, the cold was increasing and at least I was getting worked up at the apathy and indifference of the organizers.

We looked around but nothing was to come our way. My fellow musicians covered themselves with their torn and tattered cotton shawls and fell asleep. I also thought of somehow spending the night in the open but found it difficult to control my anger. A priest was sleeping near the chariot wheels and had covered himself with two heavy quilts. I pulled one quilt but this disturbed the priest's sleep and he woke up. Initially, he couldn't make out what had happened but when he saw me holding the quilt, he scowled and began to shout obscenities at me. This awakened the others and they got up as if buckets of freezing water had been poured on them. There was a huge commotion now and all eyes turned to me.

One brahmin, flames of anger and contempt shooting in his eyes, said, "You rascal, have you gone mad or lost your eyesight that you could not see the holy chariot standing right here and defiled it with your dirty touch? How did you dare do such a thing and then snatch the quilt of the brahmin?" I wasn't prepared for such a nasty turn of events and couldn't comprehend the implications of such a simple thing as taking a quilt to save myself from the biting cold. But abuses showered on me thick and fast. Before I could make out any sense of it and manage to get away from the scene, Leeladas, the chief organizer of the ceremony, appeared on the scene and I hoped that he, as the host, would pacify the angry crowd of brahmins. But he was even more furious. He turned on me like a ferocious dog and shouted, "A little bit of education seems to have gone to the heads of these low caste people and swelled their pride. How could you snatch the quilt of a pious brahmin? And what will I do with this now that you have touched it with your filthy hands?"

Leeladas seemed to be less worried about the so-called defilement of the deity than about his new quilts. Angry words and abuses were coming at me from all sides but my fellow musicians, all dalits, remained mute and motionless, so terrified were they.

I didn't notice when Pandit Narayanu, a panch of the temple, rose from the crowd and advanced menacingly towards me. He raised his hand to hit me but I held it before it could touch me. He was so taken aback by my resistance that he collapsed and fell on one of the bamboo poles that had been fixed to support the tarpaulin, with the result that a portion of it fell on him. Nobody had foreseen that things would take such an ugly turn and lead to physical scuffle. The brahmins took it as an affront to their honour but, even though abuses continued to flow unabated, they held themselves back from advancing towards me. The shower of abuses made it difficult for me to restrain myself any longer. I moved towards Leeladas who was

standing at some distance from me and said, "Pandit, so far I have
remained patient and borne with the abuses which are being showered on
me but I wish to seek an answer from all you brahmins who are here to
earn merit by participating in this holy occasion: do only brahmins feel the
fury of this freezing night or kolis and chamars also? All of you have been
comfortably snoring under two quilts each but for us you have not
arranged even dry rice-stalks or grass. Don't you feel that we are also
human beings and feel cold or heat as you people do? Our priests and
panchs may not feel ashamed but Pandit Leeladas, you organized this
occasion, you are the host and we came because you had invited us. You
have organized the jataras not of just one deity but three deities and you
should have known that there would be not only brahmins but people of
other castes also and they would need to be provided with quilts and
blankets."

I was amazed at my capacity for words and also that I could speak so
long before such a big gathering. There was complete silence while I
spoke and this in itself was ominous. Leeladas' house was three-storied
and was surrounded by other big houses, all belonging to the brahmins.
The noise had attracted women and children of these houses and they were
watching from their balconies and windows. I was upset by the fear that
the crowd might attack me. It wasn't safe for me to stay there any longer
because I knew that in that eventuality even my caste people would not
dare to come to my rescue. I collected my things and at the slightest
opportunity managed to slip away from there. I ran along the narrow path
below and climbed up the opposite slope. Some youths chased me but the
dark cold night saved me from their clutches. The crowd was stunned at
my audacity and I could hear their abuses even from the distance.

***

A night bus made its way along the road across the valley. While it
was negotiating a turn, its light fell on me and I was taken aback. For a
moment I couldn't recollect where I was and why. The light fell on me
again. I touched my forehead and found that I was sweating heavily.
Sweat-drops trickled down my body and fell on the ground. I had been
sitting there long but my mind was still reeling with what had happened at
the jatara an hour or so ago.

I stood up slowly and began walking homeward. I looked at the sky
and found that the Milky Way had moved to the north and the Saptrishi
stars had moved to the west. I guessed the morning was still a few hours

away and decided not to reach home in the dark. I walked some distance and then sat down again.

My mind was in a whirl and many things flashed before my eyes and all these pertained to what had happened a few hours ago. Whose devta is he after all, I asked myself, only of the savarnas or ours as well? Surely if he is a real devta, replica of God himself, he belongs to all, savarnas as well as dalits. Neither the priests nor the goors had ever seen him with their naked eyes and we also had not seen him. It is only a convention, a tradition that we worship these replicas as the embodied forms of God. We simply carry this tradition, like kettle-drums on our backs, from generation after generation. But in doing so, hasn't a deadly conspiracy been hatched.

Such thoughts initially shocked me and I could no longer remain sitting. I stood up and looked around but hardly anything was visible and what I could see were only my phantomized fears, taking shape and frightening me, fears of questioning the so-called sacred traditions.

The chariot procession went past my eyes once again. The deities riding the chariots are only symbols of the Divine. The chariot of the chief deity, which I had left behind, was beautifully made. It was built on two long wooden poles covered with silver. The canopy of the chariot is made of gold. Inside the chariot sits the gold mask-like replica of the chief deity. His chariot is surrounded by the chariots of other deities in smaller sizes with replicas made of silver and brass. One female deity is covered with yak-hair about whom it is said that she is a monster deity and, if left uncovered, she will wreak havoc on people. Wherever her glance falls, things are burnt down. But this is all hearsay and nobody has seen this. Four canopied chariots stand in all four directions, with silver bands on all four sides! Each chariot has a silver plate on which are embossed the names of the priests and the goors as if the deities were their personal property. A huge amount of silver has been used to decorate the chariots.

The fear of the deity is so deeply implanted in people's minds that nobody ever dares to ask any inconvenient questions as to wherefrom so much silver has come. If anyone ventures to ask such questions, they are immediately branded as atheists or heretics and punished for blasphemy. There is always the fear that if the deity becomes angry nobody can pacify him. A man's anger has remedy but when a deity is angry, he can be pleased only by prayer. The chief deity moves only in his chariot and always stays in the chariot. There is a magnificent, two-storied temple made for him. When there is no festival, the chariot is unassembled and its various parts are stored in the upper room. The deity is worshipped every day with ghee and milk, both in the morning and evening. The worship is carried out by a brahmin priest. No member of any other caste can touch the deity or enter the sanctum. It is said that the deity does not accept the offerings directly from any other caste. For generations, only one brahmin family has been supplying priests to the temple. Apart from the chief deity and his retinue, there are lesser deities who serve as his bodyguards and gatekeepers and they are placed on the outer walls and gates of the temple. They have no separate temples of their own nor do they have gold or silver masks. They have no chariots, no canopies, no palanquins. Their status is much lower than that of the deities inside the sanctum.

The chief deity has three attendant deities, who are his gatekeepers. The first dwarpal, represented by a beautifully carved black stone statue, stands near the main door of the sanctum. He is naked except for his phallus which is covered with a piece of cloth. He stands in the open without any canopy. It is believed that he doesn't like clothes and hates being enclosed in a temple and that is why he stands under the open sky. The second dwarpal has no statue because he doesn't like one. He is identified by a conical stone slab fixed in the earth with a platform built round it. An iron chain is wound round the stone slab. The third dwarpal is identified only by an iron bar, thick and long and stuck deep into the earth.

These dwarpals receive no gold or silver offerings and no earthen lamps are lighted with ghee for them. The devotees, brahmins and non-brahmins alike, who throng the temple to seek the fulfilment of their wishes, offer them coarse flour or iron bracelets. Earthen lamps of the coarsest oils are lit for them. They are also not offered tastefully cooked food but only thick rotis made of the coarsest grains. No coconuts, dates, saffron, or betel nuts are given them. All those costly things such as gold or silver or ghee lamps or ghee-cooked food routinely offered to the chief deity and his companions inside the sanctum are practically forbidden for these dwarpals and thus a strict hierarchy is maintained even in the house of gods.

Not only in this, but hierarchy is also strictly adhered to in matters of selecting the goors. For the chief deity, only a brahmin goor can be appointed because he enjoys the highest status and has a place of privilege in matters of rituals and offerings. For other deities who are housed outside the main sanctum there are non-brahmins, even dalit priests, who have the same low status in the temple affairs as the deities they are appointed to serve. The village elders say that the chief deity is the only wish-fulfilling deity and also the tutelary devata of the entire village community. But we dalits have never had the good fortune of touching even the threshold of the temple. We also wish to light a lamp before our deity, we also want to make offerings to him, but we are not permitted to enter the temple or touch the temple threshold with our foreheads. We bow to him only from the outside and seek his blessings from afar. The nearest that we can go is where the dwarpals stand, offer all our gifts to them and come back home.

Thus, there are dalits even among devtas, caste hierarchy even in the house of god. The savarnas have appropriated the gods and they swiftly climb the temple stairs without any let or hindrance as if the deities belong to their clan. And what doubt can there be? The way they swagger in claiming their right to the devta, they probably have it. The dalits are just like the dwarpals, standing outside at the gate in the open, in freezing cold or scorching sun, without any canopies or ornaments. Frost falls on them, storms cover them with dirt and dust. As for ornaments, they have only crudely made iron bracelets or waistbands. Offer them one such bracelet or waistband and the poor things are mightily pleased. But you cannot please the chief deity with such cheap offerings. He is seated in the heart of his imposing temple surrounded with every possible luxury. And who would ever dare to offer him such things and incur unremitting humiliation and disgrace by his curse!

***

I recalled the story of the deity as it was related to me by my father, how the deity appeared in the village, who had the first glimpse of him, and how a temple was built to house him, and on and on. One night, a village musician, drummer by profession, after performing at a marriage, was returning home. When he was quite near the village, he heard faint human cries in a bush. He stopped and the groans stopped, but when he started walking, the cries started again. Initially he thought it was only an illusion but the groans continued and it was quite clear to him that the cries were of a human being. He gathered courage and went close to the bush. He found that the groans were emanating from a nearby spot which was covered with stones. He moved the stones aside but the cries continued. He dug the earth with the stick of his drum and suddenly his fingers touched something hard. He felt that the object his fingers had touched was wet. He lighted a matchstick and found that blood was dripping from it. He was frightened and thought it was a miracle. He stopped digging the earth for a while, then gathering courage he moved the earth aside. His fingers again struck against the same object and again he noticed blood dripping from it. When he examined the object closely he found that the blood-dripping object was nothing but a round-shaped stone. He dug out the stone and tied his muffler round it. The groaning stopped and the bleeding also abated. He then returned home.

In the night he had a dream: A tall, handsome man dressed in white and mounted on a white horse, chandan tilak on his forehead, eyes large and shining, long and wavy hair, hands reaching down to his knees and the same muffler tied round his neck, stood before the drummer and instructed him that a temple be built on the very spot where the stone had appeared, otherwise the whole village would come to grief. He also revealed to the drummer that he is a divine being belonging to the Mahabharata period and that he had fought in the great Mahabharata war on the side of the Pandavas and now he wanted to settle down in this village.

Many unforeseen events had already taken place in the village shaking it with fears. Cows went to the forest and stood fixed at the spot where the blood-dripping stone had been discovered. Milk would pour down from their udders on that spot and they would return to the village dry. The village people were puzzled by such mysterious happenings but were unable to solve the mystery.

When the next day the drummer told the people about his dream, they all went to the forest to see that spot. They saw a round stone protruding from the earth with the drummer's muffler tied round it. In the course of time a temple was built there and that stone was placed in the inner sanctum of the temple. The deity manifested himself in the drummer. He remained the devta's goor for many years. After his death, however, the savarnas of the village managed somehow to take over the temple management and thereafter, appointed only brahmins as priests and goors.

Now the drummers, one of whose ancestors had had the first glimpse of that divine being and whose piety and devotion had been at the root of the temple, could not even enter it, to say nothing of touching the deity. The brahmins have established their absolute hold over the temple and now nobody even remembers its founder. But when on ceremonial occasions the dalit musicians perform on their various instruments, the priests would declare how much the deity was pleased with them and their music, without which he would not move even an inch during the jataras and that if ever the dalit musicians ignored their duties, the wrath of the deity would befall them. Whenever I recalled these words of the priests, the irony always pained and sometimes amused me as it was doing now.

Some nocturnal bird came and hovered over me, then almost touching my pate it flew across the valley. Its cry echoed in my ears. Then a jackal began to howl, and another joined in to compete with it. Hu ... hoo ... hu ... hoo. Then dogs began to bark somewhere afield.

What had I begun to think? ... What am I thinking? ... But what is wrong in thinking like this? Isn't it a fact that the savarnas of the village control everything, including our own lives and thrive on our sacrifices and deprivations, all in the name of the temple deity? If you look around and think seriously, you will easily discover that not just in this village but in the entire region, they wield much more power than even high government officials and ministers. They matter in everything, in wealth, in status, in influence. Moneylending on high interests is their side business. And the dalits! They are at the mercy of the brahmins and the temple priests, serving them and their whims. They are like the dwarpals at the temple gate, exposed to the vagaries of the weather as much as to the whims of the brahmins and priests. And the svaranas, they are kings in their homes and with the devta on their side, kings outside! They will not eat till they get goat meat and a bottle of liquor. All excused in the name of the devta.

Once you start thinking along these lines, you soon begin to wonder if these so-called traditions are not a conspiracy against dalits in order to keep them in perpetual bondage—clean and respectable jobs for the savarnas and unclean and degrading ones for dalits. Was it a crime to ask for warm clothes in this shivering, freezing cold? Aren't we also human beings, who feel heat and cold as others do? Father must have had similar experiences of humiliation but due to fears accumulated over the years, fear of the deity, fear of the savarnas, he never protested and took things as fixed and immutable. Your silence is your best certificate of good conduct and all your creativity and talent are recognized only so long as you remain dumb about your sufferings and degradation. The slightest desire for decency and dignity immediately reminds people of your caste and lowly social status and you are damned as kolis, chamars, dumneys, offspring of whores, bastards and shameless! And if you acquire a little bit of education, then your villainy is confirmed.

Such piercing thoughts made me feel more miserable at our plight but they also firmed up my resolve to avenge myself. I was in a rage and my blood was boiling. I hit a stone with my foot which almost injured my toe. I was so engrossed in these dark thoughts that I did not notice that it was past midnight but even now I wasn't prepared to reach home and face my father. But how long could I sit here? The morning star had appeared in the sky but it was still very dark. I knew that I would not be able to explain to my father why I had left the ceremony half-way and come away, but I could not be sitting here forever.

***

On reaching home, the first person I faced was my father. He was so taken aback by my arrival as if he had seen a wild animal standing before him.

"You....! So early!"

"Yes, Pita ji."

"But why; it was a whole night ceremony, wasn't it? Then, why have you come back so early?"

My first impulse was to dodge his question by talking about some other topic but I felt bad to lie to him. Also, I thought I hadn't committed any crime or sin, so why not come clean about the whole affair. I revealed the truth. Father was furious and turned on me:

"You consider yourself to be very clever, don't you? Don't you know your limits? All the reputation I earned over the years, you have destroyed in one stroke. God alone knows what will happen now. People will taunt me for having a son who has trampled upon his father's reputation. Your education has gone to your head and that's why you quarrelled with the priests. You should have known who you are. You should have known that a pair of shoes is fit only for the feet and not the head."

Father was disconsolate and I did not want to say anything which might hurt him more, but I found his last words too much to digest and said, "I seek your forgiveness, Pita ji, but the truth is that nobody has any respect for your musical talent. You may look upon yourself as a great artist, which you surely are, but in the eyes of the priests and other brahmins you are nothing more than a koli or a chamar and what you call respect is due to nothing but your silence with which you bear their humiliating and degrading behaviour. Whether they feed you at the temple gate or some distance away from there, you meekly accept it. You have been serving the devta for so many years but have never demanded your wages. You remain satisfied with whatever they throw at you. You never complain when they make you sleep in the open without any blankets or quilts. But are we made to only be treated like this without any regard for our basic comforts or self-respect? Can we not ask for anything beyond the pittance they give us? Have we no right to protest against ill-treatment or disrespect routinely heaped on us, but why? How long are we going to remain dumb even in the face of the worst kinds of insult and ignominy, and why?"

Father could no longer restrain himself and landed a heavy slap on my face, so heavy indeed that I almost collapsed on the ground. He was hysterical with anger, uttering all sorts of curses and abuses. It was quite a scene. Hearing the noise mother rushed out from the house and pulled me inside. Father's anger did not abate and he kept grumbling even when I was out of his sight.

***

I was unhappy the whole day. I wondered what punishment the temple committee would impose on me for my impertinence. The thought was disturbing but I was in no mood to surrender or apologise. The jatara was over in the evening and the devta returned to the temple. The sudden sounding of the temple drum disturbed me even more. Then a boy came running to my house to tell me that the temple committee had summoned my father to present himself at the temple immediately. I was utterly dismayed when I heard the message. Father's reaction was a mixture of sorrow and remorse, "I don't know what will befall me due to my own good-for-nothing son, what punishment the temple may impose on me. I may even be asked to leave the village and if this happens what will I do, where will I go?"

I was really very, very upset. I knew that my father was in no position to oppose any punishment the temple committee decided on because such punishment was deemed to have been decided by the devta himself and there was no appeal against it even in a court of law. The situation was ominous by all means and naturally my anxiety was at its peak.

What added even more to my anxiety was the memory of Shibbu Mistri and I was terribly disturbed by the thought of a similar punishment being imposed on us. The whole event flashed before me like a cinematic reel. It was two years ago that this terrible episode had taken place. The occasion was a jatara of the deity to the house of Thakur Ram Singh. The Thakur was the head of the village panchayat. Some years ago, Shibbu Mistri had sought the deity's blessings for something and in return had promised to offer a silver cap. After years of savings, he had now made the cap. He was old and his eyesight was very weak and therefore he decided to make his offering to the deity on the occasion of this jatara at the house of the Thakur. When he reached the Thakur's house the deity was being ritually worshipped. Once the rituals were over, people began to make their offerings at the deity's feet. Shibbu Mistri stood in a corner and waited for his turn. In the meantime, the crowd pressed from behind. Shibbu lost his balance and lurched forward but somehow managed to hold back; but in the process, his hand touched the wheel of the chariot and it was noticed by the Thakur. Shibbu was dragged from the crowd and mercilessly beaten as if he had touched the chariot deliberately. Blood was dripping from his mouth and nostrils but nobody came to his rescue. The crowd was furious and clamoured to punish Shibbu severely. Father was also in the crowd. He pleaded for mercy and Shibbu's life was spared. But the incident was deeply etched in my mind.

As atonement for his sin, Shibbu was ordered to sacrifice and offer a goat to the deity. When he expressed his inability to do so with folded hands, the panchayat told him that in that case he would have to offer himself for sacrifice. Father again came to his rescue and prayed to the panchayat to impose some other punishment. The panchayat ordered him to leave the village and Shibbu had no choice but to pack up his little belongings and say good-bye to his ancestral village. Nobody in the village now knew anything about Shibbu and his whereabouts.

Shibbu Mistri saved his life by accepting banishment from the village of his ancestors. Nobody came forward to help him, not even my father because he too had no courage to defy the might of the savarna people of the village or no means at his disposal to meet the demand of a goat-sacrifice. No one could say where Shibbu had gone or whether he was still alive. Whatever little property he had was transferred to the name of the temple. Now that property (a few strips of land and a small house) is in the possession of one of the brahmin priests. The silver cap offered by Shibbu still adorns the deity because it was not considered contaminated by his hands. The Brahmin who now cultivated the land that belonged to Shibbu, has no fear of defilement. But poor Shibbu! The very memory of him made me dizzy. Suppose a similar fate befalls my father, then…?

I was full of remorse for my thoughtless conduct which had turned a trifle of an event into a huge storm. What was the need? Shouldn't I have borne the whole thing as sheepishly as others of my community routinely do? Why did I think myself so different from others? I should have known my station which was no different from that of the statue of the dwarpal at the outer gate of the temple who keeps watch over the temple and its deity from outside. He never complains that he is without clothes or ornaments. Indeed, he is my devta and I salute him and implore him to give me a fraction of his composure and equanimity so that I may also keep my cool in the face of humiliation and indifference. But my remorse or repentance could not undo what I had so foolishly done. Everything now depended on the temple committee.

When father returned late in the evening, he looked extremely worried and shaken. He didn't speak to anyone in the family. He took his meal and went to bed. I thought things had not gone down well and something frightening would happen to me the next day. I couldn't sleep and my mind ceaselessly worked out the possible consequences of my wilful conduct. Perhaps, father too couldn't sleep. I heard him muttering and coughing and going out in the open all night, which all pointed to his restlessness. Probably the priest had said something so humiliating and unbearable that he was not able to digest it and it had made him so uneasy.

The situation had become critical and the news of my rash behaviour had spread all over the place. It seemed to me that it was being talked about everywhere in the locality. Bits and pieces of what people said and suggested reached me also, adding to my fears and worries. The brahmins and other upper caste people turned away their eyes when they saw me. My own community people were no different. They would avoid my contact as if I was suffering from some horribly infectious disease. I was very sorry to have caused hurt to my father but I had no means to comfort him nor courage to explain the situation and my conduct.

A few days later, another chariot-procession was to be organized in another village. A messenger had come to my village to invite the people to the festivity. He had met father also and probably asked him to attend the holy occasion. My guess was confirmed when I heard my father refreshing the tunes on his shehnai. It was after a long, long time that father had picked up the instrument and was working on it. Of late, he had practically given up his life-long habit of practicing every morning. He had probably thought that he should not exert himself anymore and take rest and pass on the shehnai to his grown-up son. But now that the son had disappointed him, he must have thought of playing again. The lilting tune of the shehnai reached my ears when he blew into it and I felt very relieved. I thought that the temple committee had taken pity on him and had not handed a heavy punishment and that father had decided to participate in the temple procession. He practiced hard that day but did not go to the temple. A messenger came several times to call him but he paid no attention to his message.

It was all very puzzling to me: his riaz after such a long time, the way he eyed me repeatedly, his composed, contented looks. I found it hard to explain his behaviour. He came out in the courtyard, scattered rice grains for the birds and poured a whole pitcher of water in the roots of the tree. Does it all mean that he has forgiven me? This thought made me happy but still I did not have the courage to look him in the face. He also said nothing to me but secretly I was on cloud nine.

Next morning, I woke up early and opened my trunk. Last week father had bought a suit-piece for me. Silently I took it out, held it under my arms and ran towards the temple. I was panting when I reached there. Nobody had seen me on the way. I looked around, took off my shoes, crossed the boundary wall and sat down at the feet of the statue of the dwarpal. I touched his feet, unfolded the suit-piece and wrapped him in it from head to foot. Pleased, I came out of the temple and wore my shoes. Initially, I thought of going back through the usual narrow track but then my heart said, today, why not take the path that passes right through the brahmin houses.

Translated by R. K. Shukla & Manjari Tiwari

SLUR

KAALIKH

Shyama called to her son Manu from the edge of the aangan. Who knows where he is busy playing. He is nowhere to be found. There is no response to her call from anywhere. Shyama's calling out in this way is not new to the villagers. But today it fell on their ears like blasts of dynamite. They all made faces. A cow came jigging down the footpath in front. It belonged to Phula panditani. Every day, instead of going straight to its cowshed after grazing, the wicked cow made her way to Shyama's house. Phula usually asked Shyama to stop the cow, but today she appeared annoyed. She was irritated more at the sight of Shyama than at the cow. She ran after the cow with a stick. Shyama didn't bother either. She took a few quick puffs of a bidi, but when the heat touched her fingers, she quickly threw it down and ground it into the soil. She called out to Manu again,

"O re Manua! Manu oye!"

When he didn't respond, she began to swear in anger,

"God knows to whose house the leper has gone. The low caste bastard is born to suck my blood. Just let him come back home and see if I don't break his legs today, change my name if I don't."

She grumbled as she turned to go inside. As she reached the door, Phula returned, having secured her cow. Instead of going straight, the cow turned towards Shyama. It hoped that as usual it would get a wheat ball or a piece of roti from her. Phula was already irritated and now her anger broke on the cow's back. She hit it several times till the stick broke. By the time Shyama came out with a roti, the cow had bolted. There were long welts wherever the stick had landed on its back. Shyama quietly watched all this from the threshold of her house. What else could she have done. She gnashed her teeth in anger as if she herself was in pain.

"The brahmani has gone mad. She doesn't even spare gau mata. I spit on you!"

She spat vehemently and crushed the piece of roti with such force that it crumbled into pieces. She flung them over her shoulder onto the roof. The crumbs spread all over the mud tiles. A few crows descended and started pecking at them. Shyama could hear their khatar-patar on the roof for a long time. Some fine crumbs also fell through the broken roof into the house. She looked at the ceiling. The weight of the tiles had twisted a few bamboo beams. In some places, there were such gaping holes that through them one could even count the stars in the sky. The ceiling was black and discoloured due to smoke. Dirt was trapped in the straw and cobwebs were hanging from these. When it rained, the roof leaked at many places and the mud wall had eroded in spots because of the damp. How much clay and cow dung could Shyama possibly plaster over it. If she plastered it on one side, it began to come apart in another. The tiles and bamboos could fall on her head at any time. Light from outside fell on the wall making it appear even more frightening. She closed the door hurriedly. Everything in the room was engulfed in the gloom.

Shyama's house consists of just the one room. It had been a cowshed once. Only she knew how she had managed to make it worth living. People said that if any cow or buffalo were kept in that cowshed it neither mated nor conceived ... But Shyama had a son. And this day, the panchayat had been called on account of him ... that ... Manu is a bastard ...! As she recalled this, it seemed as if a pitcher of cold water had been poured on her head. Life began to seep out of her body. She felt deeply embarrassed even in the solitude of her home. She became dizzy and subsided near the chulha. So much shivering in such scorching heat!

She picked up the tongs and stirred the ash. The buried embers came to life. She looked at them unblinkingly and sat absorbed in the living and dying embers. When the breeze draughted in, they glimmered like glow worms. Their warmness increased. She turned them again with the tongs. As she went on turning the embers they broke into several pieces. God knows how long she kept sitting there, caught up in this being and breaking. She didn't know what to do. Sometimes she felt as if her whole body had been burnt to ashes. The ash in the chulha was hers. It was her bones that had melted and were now glittering in the flames.

Something similar was burning inside her too. She seemed to breathe tongues of fire and was overcome with grief. Her body was terribly stiff. Her throat parched every passing moment and her tongue clung to her palate. She tried to moisten her mouth, but in vain. She didn't have strength enough to get up and take water from the pitcher.

***

The door opened with a bang and startled, Shyama almost fell into the chulha. She thought Manu had come back home and picked up the tongs in rage. But it was the panchayat's watchman.

"Why don't you come Shyama? The panchayat has been waiting for you for so long. Get up. We don't have only your case to deal with. There is other work too."

She felt as if someone had poured a basket full of filth on her head. She continued to sit and stare at the door. The watchman stood like Yama's messenger at the door. His right foot was on the threshold and his hand was on the leaf of the door. It was clear that he had kicked it open.

There was nothing new in her door being opened without a knock or call. Almost everyone treated her this way. As if she were not a human being but a stone seat at the crossroads. Anyone who took the fancy would stop there and stay for a while. They'd relax at their leisure, put down their load to rest, or sit cross-legged to play cards. They boozed and took drugs, then rolled on the ground or passed out right there. On the peg driven into the wall they would hang their tattered clothes, coat or bag, jacket or pyjama, a shirt or cap.

Shyama felt shame once again. Her past was obscured somewhere in her agony. It lay there concealed. There was thick darkness all around, as if the sun had never risen.

She tried to get up. Her body was so stiff it seemed someone had tied it up with a rope. She had to support herself with the tongs to get up. She stood up with a heavy heart. As she got up, the watchman moved from the door and stood squarely in her way. To improve the circulation of blood in her body, Shyama walked about a bit and shook her arms. When her limbs relaxed a little, she went towards the pitcher and sat down. She drew the tin can to herself and began to pour water into it. But she couldn't control the flow of the water and it spilled over as she filled the can. The stream of water flowed from between her feet into the chulha. Fire and water together made a frightening sound … chhchh ... chha.

The room filled with black-grey smoke. Bits of ash settled on her as though someone had deliberately smeared them on her face and forehead. Her eyes closed in a reflex. She tried to open her eyes when the smoke dispelled but fragments of ash made them smart. She blinked her eyes with difficulty to ease the pain. With the corner of her kurta, she wiped her hair, face, and eyes. Then she brushed off her clothes. A layer of ash had also formed on the water in the can. She flung it out the door from there itself. If the watchman had not shifted to the left, it would have splashed smack on him. "You whore!" he snapped sharply. Thankfully, Shyama did not hear him, or he would surely have had it. In her present state she was capable of anything at all.

Shyama poured out some water again and drank it in one go. As she made to get up, she felt awkward and uncomfortable, as if something had been doused inside her. Heat exuded from it seeped into all the nerves of her body, in the same way that the embers had sizzled when water flowed into the chulha. She glanced at the chulha. It had already gone cold, like washed embers in a cremation ground. With a leaden heart she went towards the door and peered outside. The afternoon was in full bloom. The shadows of roofs, trees and valleys appeared to be shrinking. The scent of animals and cow dung wafted from the nearby cowsheds. The birdbath hung from the hill lemon tree. On this sat two sparrows and their three chicks … the she-sparrow filled its beak with water to give to its chicks. Shyama suddenly remembered something. She went in and removed the steel plate placed over the basket lying beside the chulha. She was satisfied that there were two rotis from the previous night in there. These were sufficient for Manu. She herself had not eaten anything today. She picked up the sickle from the corner, put on her shoes and walked out agitatedly. She turned to look back after a couple of steps. She had left the door ajar. She walked back and latched it. The watchman had gone on ahead.

While walking, Shyama felt the embers of the fire within her begin to smoulder once again. The heat rose steadily and her whole body began to burn. She was so tense that her foot slipped backwards with every step. She flicked the dripping drops of sweat from her forehead with her fingers and then mopped it with the corner of her dupatta. The way to the school was through the aangans and backyards of many houses. Surprisingly, there was quiet everywhere. There was no sound of people talking or the noise of children playing or crying. It seemed as if a deep silence had settled over the village. If at all Shyama came across any woman, she turned her face away from Shyama; and the men gave a strange laugh when they saw her approach.

Shyama slowed down. She couldn't make out whether she was panting or palpitating. She had never before been treated like this, she thought to herself. Ordinarily, if somebody met or saw her, they would stop her and ask her to do several tasks for them. Shyama did so readily and never said no to anyone. She carried their mud and cow dung; scoured their pans and utensils; cut and fetched grass and leaves for them; and contributed in equal measure in the harvesting. She was there with them through thick and thin and participated equally in their joys and travails. In other words, she helped everyone as best as she could. It was also in her self-interest, for in return she too got something or the other from every home and this helped her to get by.

***

In her short life Shyama had hardly seen any happiness. But her whole life had become accursed after her wedding. Her parents didn't allow her to complete even class five. Marriage was forced upon her after she left school. She was young, perhaps a couple of months short of sixteen. Her carefreeness became a thing of the past; her playfulness was snatched away; and her innocence was lost. She could do nothing in the face of her parents' insistence. She swallowed their decision quietly like a bitter pill.

The man to whom Shyama was married was almost ten years older to her. Since childhood he had had a destructive mind. When his parents sent him to school, he spent the whole day hiding in the fields and the forest. He was useless at work. Hardly had the smell of his mother's milk left his mouth that he developed the habit of drinking and taking drugs. Evil deeds. Bad company. Lies and deceit flowed through every vein in his body. He was quite tall by the time he reached twenty years of age but he was thin as a stick. He never combed his hair and seldom bathed. His beard was overgrown, his nails dirty and his clothes shabby. All in all, he spelled trouble and misery for his parents.

Some people said that the boy was mentally ill. Others suggested that he was under the influence of evil spirits. His words were beyond comprehension. He talked of heaven and hell; of fairies, ghosts and ghouls. He didn't allow anybody in his bedroom. He babbled for hours behind closed doors. Sometimes, so much incense smoke billowed out the door and windows, it seemed as if a fire had broken inside. His father tried to rebuke him a few times but retreated on seeing his bloodshot horrific eyes that seemed to threaten him with mortal danger. One day, he became enraged at something. He first beat up his father severely and then smashed his mother's head before running away. A strange fear engulfed the house.

Someone advised the parents that he could be free of lunacy if he were married. When he returned home after several days, his father affectionately persuaded him to get married. He was engaged to Shyama but his parents concealed everything from her family. The deadly snake was thus wrapped around the neck of the innocent and good girl.

He was fine for a few days after the wedding. Shyama's heart was filled with the dreams of a newly-wedded bride. She began to forget the pain of parting with her parental house. But slowly, the beast inside her husband started to surface. Shyama began to be acquainted with his crazy actions. He harassed her greatly. He beat her without reason and at times he also tore her clothes. One by one, the wedding ornaments that she had kept with such care started disappearing every week. First the earrings, then the heavy silver bracelets, and after that the silver ring and anklets, all disappeared. Then, it was the turn of the symbols of marriage–the round golden hairclip and bangles. After a few days, even her clothes began to vanish one by one. Shyama was at her wit's end. Finally, she took courage and told her mother-in-law everything. The mother-in-law told her husband. In spite of being in the know, they put the blame on the daughter-in-law herself. They accused her, instead, of taking away the clothes and ornaments to her parents' home.

Her husband didn't come home for days now. And, if ever he came, he remained awake through the whole night. Shyama could not even enter her room. She had to sleep outside. He mumbled and muttered all night and kept the incense burning. He did strange and crazy things. At times, his bag was found full of bottles of wine, dead partridges, bones of cocks and animals. The hair on his head were tangled and dreadful. His dishevelled beard appeared no less than a wild bush.

Someone informed Shyama that her husband was doing some kind of sidhi to acquire supernatural powers. He went to his 'guru', a low caste chamar in a nearby village. When Shyama inquired deeply into the matter, she came to know that the 'guru' was an old enemy of their family. He had ensnared her husband with the intention of wreaking revenge. The parents, however, paid no heed to the matter despite her telling them this fact repeatedly.

One midnight, her husband came home panting heavily. His body was feverish and his forehead was smeared with vermilion. Tufts of hair of his beard and head were snipped off randomly. He stumbled inside and collapsed. His bag still slung on his shoulder. Shyama panicked. She roused her father and mother-in-law. People from nearby houses also came running. He lay unconscious. After some time, he breathed his last.

When people looked into his bag, they were flabbergasted. It contained the severed head of a child smeared with vermilion, strings of red sacred thread, dhoop, a few grains of white mustard, and some pieces of bones. More than his death, his misdeed alarmed everyone. One wise elderly person advised that all those things should be tied so cleverly to his dead body that no one would ever know what he had done. They followed his advice and everything was consigned to the flames with his dead body.

The next day, news came from the neighbouring village that the leopard had taken away a small child from a house of the pandits.

Shyama's state was worth seeing. Surely, her husband had killed that innocent child. She was more distressed at the child's murder than her husband's death. She cursed her parents for tying her to that man and reviled God for punishing her unduly.

She wanted, nevertheless, to remain at her in-laws' house and care for them, but that was not to be. One day she suddenly fell ill. No one bothered to ask her what was wrong. Instead, in that very state, her father-in-law reached her to her parents' home.

Shyama's health deteriorated considerably. Her parents were shocked to see her condition. Their flower-like daughter had dried up like a stick. Her eyes were deeply sunken and appeared as if someone had fixed glass marbles in the two sockets. Blood oozed from her chapped lips and her face splotched with dark patches appeared frightful. At the hospital, she was diagnosed with tuberculosis. She was admitted there for months to undergo long treatment. After discharge, she started living with her parents.

Shyama stayed quite happily with her parents till they were alive. But after them, her misfortunes returned. The taunts of her sisters-in-law became intolerable. Her brothers too didn't care for her. Her alienation in her parents' house began to rankle. She was greatly disheartened and couldn't sleep for many nights. She often got up from her bed and either made her way out into the aangan or sat down to cry on the low wall of the granary. Sometimes, she even slept there.

***

Shyama was extremely distressed and dismayed. She couldn't find a purpose to live and thought of ending her life. But then the injustice of her in-laws streamed into her eyes. She mustered courage and made a resolution. Then, she gathered up her few clothes and without telling anyone she went back to her in-laws' house.

Her sudden return was a misfortune for them. They were shocked into silence by their anxiety. No one talked to her properly. They were aware that it was not easy to legally turn her out of the house. So, they began to trouble her in various other ways. She, however, bore their offensive behaviour stoically. She didn't lose courage and endured everything they did resolutely. In the end, they had to give Shyama a couple of fields as her share of the property. And in order to drive the burdensome woman out of their way they gave her one room in the cowshed to live. She accepted this without demur. At least, she had a roof over her head. She worked day and night in her fields and also strove to make her room liveable.

The real problem for her was to get two square meals. To avoid disrepute among the villagers, sometimes the mother-in-law gave her a little flour and rice. But this was not enough. Shyama laboured day and night. She pounded stones and gravel. From this, she managed to secure some food and clothing. At times, she had to take credit from the shopkeeper. There was only one shop in the village. Lala Dhari Singh was a very influential moneylender. Whenever any big politician or officer came to the village; they stayed in his house. Generally, the pradhan, patwari and teachers gathered in his house. He never lent money without a selfish motive. Whenever he saw Shyama, he swaggered a little too much. He was insolent and even obscene with her. In need of credit, she was compelled to put up with all this.

One day the lala said to Shyama that he would talk to the pradhan to grant widow pension to her and get some amount sanctioned for her to build a house. He would also help her to get a ration card so that she could get cheap and free rations. In this hope, Shyama began to go to the pradhan's house every day.

After a few days, her pension came through. The ration card too was made. Fifteen thousand rupees were also sanctioned to Shyama to construct a house. When her father-in-law came to know about all this, he began to pay close attention to her. He became excessively affectionate towards her. While passing by he now stopped to ask about her wellbeing. At times, he even drank and sprawled right there in her room. Occasionally, her brother-in-law too would come around.

The pradhan had taken the responsibility of constructing her house upon himself. Although, she well knew that he was devious and shrewd, what else could she do but agree. She had to get the work done somehow. Her father-in-law also wanted it that way. A two-room house was built, but the material used was so inferior that hardly seven or eight thousand rupees would have been spent on it. The rest of the money was misspent in the name of Shyama's house.

One day the temple priest also came with the pradhan to Shyama's house. She was astonished. He bathed at least twice if he touched an outcaste by chance. And here he was in the house of a dalit widow, Shyama …?

She understood that there was something amiss. There was evil in every heart, whether of a politician or a pradhan, a pandit or a thakur, a teacher or a patwari. What to say about her family. Relationships were only illusions or pretence. No one cared for anyone. Everyone had ulterior motives and purposes. They thrived only by exploiting the poor. And if they saw a woman, they neither feared the devata nor cared for religion; not even for caste or untouchability. Even useless decrepit old men, having many daughters and daughters-in-law, go wild with lechery once they are under the influence of liquor or cannabis.

Shyama plastered her new house with cow dung and clay and somehow made it habitable. But one of the walls fell down in the very first rains. She appealed to everyone for help but no one came to her aid. After many seasons, the house had crumbled in several places. Her in-laws continually tried hard to oust Shyama from the cowshed but she stayed strong and did not leave.

***

When word spread that Shyama was pregnant, the villagers were filled with curiosity. Whenever she went out or set off to fetch water, both the young and the old watched her closely. Everyone's eyes were drawn to her stomach. Slowly, her belly swelled. The suspicion of the villagers was confirmed. Her in-laws raised a veritable storm. For the people of the village, she was now a fallen woman. But Shyama closed her ears to the gossip. She shut her eyes to the people. She was tired of hearing abuses. Many a times she thought of killing herself by jumping off the hill, but she didn't have the nerve to do so. The mother's love grew with the child in her womb. A hope was kindled … a release from loneliness. A support for the future. … And Shyama's eyes were set on welcoming her baby. After nine months, when the baby was born, it was a boy. Putting everything aside, the village women had tended to her at the time of delivery.

The child started to grow. People tried constantly to match his face with the youngsters of the village. Everyone had their opinion, but no one could guess at the truth. For Shyama's in-laws, the birth of the boy was calamitous. The father-in-law knew that if the child was registered in the panchayat register, he would become heir to his whole share in the property. Shyama herself had never thought so far.

A few years went by quickly without Shyama being aware of time passing. Her dreams also grew over time. One day she took her child to the headmaster of the primary school to get him admitted there. The headmaster filled in the documents. When he asked her the name of the boy's father, Shyama was embarrassed. But the very next moment, she took hold of herself and gave her husband's name. The child was enrolled. The very next day, however, the headmaster called her to the school and told her that she had given the wrong name as the child's father. Her father-in-law had complained that the child was born after many years of her husband's death. The headmaster was in a quandary. Shyama suppressed her feelings with great difficulty. All her dreams evaporated. Absorbed in her dreams, she had traversed so far that she had all but forgotten her past. ... But now, her son would not be able to study. Everywhere he goes, people will ask him his father's name. She wondered what to do, where to go. Who to turn to for help? Her sorrow knew no bounds. Her blood ran cold. She came back home dejected.

The matter was not confined only to the precincts of the school. Her father-in-law created one more problem for her. He filed a case in the panchayat that this immoral woman had brought dishonour to their family. She was so audacious as to foist any riff raff's son on them. Now it was no longer a matter only of cancelling the admission of the child, but an appeal to expel Shyama from the village. As the matter had begun from the primary school, so the panchayat was called there.

***

Shyama read her whole life through on her way to the school. She measured it all with her footsteps. She felt extremely alone today. It seemed as if she was thrown into the wilderness where there was neither a pathway, nor a place to sit. Neither sunshine nor shade. Neither succour nor shelter. Any wild animal could pounce on her and tear her to pieces. But where else was there to go? It could well be her last day in the village!

Many different thoughts arose in her mind. They flashed like lightning within her. The flash fanned the fire inside her and the cinders started to blaze fiercely just like the embers in the chulha burst into flames when air was blown on them. Drops of sweat flowed down from her brow to her cheeks, she wiped them away calmly with a corner of her dupatta.

Six or seven steps led to the school ground. Shyama heard noises as she climbed up the steps. People were talking to each other. Every now and then, somebody guffawed and the sound pierced Shyama's ears like drops of scorching oil. Her feet became leaden. She stumbled a few times as she laboured to climb the steps.

She turned back abruptly, hurried down the steps and leaned against the wall. The noise increased. She stuffed her fingers in her ears, only to realise that the noise was more inside her than in the world outside. She took her fingers out of her ears and stood looking all around for long. Then she turned her eyes to the sky. Gangs of dark clouds were gathering from the west. They collided and broke apart into fearful figures. The sun ran helter-skelter from them. The clouds sought to swallow it like eclipse-causing Rahu. This sport of the clouds continued momently and then the sun made good its escape. Where patches of gloom had covered fields and valleys a minute ago now the sun reigned supreme. Shyama gathered the sun to her heart.

Shyama climbed up the stairs in one go. A hush fell on the ground as soon as people saw her arrive. There was no chatter and no movement, no noise and no guffaws. As if time had stood still. Shyama took in the ground at a glance. People from the entire village and also from neighbouring villages had poured in. There were some people there who she had never seen before. Women, youngsters, elders and children had all gathered as if a tamasha were going to take place.

The pradhan looked at Shyama's face. Fearful face! A raging storm in her eyes. Breasts hanging over her belly in a grubby kurta as those of a zombie. Although she was still far from the pradhan, her long shadow sliced through the crowd and fell on him. Something strange overcame him and he trembled with an unknown fear. He stood up. Her father-in-law turned to look at her from where he sat but he could not look her in the eye. She kept walking…. The pradhan sat down but the uncertainty and anxiety in his mind were evident on his face. No one else noticed any of this.

By the time Shyama reached halfway through the crowd, the last vestiges of her fear vanished from her mind. Once again, she looked all around. There was a big crowd. People were sitting as far as the school veranda and under the shadow of trees and bushes, as if it was the occasion of the processional visit of the deity or the official visit of an MLA or minister. All of a sudden, a swift gust of wind rose from the east and swirled in the middle of the ground. It rolled like a watermill, clutching piles of soil and bits of grass and leaves, before settling on the crowd. The faces of the pradhan and many well-known people became smeared with dust. Pieces of grass stuck to their hair and clothes. Shyama burst into laughter at the sight, covering her mouth with her dupatta. The wind was so fierce that even the dogs lying nearby had started to bark in fear.

A murder of crows flew in from somewhere and sat down on the roof of the school. A few of them let out caws but then all became quiet. A number of dogs ran back and forth. Perhaps, they had all harboured the delusion that a feast or the devata's bhandara would be hosted there that day.

Shyama came and stood right in front of the panchs. She looked to each side. There was only one unoccupied seat. Her father-in-law sat next to it. She went and sat down to his right. He made as if to leave but she caught his arm and wrenched him back into the chair. She placed the sickle just in front of her. Her father-in-law almost choked. He feared for his life. He looked at the sickle and then at the pradhan occupying his high chair. He shrank away from Shyama and his arms clung to his legs. His lips and mouth were dry. There was utter silence for a very long time. No one said anything.

Shyama bolstered her courage and firmed up her resolve. She also took it upon herself to initiate the talk.

"Why have I been called here?"

Everyone gazed blankly at each other.

The pradhan controlled his annoyance with great difficulty. Irritated, he said, "Your father-in-law says that you have entered a false name as the father of your child."

She broke into a laugh. As peals of her laughter rang out, the crows sitting on the roof flurried away. Nobody understood the import of her laughter; but the pradhan was infuriated, as if a storm had come down on his head.

"Then you could have asked my father-in-law himself whose name to write against the father's name?"

She glanced sideways at her father-in-law. He squirmed and stood up. In a trembling voice, he said,

"Pradhan ji, my son has died long ago. This boy was born many years after his death."

"Ramdutt, don't you dare abuse my child...."

Brushing aside all decorum, Shyama warned her father-in-law by directly calling him by his name. He felt as if a tight slap had landed on his face. He was taken aback.

Shyama's eyes became bloodshot as she said this. Her hand spontaneously reached out for her sickle.

Her father-in-law's legs trembled as he stood there.

The pradhan tried to handle the situation.

"Ramdutt, this is not your home. Say whatever you have to properly."

The pradhan was obviously on his side. So were the other panchs. They also did not choose to see the truth. The liquor poured into their bellies and the money stuffed into their pockets were showing their efficacy today.

The father-in-law spoke with folded hands,

"What can I say pradhan ji. You know about it yourself. You alone can deliver justice."

After saying this, he went and sat far away from Shyama.

The pradhan leaned forward.

"Look Shyama! The whole area knows that your husband had died quite a while ago. How then can you get his name entered in the register!

In the panchayat you have to speak the truth, otherwise, we will expel you from the village. Think about it."

Although the pradhan managed to say this much but he had begun to perspire even as he spoke.

"So, you want to write the correct name of this child's father…?"

Shyama had resolved and settled the anguish in her mind. Now a detached expression showed in her eyes and on her face. She picked up the sickle and stood up. The panchs became a little restless. People pricked up their ears,

"So, master ji?"

She turned towards the headmaster. He was sitting on the chair with his head bowed. A small table was placed in front of him. On that were placed an attendance register, an inkpot, and a penholder. These things appeared to mock at the master.

"What are you thinking! Pick up the holder and write down the name of the child's father."

On hearing the words, 'name of the child's father', many of those present were filled with dread. She stood by the headmaster.

Shyama's eyes were on the pradhan. He was too arrogant to perceive what was happening. When he finally grasped the import of her look, his face turned ashen as if he had been beaten with a shoe a hundred times. Utterly abased, he didn't know whether to keep sitting or to go. He was shaken and in complete disarray as if he had run into a hedge while walking down a straight path. The lines of disgrace were etched on his face. He was terrified. The few strands of hair on his bald head bristled. His face was that of an opium addict denied his dope. He rolled his eyeballs without moving at all. He scratched his head with his right hand. He wanted to wipe off the sweat on his brow but couldn't muster the strength to do so. He picked up his bag from the back of the chair and crept away. Everyone's eyes followed him, but Shyama called out,

"Pradhan ji, take your official seal along."

He stopped and groped the pockets of his jacket urgently. He turned back with such hurry as though afraid that someone would hit him on the head with a stick. He picked up the seal from the table and ran away. The condition of the panchs was worth watching.

Shyama now turned to gaze at the temple priest. Everyone was astounded. Suddenly, his cap slipped off his head. Although he caught it, he couldn't put it back on. He pushed it into the pocket of his jacket. His hand went to the crown of his head and he wound the long tuft of hair, which indicated his high caste, around his fingers as if he would yank it off. The breeze dishevelled his long hair. His whole face was instantaneously drenched in sweat. The vermilion tilak on his forehead ran down his forehead and besmirched his cheeks, nose, and lips. When he wiped off the sweat with the scarf on his shoulder, his whole face was covered in red. Shyama's gaze was still fixed on him. Many people laughed at the priest's face. The laughter pierced his heart like a lance. He gathered his dhoti and sidled away barefoot. He even forgot to wear his slippers. As he broke into a run, his hand fell on the sacred thread across his torso. God knows why, but he slung it over his ear as pandits do when they answer nature's call.

Thirdly, Shyama looked at the village shopkeeper. His hidden guilt had already accosted him. With bowed head, he seemed to sink completely into the ground. The bidi was stuck in his lips but he did not puff at it. His lips might even be scorched but the sting of losing his reputation set his innards on fire. The conceit of the rich moneylender vanished in a flash. He flopped on the chair half-dead.

Now Shyama turned towards the patwari. Lord of the lands! He blanched with dread. The grandeur of being a revenue officer was all but gone. He stared as intently at the coach grass near his feet as he did when reading the permanent record etched on cloth to make the revenue papers. He staggered to his feet and slinked away with his head lowered.

Shyama's father-in-law was sinking into the ground. He wanted to slip away unnoticed, but Shyama stopped him,

"Sasur ji, the list of names is not yet complete...."

She threw a contemptuous look at her father-in-law. A slight rustling sound was heard. Shyama saw that drops of urine were falling on the ground through his pyjama. He hung his head and his cap slipped down to his forehead.

Gradually, the school courtyard emptied. Everyone left in a hush as though they had all been disgraced.

The headmaster opened the register. He turned a few pages and vehemently dipped the nib of the holder in the inkpot. Then he shook off the excess ink and stroked out the name of the child's father. He now wrote a new name ... Manu Dutt, son of Smt. Shyama Devi.

Shyama looked back on her way out. The father-in-law was still standing there like a statue as if he was waiting for the earth to gape open. Her heart was overcome with bitterness. She wanted to spit at him but could not. ... While descending the steps of the schoolground, she felt as if she had emerged from a soot-filled cell.

People say that Ramdutt stood frozen there till dark.

***

So long as the headmaster remained at the school, the mother's name continued to be written in place of the child's father. After his transfer, another headmaster joined the school. When he saw the register, he had a hearty laugh at finding the father's name entered as "Smt. Shyama Devi". He swore freely at the incompetence of the former headmaster. Then very neatly, he rectified the entry in the register: Father's name – "Sh. Sham Dev."

Translated by Khem Raj Sharma and Meenakshi F. Paul

IN THE NAME OF GODS

DEVATAON KE BAHANE

Somdhar completed twenty-five years of age in January. Five years ago, he had got a government job but his village is still the same: the primary school is still a primary school and nothing has been done to upgrade it. There is no piped water supply to the village and people are forced to draw water from the old village well. There is no post-office or medical dispensary. Electricity is still a dream for the villagers. To reach the nearest town one has still to walk fifteen or twenty miles. When anyone in the village is ill, the only source of comfort to him or her is the village priest or the ojha and when that fails and the patient has to be taken to the town hospital, the family members have to transport him on their shoulders in a makeshift palki.

When Som visits his family in the village, he has to trudge a bumpy hilly track of over ten miles on foot. He reaches his village hours after sunset. Nobody in the family has any idea about his visit because there is no means to inform them in advance. Every Saturday his parents, uncles and aunts wait for him even though they feel that there is no point in his taking so much trouble just for one day's stay at home. So, they all go to bed. But when he does come and reaches near the house, it is Jimmy who is the first to know it and his loud barking awakens the entire family and before Som steps into the courtyard the two-room house is illuminated with the light of the solitary lantern. Mother rises, coughing and rubbing her eyes and scratches up the ambers thickly covered with ash in the hearth and puts some firewood on it to kindle the fire. Som knows that mother's coughing is no disease but a kind of secret language that encodes all her miseries and hardships that usually go with life in these hilly regions. The news of Som's arrival is like the arrival of the new crops. He just sits on his bed, puffing at his hookah and the sound of the hookah mingles with mother's coughing and spreads all over the courtyard. His younger sister, Chhoti, rushes to the courtyard with Jimmy, shouting 'bhaiya, bhaiya' with joy. An air of festivity wafts through the house even in the thick of the night.

***

Father was not in favour of allowing Som to continue his studies beyond class eight. He wanted him to marry and settle down in life. He also wanted that Som should now relieve him and take over the household responsibilities and look after the crops and cattle. He himself was a famous weaver of that area, who had his own handloom and was known all over the place for his unmatched skill in weaving woollen wrappers, mufflers and coat-patti lengths. He was respectfully called 'master' by other weavers. He wanted Som to follow in his footsteps and make a name for himself as the able son of an able father. Som acknowledged his father's expertise but was unwilling to spend his entire life sitting at an old decrepit loom unravelling knots and disentangling entwined threads of wool. He couldn't see any future in it. He would often wonder at the fact that a large shawl that took about a fortnight for his father to finish would not earn more than fifteen rupees as the price of his labours. The village head or the landlord would not pay even this much and father would never ever dare to ask them for his wages. He would regularly pay off the interest on his borrowings but the amount seemed always on the increase even after he had paid thousands of rupees as interest.

Som managed to pass high school in extremely trying circumstances. He could never have enough money for books and stationery and then there was the time wasted in commuting back and forth between home and school on foot. The village school was only up to the fifth standard and because the junior high school was about eight kilometres away so the boys and girls of the village would not continue their studies any further. Moreover, the road to the junior school was stony and bumpy and passed through a patch of thick forest. Apart from the fear of slipping into a gorge, there was also the fear of wild animals. Then there flowed a hilly river close to the school which remained practically dry in the summer months but became a terror during monsoons and the students had to cross it to reach the school. Even those children who could somehow afford to enrol in the junior school were thus forced to stay at home during the monsoon. The village panchayat taxed the villagers for constructing a bridge over the river several times but the bridge remained only a dream.

Som insisted on studying further. Some village elders told the father that the boy was intelligent and hardworking and should not be taken out of school, and father relented. He prevailed upon a relative to lodge his son in his house and the relative agreed but Som didn't feel at home in the relative's house and he decided to daily trudge the distance from home to school and back. He passed the junior high school in the first division and expressed his desire to go on to pass the high school but the high school was over ten kilometres from the village and it was not possible for father to bear the expense of his schooling, boarding, and lodging but he also did not want to discourage Som in realising his ambition to pass the high school. In the first year, Som would start for the school quite early in the morning and reach the school on time. He would reach back home very late in the evening. His passion for education had the better of all his fears of the dark and the lonely forest road and the wild animals. He would manage to do the school assignments in the light of the sun someplace on his way back from the school and cram his lessons as he walked home. The total distance that he covered on foot every day was about twenty kilometres but this did not deter him and he passed the high school in the first division. This was news for the whole region because he was the first to have passed the high school and that too in the first division! His father's pride in his son's abilities was beyond words.

In those days high school with first division was considered a sure gateway to a good and respectable job. Jobs back then were easy to come by and had not become scarce like these days. One of Som's uncles lived in the town and was employed as a mason in a government department. Father requested him to accommodate Som in his quarters which he gladly did and on his recommendation, Som was able to get a job on daily wages in the municipal corporation. In the mornings and evenings, he would help his uncle in household work and then go to his own job, which involved digging the road and cleaning the streets. The uncle had got a good servant in Som and that too for free. Som had no choice but to carry out whatever his uncle asked him to do. He knew that his uncle was taking advantage of his circumstances but he could not talk back to him or protest because that would mean an end to his dream of being of some use to his family.

He had already registered his name in the employment bureau and after a few days, he got a call letter from a government department. He was overjoyed at the prospect of being selected to the post of a clerk. He informed his parents immediately for whom the news was a real god-send. But it didn't go down well with the so-called big people of the village who were not prepared to believe that a weaver's son would succeed where their own sons had failed. They became jealous but they couldn't do anything openly. As for Som's parents and his sister, they too couldn't believe that fate could be so generous and bountiful. They were overjoyed.

Som's father had borrowed money from the village pradhan and other moneylenders to meet the expenses of Som's education. By the time he got a job, the amount had increased to about thirty-five thousand. In those times this was a huge amount but Som started paying off their debts right from his first salary. He also managed to get released the agricultural and pasture lands which his father had mortgaged while he was studying. This naturally sent out a good message to his community and others in the village and he was regarded as a model son. People began to trust him and he earned their respect and goodwill. Those who were feeling crushed under debt gained the confidence of paying it off through hard work and patience. But there were families which were so poor that freedom from debt for them was beyond the realm of possibility, although Som's example did kindle a distant hope in their hearts.

***

Som was happy and relieved but not satisfied because he thought he had not reached his final destination as yet. He did not want to slacken his struggle and sit back enjoying the little he had achieved. He continued his studies even after he had got the job. He managed to pass BA then MA and then a few diploma courses. By now he had reached a good position. But he had not forgotten his native village and was determined to improve conditions there. Many ideas came to his mind but to put them in practice was not all that easy.

There were some persons from his village who were employed in the city. They were from various castes but none of them was adequately educated. They were all engaged in petty jobs and could not look beyond their immediate needs and requirements. Two or three of them were practically illiterate. But Som talked to them and formed a society and got it registered. Initially, they were sceptical but they all were impressed by Som's abilities and pledged their full support to him. Whenever he visited his village he would go to their homes and explain his plans for the improvement of the village. Not everybody in the village showed equal enthusiasm and sometimes they ridiculed his ideas. They were not prepared to believe that village life could be changed by such fancy ideas of a person who had just got a job in the city and was ignorant about the village ways that had persisted for centuries. Only political persons could bring about changes because they are resourceful people and can influence the leaders in the capital, they thought.

The village was small and the dominant people, though numerically a minority, were either brahmins or thakurs whose writ ran unchallenged in the village panchayat. They had money, they owned most of the agricultural land and they were also in the moneylending business but they were self-centred and could not think beyond their petty selfish interests. They took full advantage of the poor dalits' misery and illiteracy. The dalits, though a majority, were divided into numerous sub-castes. They were always at the mercy of the savarnas who exploited them in every conceivable manner.

The head of the village panchayat was an illiterate Thakur who was also the wealthiest person of the area. He owned over one hundred bighas of cultivable land and also ran a shop. He was the landlord of two villages and had two wives. He was a well-known moneylender and his clients were spread all over the area. Most of his borrowers could never pay off the debt and the interest kept on rising. Quite a few of his debtors had died without clearing his debt after mortgaging their lands and other properties. This was a boon to the Thakur and his coffers swelled in no time. Whenever panchayat elections were held, he was elected unopposed because no one came forward to challenge his candidature. Whatever financial grants came from the government for development purposes he sat over them and with the connivance of the officials, siphoned off the money. Many other people of the village were his accomplices in these dark deals.

Som's village was the largest dalit majority village of the whole area. Many plans had been sanctioned for dalit-upliftment and huge amounts had been sanctioned for this purpose but not a rupee was spent on this account. Som had all the details about these plans and financial amounts but he did not want to bell the cat without carefully examining all the details. His father used to tell him that in order to make a line shorter you need not cross out or erase it but only to draw a bigger line beside it. Som took this advice to heart and waited for an opportune moment to launch his plan. When the village pradhan and his henchmen came to know that the son of the weaver had dared to found an organisation called the Village Development Committee, they were angry and took it as an affront to their authority and prestige. They simply couldn't digest the fact that somebody else should take the initiative of developing the village while they were still around. They took it as an open challenge to their hold over the village. But Som was not interested in going to them and to seek their advice or suggestions. He had decided not to bother about what such people did or said about him. The village pradhan was however not going to take things lying down because he knew in the heart of his hearts that it was the beginning of his end, unless he did something to nip the threat in the bud.

Som himself knew that he had jolted the bee-hive and should be ready to face the bees' assault. But he did not allow such thoughts to overtake his enthusiasm for his mission. He never openly challenged his adversaries because that would distract his attention and energy. He had won the confidence of many young men of the village, especially those who were employed in jobs in the city. Thus, he had behind him a band of like-minded persons who were interested in the development of the village. Due to their jobs they had become acquainted with new models of development and were keen to replicate those models on a small scale in the village and they were all with Som and were prepared to stand by him through thick and thin.

He made many attempts to prevail upon the high district officials to visit the village to see for themselves the progress of the government projects sanctioned for the development of the village but nothing came of these attempts and the reasons were not far to seek. First of all, no officer was ready to visit the village because there was no transport and they were not prepared to walk the distance. Som had no immediate solution to this problem but he wasn't the one to give in so easily and he continued writing to government departments seeking one information or the other about the development projects for his village. So much so that even the otherwise impervious bureaucrats could no longer dodge his enquiries.

Very soon a sub-post office was opened in the village for which Som and his friends had been fighting for long. One of his friends was employed in the postal department and he was a great help in this matter. Now letters came to the village and went from there with so much speed that people were surprised and spoke highly of the perseverance of Som and his friends. This was followed by the opening of a primary school in the panchayat. The school was the effort of the Village Development Committee but the pradhan and his henchmen boasted about it as their achievement. The people, however, now knew well the work of the committee and Som's actions.

***

The local MLA was a difficult person to tackle. It was well-known that he hardly ever met his voters. In fact, Som did not remember having ever seen the MLA even during the elections because the number of voters in that village was not more than a few hundred and he did not bother to come to that decrepit village to seek their support. Local leaders and officials did visit the village once in a blue moon but they always stayed either with the pradhan or other landlords and never bothered to visit the hutments of ordinary people of the village. Huge quantities of mutton and wine were arranged by the hosts for them; meetings were held in their honour where they would announce plans and projects, such as various kinds of subsidies and loan waivers especially for the welfare of the local dalits; which always, however, remained on paper and the real beneficiaries would be the pradhan or the landlords. They would invite a few of their debtors, especially dalits and take their thumb impressions on plain papers, telling them that it would help them financially in buying a cow or buffalo. Cows and buffalos were indeed bought but their real owners were the landlords themselves. All the money meant for the welfare of the dalits would be appropriated by these influential people. Thus, dalit upliftment would be carried out on paper and the dalits would never know anything about it. And in a year or two when they received recovery notices from banks, they would be shocked and go to the pradhan or the landlords who would lend them money to pay off the loans. Thus, the debtors would remain debtors and the tiny amounts thus borrowed would pile up to thousands without the knowledge of the borrowers.

Time passed and even more changes began to take place in the village. Initially, no one from the opposition parties came forward to contest against the out-going MLA but this time three other candidates from his own party staked their claims to the ticket. The MLA felt threatened to find his traditional support base slipping from under his feet. Previously, he had never bothered to keep in touch with the voters in the village and confidently depended on the pradhan and other influential people to manage the votes for him. But now he could not afford to be so complacent. He had never felt so challenged in his constituency but he was quite close to the party high command and the government. His seniority in the party and his experience as a seasoned politician had always stood him in good stead. Now he was past sixty years of age and his defeat would ruin him forever. Therefore, he began to contact such persons in the village who were relatively young and had impressed the people with their activities and he found Som's name at the top of the list.

Som was very surprised when one day he got the message to meet the MLA. In fact, he was looking for an opportunity to meet him in connection with his plans but never expected such good turn of events. Meanwhile, the activities of his Village Development Committee had stirred the people not only in his village but in the surrounding villages as well and he was happy that his efforts had started to have some impact. The MLA had also heard about him and wanted to meet him. Som decided not to meet the MLA at once but when he did finally go to the MLA's, the latter behaved so warmly with him as if the two had known each other for very long. They talked about many things and Som was excited. In the election, nearly sixty percent of the village votes went in favour of the MLA despite the all-out efforts of the opposition candidate. The ruling party was not very hopeful this time but it managed to form the government in the state. The MLA was all praise for Som and the kind of work he and his committee were doing. He was very close to the chief minister who always sought his opinion on matters of policy and political decisions. There was a rumour that he might be made the deputy chief minister. Som expected that the MLA would help him in his village development programmes.

Som was as passionate about his village work as he was about his studies and naturally he won the acclaim and admiration of the village people. And now that he had become close to the MLA, his stature grew overnight in their eyes.

***

Som was in the village on holiday. His father told him that there was a jatara ceremony in the house of a village brahmin, Pandit Motiram and that he was also invited. Som thought it would be a good opportunity for him to meet the people of the village at one place. Next day he attended the ceremony with his father. He was dressed in shirt and trousers but he noticed that his father was a little uneasy about his fancy dress on a ceremonial occasion. But he couldn't clearly guess the real reason, therefore he asked his father who tried to dodge the question but when Som insisted, he told him that the brahmins and thakurs assembled there would take offence when they noticed that Som had belted his trousers over the loose ends of his shirt. Som was shocked and infuriated but controlled his temper and took out the loose ends of his shirt from the trousers. Father was relieved but Som was seething with anger.

Motiram Pandit was pleased to see Som when he reached there with his father. He was a poor brahmin but had made elaborate arrangements for the visit of the devatas. Som was surprised. Motiram had invited a large number of guests from all communities. Arranging jatara of two devatas was considered expensive but the poor brahmin had managed things to give a grand look to the ceremony. Two huge goats had been slaughtered to please the devatas.

Motiram's son Karamchand came to greet Som the moment he saw him. They had been classmates up to the junior level in school and were meeting after a long time. Both were very happy. But Som was stunned to notice that Karamchand, though of his age, looked much older. Som was still a bachelor but Karamchand was already the father of five children.

'Karam, what has happened to you?' asked Som in disbelief.

Karamchand was deeply touched and his pent-up pain rose to his lips and tears filled his eyes.

Som made him sit close to him. Even though Karam had plenty to do, he disregarded everything and sat down with his friend.

'You know we are poor people and find it difficult to manage two square meals for the family. I also wanted to continue my studies but poverty forced me to give up. Father works hard even in old age and performs his priestly duties at the households of his fixed patrons. I work as a labourer in the road construction project. I was keen about my children's education but found it impossible to manage the expenses.

'But this grand jatara must have cost a good deal of money,' Som couldn't help asking.

Karamchand took a deep breath, looking downward at the tiny blades of grass on the surface of the earth and then said, 'This pomp and show which you see has all been arranged by borrowing from the moneylenders. Father had promised that he would arrange two jataras if gods were pleased to rid me of my illness.'

'To rid you of illness! What do you mean? Are you ill?'

'You probably do not know that sometime back I was seriously ill. Initially, father visited the temple regularly hoping that his prayers would be answered but my condition went on deteriorating and father was advised to take me to the hospital. Father relented and took me to the hospital where the doctor examined me and scolded father for wasting so much time before hospitalising me. I stayed in the hospital for several days and came home only when I had fully recovered. Now I am well.'

Before Som could say anything further, Karam was called away by his father. Meanwhile Som was still amazed by what Karam had told him and several questions arose in his mind: had Karam not gone to the hospital, he would not have recovered and there was no role of any gods or devatas in his recovery but here was his father who had organised such a grand ceremony to express his gratitude to the devatas for his son's release from illness. He had borrowed money on interest for the jatara but Karam's children could not go to school for lack of money! Even Som's father had lent some money to Karam's father for the jatara but had kept it a secret from him. After the jatara ceremony, Motiram would perform the ritual marriage of a peepal tree which would again cost him a fortune. Som was greatly agitated at the ignorance and foolishness of Karam's father.

He thought that the money Motiram was spending on the entire ceremony, including the wedding ceremony of the peepal, could be better spent on his grandchildren's education. But Motiram was more interested in impressing the people by spending money on the ceremonies so that his social prestige might go up. Som was sad to reflect that poor people were so trapped in superstitions and blind faith that they did not realise how they were ruining their own and their families' lives. Their own children did not agree with all this but they thought it better to keep their thoughts to themselves.

A little while later the jatara ceremony began. Men and women of the nearby villages had come to watch it. All of them were keenly and devotedly involved in the ceremony although they had not forgotten their caste divisions and had eaten the feast separately. Som's mind was reeling with various thoughts but he was deeply affected by the grand spectacle on the occasion, spellbound by the dancing and singing that was going on around him. One devata had come in a procession from his own village and another one from a neighbouring panchayat. In the procession from his village, the kettle drum was played by Parshotam, an elderly man from his village, while his son, Baburam played the dholak. He was very young but had acquired complete command over the traditional instrument. There were three other drums which were also played by the low castes. Som's uncle played the shehnai. It pained Som to think that because of their low caste the drummers and other musicians could not go inside the temple. Even when the devatas rode out of their temples on their raths they could neither touch the devatas nor their richly decorated palanquins. Even so, their music was considered sacred and even the devatas would dance madly to their tunes.

Som was deeply disturbed by such thoughts. People believed in these devatas and looked to them for relief in times of difficulties. This belief was their only support. The landlords and moneylenders were also looked upon with the same reverence and awe. The only difference was that the landlords and moneylenders were humans and the poor people looked to them for their material needs whereas the devatas were superhuman who saved them from unforeseen calamities. People depended more on the pradhan and the moneylender who 'helped' them when they had nothing or nobody else to fall back upon for their living and the pradhan and the moneylender took full advantage of their helplessness. But another thought came to Som. If so many people could come together in the name of just two devatas, then it means that if the number of devatas were increased, the gathering would also increase manifold. But the problem was how to go about it and mould it to some useful purpose without hurting the religious beliefs of the people.

Som spent the whole night brooding over it. Sleep came over him only late in the morning but it was broken by the morning noise, especially by the loud chatter of the birds that had ensconced themselves at the tree in front of his house. He left his bed and walked into the courtyard. His eyes travelled through the zigzag paths of the fields to the eastern peaks covered with garland-like clouds and the early morning sun looked as if it was encircled by those clouds. Som felt those many-coloured clouds and sun rays entering into the pores of his entire being. He fixed his eyes on that red ball slowly emerging from behind the mountain peaks and allowed the cool morning breeze to fold itself around him. But soon as the sun rose further, the coolness of the morning began to turn warm. He came back to his room and washed his face with water to feel fresh. Then his mother called him for tea and he sat near the hearth and began to sip it.

As he sipped the tea he felt an urge to go to the temple and immediately set out for it. He could hear the chanting of the sacred verses interspersed with the pealing of the temple bells. Then he heard the long-drawn sound of the conch shell. The priest was performing puja. Som addressed the pujari as Kaka with affectionate respect. The pujari was quite old and incapable of hard physical work and therefore he spent his entire time in the temple. When Som reached the temple, the pujari had finished the morning rituals and was now sitting on a mat in the temple courtyard. Som touched his feet and sat down beside him. The pujari took some time to recognise him but when he did, his face beamed happily and he asked Som to sit on the mat with him. He put his right arm on Som's shoulder and asked,

'How are you, son and how is your job going?'

'It's all well with your blessings, Kaka.'

'And what about that committee of yours?'

'That's also doing well.'

Then both remained silent for some time. It was Som who broke the silence.

'Kaka, can you see over yonder?'

The pujari turned his head towards where Som had pointed.

'The road that you see over there is now busy with buses and cars plying on it. When as a kid I went to school, the road construction had just started. Now, this road goes up to Kinnaur.'

'You are right son, but I have spent my whole life trudging the narrow hilly tracks. To tell you the truth, I've never sat on a bus. I've seen it only from a distance from where it always looks like a small mobile house. I wonder if in the very short time that I have in this world I will ever be lucky enough to sit on a bus.'

'No, no, Kaka don't think like that, I promise you that the day the bus service starts from our village, I'll myself take you to the town on the bus. But for that you will have to bless me and make a promise.'

'Promise! What's that promise?'

'Promise your vote to me.'

The pujari was taken aback by Som's words. He moved back a little. He looked astonished. He scrutinised Som from top to toe and noticed an unusual shine in his eyes. He removed his cap from his head and scratching it he asked:

'Are you going to contest any elections or what?'

'Oh, no, Kaka, no elections. But I want to invite the Chief Minister to visit our village.'

The pujari stood up when he heard this. Som also stood up. He knew he had said something which no one in the village could ever imagine or think. The Chief Minister had never visited the tehsil, to say nothing of the village. Even the MLA of the area visited only those places which were well connected with roads. Even though the area was not otherwise very far away from the state capital, the lack of roads and means of transport had turned it into a backyard of the state.

Both of them kept pacing up and down in the temple courtyard. It was the pujari who broke the silence.

'But how can a man like me help you in this matter? It's a big undertaking and if by God's grace it succeeds, then I'll think that my life has been worth it. It will be a boon for our children as well'.

The pujari's words were a great relief to Som because it meant the co-operation of the entire brahmin community of the village. He called a meeting of his committee but invited to it only those who worked with him in the city. They couldn't believe when Som told them what had transpired between him and the pujari but they had so much confidence in Som that they did not question him on the whats and whys of the matter. They all believed that if everything went as planned then it would bring about a big change in the village. It was unanimously decided not to ask for any monetary contribution from anyone in the village and all the expenditure should be managed by the employed committee members themselves.

***

Som did not want to make his plans public nor did he want to tell people that all this was being done in the name of the gods. He had approached the pujari precisely for this reason because he knew that the people around there had immense faith in the temple and whenever there was any problem, they would all troop to the temple to seek relief from the devata. Even if somebody had a minor headache the devata would be approached. If someone was seriously ill and needed to be hospitalised, the first door to be knocked on was that of the temple and the few sanctified grains of rice given by the pujari were considered the most effective medicine. No doubt this was pure superstition but people had nothing else to look to. The road was far away and the hospital still further away. The problem of money was of course always there. Therefore, the village devatas were their only succour in times of crises. In point of fact, they lived their lives in their cave-like houses in those far off hilly regions and bore patiently with all the day to day hardships only because of their deep faith in the devatas, whom they venerated as their saviours and guardians. Som's target was this faith itself which he wished to use for the welfare of the village. He dreamt of bringing development to the area in the name of the gods.

Somehow, the local MLA managed to get an inkling of Som's plan. When asked, Som told him that the people of the village had prayed to the village devata not only for the MLA's victory in the elections but also for his party to form the government and as an expression of their thanks to the gods they were planning to hold a jatara of eleven devatas at the temple to which they wished to invite the state chief minister. The MLA was pleasantly surprised. In his entire political career, this was the first time that he came to realise how much the village people were pleased with his victory and that they had made such an incredible promise to the gods. Som also told the MLA that they did not want any material help from the government in holding the ceremony and were prepared to manage the whole thing on their own. Their only wish was, Som told the MLA, that he should also participate in this sacred ceremony. And since the matter was one of the people's religious beliefs, the MLA had no choice but to say yes.

The next day the MLA met the chief minister and told him about the ceremony. The CM too was astonished. His experience had been that such occasions were mostly used by unscrupulous people to extract money from the government and then misuse that money for some other purpose. But here the villagers were willing to spend lakhs of their own hard-earned money and organise a jatara of eleven devatas merely for his victory. It would be a grand occasion and a large gathering of people was expected to participate in the jatara. So why not take full political advantage of the occasion by being present in the village on that day, thought the CM. Therefore, he took no time in saying yes to the MLA. Som and his friends in the committee knew very well that the villagers had not prayed to the gods for the CM's victory but it was their ruse to bring the chief minister to the village which he would otherwise not care to visit. It was decided to hold the jatara sometime in April. The district administration was taken aback when informed of the CM's proposed visit to the village but began to prepare for the occasion in right earnest.

It was but natural that the news would become a talking point in the entire area. People would not easily believe that a mere handful of youngsters could be behind such a seemingly incredible event but the truth was precisely this. Som and his friends as well as the people of his village were excited and plunged into the preparations in full swing. There was excitement all around and the atmosphere was truly charged but for the pradhan and his cronies, the news was a big blow. They just couldn't swallow the fact that all this was the brainchild of Som, the son of a village weaver who counted for nothing in the affairs of the village.

On his part, Som knew that he had bitten more than he could chew but he didn't allow this despondency to overwhelm him. He knew that it wasn't going to be easy to manage everything in that backward village but a greater challenge was inviting the eleven devatas from across the whole area to his village and arranging the ceremony in a way so that everything passed off smoothly. This was going to be the first time in the history of the village that eleven processions with eleven raths would arrive there. No doubt jataras were held almost every year but only after somebody's wish had been fulfilled. There was always a selfish reason behind these jataras: either someone had been blessed with a child or somebody was cured of a disease. Jataras were held when somebody's business had prospered or somebody's family had come out of some difficult situation. But jatara for the construction of a road or the opening of a primary school or the election victory of a candidate or party was unheard of. Moreover, organising a jatara is not everybody's cup of tea. Apart from other things, you have to make arrangements for goats for sacrifice which is an extremely costly affair; and this done, you have to invite people from your and neighbouring villages. Every rath is accompanied by thirty or forty persons who need to be looked after with special care in matters of food and clothes. And then there was the expenditure on a number of workers who were temporarily employed during the ceremony, apart from the routine pujaris and temple employees. Each village had its own temple committee and the members of these committees had to be approached for participating in the ceremony along with the rath procession of their village devata. It was really a very complex and expensive affair.

Som and his friends visited all the temple committees and ceremonially invited all the devatas to the jatara. They removed all the doubts and reservations that were raised by the several temple committees. They all were highly impressed by Som's approach and his behaviour. In fact, they were all surprised by his sharpness and modesty and all of them accepted his invitation, that too without insisting on animal sacrifice. This was a big relief because if even three goats each were to be offered to the devatas then Som would have to make arrangements for at least thirty-three goats. Som was against animal sacrifice on such pious occasions and thus had saved thirty-three animal lives.

As time passed everything fell into place and preparations continued unabated. Som and his friends collected funds from among themselves and did not bother anyone in the village so far as money was concerned. They ensured the participation of the entire village and took care that nobody felt left out or ignored. They also saw to it that the entire programme should reflect the collective effort of the people of the village. Everybody was excited, women in particular. The women made a point to meet every day and discuss the progress of the preparations. As the day of the ceremony approached, the excitement of the people also increased and the usually care-worn faces of the hard-working people of the villages acquired a new glow and an air of expectancy was clearly visible on them.

***

When the ceremony was only twenty days away, the tehsildar and officials from other government departments began to descend on the village to take stock of the preparations. For the people of the village, this was a momentous occurrence. And no less surprising for the officials was the spectacle of watching all the villagers working together for the occasion. The main ceremony was to be held in the ground of the local primary school. The ground was small and the people worked together to widen it. They would work from morning till evening. This impressed the tehsildar who asked Som several questions and Som explained everything to him in detail. He was pleased to think that the officials who never cared to visit the village otherwise had come on their own without anybody inviting them. And this was no miracle of any god or devata but because of the visit of the CM. These officials had no interest in the devatas or religious rituals but only in their jobs. Political leaders were their gods. From now on one officer or the other came to the village every day. For the local MLA, the visit of the CM was a matter of pride. Even the slightest oversight in the preparations could cost him his political future. He knew the village was in a backward region where even basic facilities were lacking. Therefore, he had instructed the district officials to keep in touch with Som and other committee members.

The public works department had assigned twenty persons from its own labour force for widening the path. Good fortune had smiled on the road after many years. The water project which had been sanctioned some thirty years ago was now taken up to be completed before the CM's visit.

When work started on the water storage tank, people were aghast to see that they had been drinking water from this tank which was filled with silt. It took five days to clean the tank and then fresh water was filled into it. Two hand pumps were also bored in the school compound. The old school building with its mud walls and leaking ceiling, its mud floors and broken chairs, took quite some time to be repaired. Its walls were cemented, new doors and windows were put in and new chairs and tables were bought. The school now looked completely new and the people were pleased by all this. Many officials of the district administration had visited the village to see that everything was in place before the CM's arrival. Som was the centre of everybody's attention and even the officials consulted him and sought his opinion on the arrangements. But Som neither interfered in their affairs nor did he allow them to interfere in his. He thought that development came neither as the will of gods nor on the demands of the people but only when the politicians wanted it. If they put their foot down, nothing could happen.

Two platforms were erected on one side of the ground. Another platform was erected for the devatas, on which were placed eleven ceremonial seats. Yet another platform was erected for the CM and other guests. This was decked with flowers and green leaves and looked grand.

However, the biggest problem was the preparation of food for the guests and the large number of devotees who were expected to turn up. Som had made special preparations for it. He saw to it that nothing was brought from the market. It was the month of April and whatever was available in the village was to be cooked and served to the guests. There were three or four persons in the village who worked as cooks on the occasions of weddings or other festivities. They were entrusted with the kitchen. The food was to be prepared from locally available materials in local culinary styles which would be served to the guests. There were many items about which the city people had not even heard ... sweet dish and raita of chhuro, vegetable dishes of dagla, kachnar, shimble phali and tyamble, sour dish of kwarpatha, chhuchh and sarson ka saag, makki ki rotiyan, chhachh, madri rongi, etc. etc. Some ten or twelve such dishes were prepared.

***

It was the first evening of the jatara. The devatas were about to arrive. The route through which the procession had to pass had been cleaned and cow urine had been sprinkled on it to purify it so that the devatas would not be polluted. People were waiting for the devatas. Birds seemed to have taken a cue from the humans and had ensconced themselves on the trees around. In their own way they sang the welcome songs as the old women sang on auspicious moments. The sun was slowly climbing down from his golden ladder over the hills in the west. It seemed as though the sun was standing on the last step of the ladder in order to have a glimpse of the devatas and watch them greet each other. He seemed to be sending his golden rays to convey his regards to them. The golden colour of the ripe wheat crop in the fields added a new glow to the air. A gentle breeze was blowing and the waving wheat stalks seemed to be nodding their participation in the ceremony. In the field where the crop had been harvested, small bundles of the wheat stalks glowing in the evening sunlight looked like honoured guests waiting to be feted by the hosts. As for the residents of the village, their joy was overflowing. The village had become one family. There was no community, no brahmin, no kanait, no lohar, just one whole village. Only the pradhan and his henchmen were indifferent and kept themselves aloof from the ceremony. There was more bitterness and anger in their hearts than joy and enthusiasm in the hearts of all the people. The success of the committee did not go down well with them at all. They could neither accept it nor show their resentment.

The devatas' raths began to arrive. The melody of their instruments wafted in the air. The whole village came out in their welcome. The members of the committee were standing at the gate of the jatara ground. For each devata, there was a separate plate with thick sweetened rotis as prasad, incense and garlands. The deep sound of the narsinga filled the air with thrill and excitement. The village devata, Harshing was the first to arrive. He was the host to the other invited devatas. The moment the rath entered the ground his musicians played the invocatory tribute to him. Music filled the air and at that moment the devata entered into the pujari. The panchs offered him support and he waved his hand towards the musicians to stop the music. His whole body was in a state of convulsion and his eyes were red with frenzy. He called Som to himself. Meanwhile, the panchs put a handful of sacred rice grains in his right hand. He closed his fist, shook it for some time, opened it and gave some grains to the people standing near him. Then he gave five grains to Som, then seven and finally five more. This denoted the blessings of the devata. Som understood part of the ritual language which at the moment meant that the devata was pleased and had given his blessings for the success of the ceremony. Som offered the garland to the pujari who placed it on the devata's rath. The devata now departed from the pujari.

The committee members were happy. The village people were happy. The devata had given his blessings. Just then three other raths were seen

approaching the ground. Dev Harshing on his rath and everyone else
present moved forward to welcome them. The musicians accompanying
the devatas played rousing music on their instruments for a long while to
announce their arrival. Then Dev Harshing welcomed them in the
traditional manner and his rath touched each arriving devata's rath one by
one. It was a poignant moment and the devotees were moved to tears. Few
more devatas arrived and they too were welcomed in turn. The sun, having
witnessed the meeting of the devatas from his golden chariot, was now
slowly descending into his nocturnal home below the horizons. The ten
invited devatas sat together.

Just then, the eleventh devata was seen arriving. His music was very
different from the others. The devata had arrived from a far-off distance.
He is known as Mahunag, an incarnation of the Mahabharat warrior,
Karna. As soon as he reached the festival ground he grew furious and his
fury was unleashed on the bearers of the rath. The rath became very heavy.
The bearers began to sweat profusely. The devata made the rath carriers
run around the ground. The rath moved forward and backward. It tilted
down and righted itself. The carriers found it immensely difficult to keep
their hold on the rath amidst the frenzied sounds of the folk instruments.
The accompanying pujari tried to pacify the devata and sought his
forgiveness. The crowd and the temple workers were anxious. Standing in
a corner Som watched the spectacle, nervous and perplexed. He moved in
front of the rath and stood before the devata with his hands folded.
Suddenly the rath turned to the west and the bearers rushed it out of the
festivity ground and ascended towards a hillock. Before anybody could
realise the rath entered the compound of the Shiva temple on the hillock.
The two silver plated poles of the rath came to rest at the temple door.
Mahunag had come to greet Lord Shiva before meeting the other devatas.
After meeting Lord Shiva, the devata became calm. Then Mahunag came
down and met the other devatas. After this, all the devatas began to dance.
The village and the entire valley was filled with divine music. It appeared
as if all around there were only devatas this evening. The thrill of the
music seeped like sweet sap into the hearts of all the people and the sound
of the instruments fell on them like hail on a tin roof. After this, all the
devatas were seated in their appointed places. Of the eleven devatas, three
are Harshing, they are blood brothers and bear the same name. Seven other
devatas are known as Kurgan Prakash. And one is Mahunag.

***

On the day of the ceremony, people from the nearby villages had
begun to arrive in bunches since the morning itself. They were excited

about having a glimpse of the devatas as also about the visit of the chief minister. The raths of the devatas accompanied by their pujaris, attendants, and musicians were arranged in a line on one side of the compound and could be seen from a long distance. As soon as the people arrived they would first go to the devatas, touch the raths with their foreheads, place their presents before the devatas, collect the sacred rice grains from the pujaris and then turn to the ground. Meanwhile, the members of the gram-sabha along with Som and his friends were waiting for the arrival of the CM. The news came that the chief minister with his entourage was just about to reach the venue. For a time, the people assembled there forgot all about the devatas and their ceremonies and began to look for the CM's party.

As soon as the chief minister arrived, the horns and drums were sounded and the atmosphere became charged. People with garlands in their hands were standing in a line. The CM had not expected such a colourful and tempestuous welcome in that backward and remote region. Apart from others, he was accompanied by the local MLA, many political leaders of the area and a large number of administrative officials of two districts. He was given a traditional welcome with flowers and garlands as grandly as the one given to a bridegroom by the bride's mother and aunt at a wedding. Four women stood in welcome with bell metal plates in their hands on which were placed lighted lamps made of wheat dough, many different flowers and vermilion powder. One pandit was chanting the mantras.

The opening ceremony was also not done in the usual way. A ten-foot long and five inches wide 'ribbon' of palm leaves was prepared which the CM cut open with a sickle to mark the opening of the ceremony. No one could recall any such traditional inauguration of a jatara in the past. The CM and the MLA removed their shoes and bowed their heads before every rath to seek the blessings of the devatas before occupying their seats on the raised dais. As they ascended the dais, people showered flower petals on them. For a moment they were spellbound with the decorations of the dais and the compound and forgot that they were VIPs. They were deeply moved by the emotionally charged atmosphere and the air of sacredness that prevailed all over. The MLA was very pleased because, somehow, he thought that the credit for the grandeur of the occasion belonged to him. On his part, Som was pleased and satisfied even though the strain of arranging the show was clearly visible on his face.

Som had taken upon himself the responsibility of conducting the proceedings. The list of speakers was pretty long. Many people of the surrounding areas had approached Som with demands and memorandums and wanted to present them to the chief minister. These demands and memorandums reflected the pains and miseries of the common people and they believed that once the CM came to know of their problems, he would solve them all. They all wanted Som to apprise the CM of their demands in public from the dais and hand over their representations right there before the gathering. This was a perfectly legitimate wish of the people because it was the first time ever after independence that the head of the government had come to the village. For them, it was a momentous occasion in the sense that the chief minister himself had come to the place which even a petty government official of the rank of a tehsildar never cared to visit. Som first welcomed the devatas as befits a deeply religious person and then expressed his and the villagers' gratitude to the CM, the local MLA, and the administrative officials. He was brief and to the point and did not waste words. He chose his words carefully and precisely to bring home the real purpose in a veiled but effective manner. He said,

"Whenever I meet the elderly men and women of the village, they often ask me if I had ever seen a chief minister with my eyes and how a chief minister looked and dressed and spoke…. Their simplicity and guilelessness always touched me and I often fumbled with words in replying to their simple queries. Their long-cherished demand and wish was to see their chief minister in person. This day has become memorable to them because their wish is now fulfilled. They don't want anything else. Thank you."

The crowd could hardly make out what Som had said but his words were greeted with loud clapping by the chief minister and the MLA and this assured the crowd that their demands and aspirations were taken note of by the government. The local MLA stood up to request the chief minister to say a few words on the occasion.

The chief minister simply smiled and did not utter anything for some time. His eyes were moist and he was deeply moved by the people's expectations and their belief that their long-standing grievances would now be redressed. Before him were eleven devatas and their colourful raths and canopies decorated with silver and gold. Complete silence descended on the ground filled with thousands of people. The chief minister wiped his tears and took Som in a tight embrace. The crowd clapped and the chief minister's speech began:

"In my political career I have never ever seen such a grand occasion where there are no chairs, no tables, no pavilions, no sofa sets! No people who always run around us looking for favours to hog the limelight. Nor any demands by the people. What I see here is only the affection of the people and the sacred presence of the gods and their blessings. It is true that I could reach here with much difficulty and my officers must also have found it extremely difficult to reach here. I also know that these officers are here because I am here. I wonder if they have ever come here before even though they are supposed to keep in touch with the people, especially in the remote regions of the state. I wish that next year when I come here, my car should stop right at the gate of the temple. Officers of the PWD should please note that a similar programme will be held next year also. I notice that the votes are here but the government that runs on these votes is somewhere else; at least I don't see it here. The place is backward and not easily accessible. Our development projects worked out in the secretariat dry up before they can be implemented on the ground. This is obvious here. I announce the upgrading of the village primary school to the junior level in addition to two more primary schools and a primary health centre. The electricity department is directed to ensure power supply to the village within three months. I also announce that a government ration shop be opened forthwith in the village". After saying this much he sat down.

The crowd was so overwhelmed by these announcements that for a few moments it was dumbfounded. The people simply couldn't believe their ears that they had got such a huge bounty without even asking for it. At that moment a question lit up in their minds about who was the real devata ...? Then Som clapped and broke the stunned silence.

Then the jatara started. The devatas danced. The music of the dhols, nagaras, narsingas, karnals, shehnais, etc. rose to a crescendo. Despite this, to the people today the chief minister appeared to be the lord of all the devatas. Their hearts danced, not to the sacred music but to the tune of development. They felt as if they had been roused from deep and blind slumber to a new dawn in a new world. The chief minister was happy and so were the local MLA and others who had come to witness the jatara.

The panchayat pradhan had come with his cronies hoping that he would be asked to sit on the dais with the chief minister but Som did not allow him the opportunity. He wasn't even asked to speak on behalf of the panchayat. In any case, he was illiterate and what could he have really said on the occasion. Feeling ignored, he stood somewhere at the back in the crowd. He felt alienated and humiliated as though he had been hit with a shoe on the head a hundred times. He felt grossly insulted as never before. The arrogance of being respected and honoured as the pradhan and moneylender flew away in an instant; in the way a tiger flees like a jackal when scared with the sudden sound of blasting for tunnels in the mountains. Or like the bird of prey, kuhi takes off from a branch. His reputation, built over years, was undone. He thought it best to quietly slip away from there. He felt his legs had no life in them as he walked home. His body trembled and his heart was in turmoil.

His condition was like that of a mad man. His humiliation struck him like hammer strokes. There were a few others too who found themselves in a similar situation. Their long-established empires seemed to be crumbling. It is said that the pradhan had not slept that night. Strange things began to happen to him. Dhol-nagaras clamoured in his ears. The cries of the impoverished also rang in them. He saw his jersey cows, bought with the subsidies meant for harijans, running away with uprooted stakes. From his safe crammed with ledgers bearing the thumb prints of the poor, he felt the thumbs emerge and bear down on his neck. It seemed to him that all the scarecrows from the fields had climbed the wall of the yard to laugh and jeer at him.

***

The chief minister, the MLA, and the officials left after lunch. Then the devatas also departed one by one. When Som returned after seeing off all of them, the sun was on the last rung of his golden staircase. The village, fields, and the entire valley seemed to be enveloped in a golden sheet. Small children with their toys and sweets were running home. Multi-coloured ribbons were braided in the hair of the girls. Carefree young boys swayed to the nati and film songs. Women had dozens of coloured bangles on their wrists and their tinkling filled the air with sweet melody. The bangle-sellers and vendors of ribbons, cosmetics, etc. were winding up their wares and preparing to go back home but a few tea stalls and mithai shops were still running on the hill above the festival ground. A number of village elders sat in clusters and puffed at their bidis. They lounged relaxing after the exertions of the festival and sang praises of Som. The older women were happy and contented because they had seen the chief minister in addition to having the darshan of the devatas. For them, it was a dream come true. They felt young again and their hill feet walked with renewed enthusiasm.

Som was surrounded by a number of people, but even after his grand success, there was emptiness in his eyes. Suddenly, his gaze went to the right of the stage. A girl stood there hesitatingly behind the wild pomegranate tree. Som quietly went over. The sun had climbed down the last step and had bestowed a red glow on the dusk. For a moment, Som felt as if the rosy hues had come together on the girl's beautiful face. On seeing Som standing before her, the girl's face lit up with the joy of the festival. She was the pujari's daughter, Krishna. God knows for how long she had been waiting for Som. She looked all around and hurriedly handed a packet to him before running away. When Som opened it, there was a red silk handkerchief and some mithai in it. Before he could enjoy this unexpected affection for a little longer, his sister, Chhoti called out to him, "Bhaiya, we are here too."

Som was caught red handed. He pulled Chhoti's ear and rapped her lightly on her cheek. Baba and Amma were standing nearby. He touched their feet in turn and took their blessings on his success. Jimmy also came wagging his tail to ask for mithai. Som gave him a piece of jalebi from the packet that Krishna had given him. Baba held Som to his bosom for a long time. The village devata was still there. The pujari witnessed all this while sitting beside the rath of the devata. Som went towards him. The pujari was thrilled even more than when the devata had descended upon him. He embraced Som. For a moment he wished that Som belonged to his caste, then he would have wed his daughter to him.

Everyone's eyes were moist ... how sweet are the tears of happiness .... this they had realised only today.

The village pradhan was now confined to his room. He kept rummaging in his safe. His family members were convinced that he was possessed by an evil spirit. They decided to hold a puja at the chief devata's temple on the first day of the month to drive away the evil spirit but when the pradhan heard about it, he lapsed into a strange frenzy. He raved loudly that the son of the blacksmith had defiled and ruined the devata.

Translated by Manjari Tiwari and R. K. Shukla

THE RIVER HAS VANISHED

NADI GHAYAB HAI

Teekam ran up panting to the edge of the field below the house and cried, "Pita! Dada! Tau! Come out. The river has vanished."

He cried in such a loud voice that whoever heard it, came out.

Taking a footpath going up to the house, Teekam had reached the courtyard now. His forehead and face were covered with sweat. Drops of perspiration slid through his soft beard towards his neck. There was fear and surprise in his eyes that made them take a deep red colour. His father and grandfather were the first to come out and walking up to him asked, "Teeku beta, what happened? Why are you shouting like this? What has vanished so early in the morning?"

He was breathing hard and his lips had gone dry. He felt his tongue sticking to his palate. He tried hard to say something but no words came out of his mouth. He could not move his lips. At that time, carrying a lota his mother came out of the house. With great affection, she touched his head and extended her hand toward him with the lota in it. Teekam snatched the lota from her hand and drank all the water, as if he'd been thirsty for years. Then he felt better. By then some more people from adjoining houses had assembled in the courtyard and were eager to know what had happened.

The rainy season had just started. It was about seven in the morning. By this time, despite the sun still being behind the mountains in the east, its glow could be seen everywhere lying like a golden sheet over the village. But today black clouds covered the mountains. The mountains looked as if they were a part of the sky. Over the mountains in the northern corner of the sky, clouds with frightening shapes could be seen. When the wind scattered the clouds in the east the redness of the morning became visible, making the clouds look as if they were on fire. It was then that a number of explosions were heard in the distance, startling the people gathered in the courtyard. They were not clear whether the sound was that of the thunder, or of something else. The glass window panes of many houses had cracked. The sound of the lowing and bleating of the cattle, sheep, and goats could be heard from the cattle-shed.

More composed now, Teekam was telling everyone, "Like every day, I reached the gharat on the river bank. I put down the sack of wheat and went down to turn the kuhal to start the mill, but I saw that there was no water in it. I thought the kuhal must have breached somewhere. I moved further towards the river. When I reached there, I was confused. I could not understand why the river that is never without water had gone completely dry. For some time, I stood there not knowing what to do. I wiped my eyes a number of times to make sure that what I was seeing was true. The river had really vanished. Its water had dried up."

Hearing Teekam's explanation, everyone was speechless. Coming closer to him his mother said, "Look, Teeku! Last night, you were awake till late in the night. How many times I've told you not to watch the television till that late! You did not sleep well, and I woke you up quite early in the morning. You must surely have missed something on the river bank."

Meanwhile, the pujari had also arrived, and was paying close attention to what Teekam was saying. The pujari, taking the lead, told everyone that there was no point in standing there and discussing the matter. They should all go to the river bank and see for themselves what had happened. All agreed with him and set out for the river.

Soon they were all standing on the river bank. Teekam was right. There was no water in the river. It seemed as if someone had stolen the entire water of the river during the night. No one knew what to do. Meanwhile, some people were seen walking up from below. They too were wondering where the river's water had disappeared.

Walking along the river, people began to climb towards the mountains. The river flowed down from there. It was a small river but until that day, its water had never dried up. However hot it was, there was always water in it. The high mountains from which the river started were always covered with glaciers. Some of the blocks of ice on the mountain were even centuries old. The small river was the source of livelihood for the people of many villages. On the other sides of the river, the farmers had their fields in which they grew paddy, wheat, and vegetables. Even today there was no water supply system in those villages in the hills and so water required for the villages had to be drawn from small kuhals. But that day it seemed as if misfortune had struck them.

They had walked about a kilometre when the pradhan of the area was seen coming down the footpath. There were some strangers with him who did not appear to belong to the mountains. When the people saw him, they had some hope. He was indeed the protector of the entire area. The pradhan was surprised to see so many people assembled there. He asked the priest, "Pujari ji, where are you going so early in the morning? Is everything all right?"

When people accompanying the priest saw the pradhan they felt slightly better. The priest replied, "Pradhan Sahib! We are lucky to have met you. What is there to say? You see for yourself, the water in our river has dried up. Only God knows whether our devta is angry with us."

The pradhan burst out laughing when he heard that. The strangers with him also began to laugh. Someone else might not have seen anything in this laughter but Teekam did not like it at all. There was something in it that pierced him deep down. He was a young man of twenty-one who had passed his matriculation and was trying hard to join the police force. He belonged to a poor family so he could not go to the city for his higher education. But he was studying at home for his B.A. through correspondence. Not only that, people of the village called him the 'pradhan' as he was always busy doing something for the village. Occasionally he would write a letter or an application for someone. He would often help a villager. He kept telling the people about their rights. No one in the village could talk as well as he did. People had begun to see him as the future headman of the village. They wondered why he was so keen to join the police force.

Taking a cigarette from his pocket and lighting it with a lighter the pradhan began to talk to the priest.

"Pujari ji, it is not necessary to get so worked up early in the morning. Your river hasn't gone anywhere. Now it has turned into electricity. It will shine in the region as electric lights. It will bring new jobs for you. The village people are always telling me that the pradhan has done nothing for them. Today the company is giving a job to one person in every family. It was for this purpose alone that I was coming to you."

"You mean…"

Teekam interrupted the pradhan. He was somewhat taken aback. He had never liked Teekam at all. And why would he like him? He was educated and could have claimed his job anytime.

"I mean, son, that you are an educated man. Don't you read the newspapers? And you dream of becoming a thanedar. And pujari ji, on the border of the district adjoining the mountains the chief minister has recently inaugurated a new power project. That river of yours has gone there through a tunnel. It will generate electricity there."

"But what will happen to us, pradhan ji. All the fields in these villages will dry up. The gharats will close down."

"There will certainly be water for you, pujari ji. It will be there. The rain water will remain in the river. It will not climb up the mountains, will it? Now these days who runs a gharat? The mills will be run by electricity. Well Teekam, why don't you set up one or two mills? The government is giving loan for it. Why are you bothered about getting a job in the police force?"

Saying that the pradhan thought it would be wise to go away from there. Teekam might have understood everything, but the others did not understand what the pradhan was trying to say. Then it was Teekam himself who explained to everyone that the river has been taken to the other side of the mountain through a tunnel and it would never return. There its water will be used to generate electricity.

With the disappearance of the river, another problem cropped up before the village. Their village was located in those foothills of the mountains where there was always a danger of avalanches of the glacier. Now because of daily blastings, tons of rocks began to rain into the river and the gharats located on the bank were completely destroyed. The river in which blue and clear water flowed at one time began to fill up with earth and rocks. The greatest danger was to Teekam's village. People knew that if the blastings woke up the glaciers sleeping for centuries, they would engulf the entire village. That is why no one else but only they had to do something about it. Whatever work that had to be done on that project was done, but now they had to stop that project.

Teekam formed a committee of his villagers and wrote an application to the authorities on which he got their signatures. He believed that going to the pradhan would serve no purpose. They would have to meet the legislator of that area and also the chief minister. That is why the first thing he did was to take about ten people to the legislator to meet him. But instead of showing concern for their plight, the legislator delivered a long lecture on the importance of development. When nothing happened there, they somehow managed to meet the chief minister. But they had to return empty handed from there also.

Disappointed and frustrated, they returned to the village. The work on the power project was going on in full swing. Now even a road had been constructed passing at a point below their village and because of the digging and the blasting, the hills began to sink. Many acres of land had already sunk. Now their priority was to stop the work.

Everyone knew that from the pradhan and the legislator up to the top, no one would help them. It was because the company that was given the work was very big and had put in billions of rupees into the project. It was not concerned with the fact that because of its work the river was disappearing, or that the forests were being destroyed, or that the land of the village was sinking, or that people were losing their livelihoods. For the company those mountains were gold, and the government of the state was also very kind to them. But the people now had nowhere to go.

It was the priest who suggested that they should seek the blessings of the deity. In any case, the deity of that village was known far and wide for his divine power. So much so that before elections, even the chief minister never forgot to bow before the deity. The temple of the deity was ancient, and extremely impressive. It had two floors, one of which was the basement where things worth lakhs of rupees were stored. Almost all the kalashas and the statues of the temple were made of gold. On its door, there were exceptionally beautiful engravings. In other words, it was the most imposing temple in the area. The deity too was considered to be very powerful.

When a group of holy men invoked the deity, he was angry. The pradhan, legislator, and the chief minister bore the brunt of his anger. Talk of total destruction was in the air. It was decided that the legislator be called before the deity. An order on behalf of the deity was issued but the legislator did not appear before him. Then an order was sent to the chief minister. In a very balanced tone, the chief minister replied that he had great respect for the deity but to bring the deity in matters of development was some kind of opposition politics. People lost hope.

Then they decided that now they would fight the battle together. The work of the company had to be stopped. So, along with the people of that village, people of many other villages too came together and protesting in a large group they stopped the company's work. They continued to stay on and hold a sit-in. The next day they heard that thousands of policemen were coming from the city. Teekam was aware of the atrocities of the police. A conference took place. It was decided to seek the help of the deity. A few people went back and ritually decorated the chariot of the deity in the traditional manner. That was their last option to save their village, river, and their land.

Accompanied by people playing music, the deity came out to launch this unusual campaign for the first time. That day it was neither a Dev Jatra nor a festival of the deity anywhere. Neither was there a marriage in someone's house, nor had anyone's wish been fulfilled. By noon, the deity reached the place of protest. Accompanying the deity were innumerable people. More than a hundred were already there obstructing the work of the company. The deity and the government's police force reached the spot almost at the same time. People had the belief that now no powers that be could crush their protest. They had the deity with them and they had the deity's might with them.

The situation was turning grave, but the company was not ready to stop work at any cost. If work on the road construction was halted the company would incur a loss of billions. That is why the government had passed orders that whatever it took, people were to be driven away from there.

On a loudspeaker, a senior police officer repeatedly asked the people to disperse. But the number of people accompanying the deity continued to grow. Leading the procession was the deity's rath, decorated with coins of gold and silver. People carried the flags of the deity and played music. When the situation could not be controlled, the police were ordered to resort to lathi charge. Like hunting dogs, they pounced upon the people. In that protest there were men, women, young, old and also children.

The police lathis were raining down on the people. But they did not seem to have any effect on them. When lathis proved ineffective on the bodies of those mountain people, grown strong working in mud and dung, guns were taken out. Then suddenly the firing began. The first bullet struck an old custodian of the deity's rath. He stumbled down the hill. The second bullet hit the main priest. He cried out. The plate of flowers, rice and vermilion fell from his hand and he collapsed on the ground losing consciousness. People were in a state of panic. Now it was becoming difficult to continue facing the bullets. They began to retreat. They began to run away. But that too was not easy. They had to run on a very narrow path on both sides of which were ditches. On the right side, there was a deep ravine. Countless policemen holding lathis and aiming their guns at the crowd were climbing up the path from below. Two young men were also hit by bullets. They died on the spot. A girl was counting her last breaths. Many people had been injured. They were lying sprawled on the path and among the bushes.

Teekam was trying hard to save the deity somehow. Turning the face of the rath back, he shouted at the priest of the temple to run from there. The deity was fully decorated. He was on the shoulders of the people. For the people, it was difficult to decide whether to leave the deity there and run away, or to carry him on their shoulders. Even the deity could not stop the lathis and the bullets. With great faith people had brought him there so that he would fight for their rights. It was a unique protest with the deity, but even he was helpless against bullets. Because of the presence of the deity people had felt a great confidence. They had the power of the deity with them, no one could do anything to them. That belief was proved wrong. The deity watched all that silently. His power was not revealed. The oracle did not speak. The assistant oracles too were silent. There was no meeting of the village elders. The drums rolled down the hillsides. The deity could neither stop the bullets nor save the lives of his priests. Showing courage, some young men had carried away the bodies.

In dismay people returned to the village. Women and children were waiting for them in their homes. They had reached the village with great difficulty. When they saw the dead bodies of the priest, the keeper of the rath and two young men, everyone lost hope. That incident had shaken the whole village and the entire area. The priest of the deity did not know what to do next. The young men were angry. They snatched the rath of the deity from the carriers and placed it in the courtyard of the temple. They also placed the drums and other musical instruments near it. One young man brought kerosene from his house. It was only a matter of minutes before the rath of the deity would have been burnt when Teekam stopped them and persuaded them not to do so. Somehow the people were pacified and then the deity was locked up in the temple. That was the limit of their faithlessness. That day a number of illusions had come to an end. A number of beliefs had died. The deity was lying silent in the temple. He had lost all his power. Where had all his power gone? Why did he not help the people? Why had no miracle taken place? Why did the deity not show his gigantic form? Then why had the people of the village and of the entire area carried his burden? ... Such questions confronted the people again and again.

Like a forest fire, news of the incident spread throughout the area. People were disturbed by the atrocities of the police. They were also stunned. They were shocked to see what had happened, although the deity was with them. When even the deity could do nothing, who could help them? A mood of grim sadness pervaded the whole area. There was darkness everywhere. Their village would be consumed by the project. Then there would be no water, neither for their cattle, nor for their fields. There would neither be the greenery of the forest nor the sound of the river. There would be nothing left. What would remain would be the thunder of dynamite blasts ... the cracking, collapsing mountains ... the melting glaciers.

Now the policemen had no worries. Before their bullets, even the deity could not stand. They were eating and drinking. They had pleased the government and also the company people. Goats were being slaughtered. The officers of the company had arranged everything for them. In the beginning, the policemen and the company people were surely afraid of the deity. They were afraid of the miracles they had heard performed by him, but now those were merely stories. When the police had fired, that all-powerful deity ran away, carried on the backs of people.

But the next day the newspaper headlines broke the news that people who had been the victims of oppression that day had attacked intoxicated policemen and company people who were celebrating their success with meat and drink, and also that in the morning, there was no trace of them left behind. At the scene, lay only some guns, a few lathis, dozens of broken liquor bottles, goats' heads and skin, and some torn pieces of khaki uniforms. Perhaps the deity, whom the oppression of the police had turned into a deserter, appeared collectively in the villagers and the anger of the people destroyed the oppressive arm of the government.

Translated by Ravi Nandan Sinha

AABHI

AABHI

AABHI

Situated at an altitude of 11,500 feet above sea level, Serolsar Lake lies in the remote Anni area of Kullu district in Himachal Pradesh. The lake is about five kilometres away from Jalori Pass. Beside the lake is situated an old temple of Budhi Nagin Ma, the Mother Serpent Goddess. A bird, which the locals call 'Aabhi', keeps the lake clean by removing bits of straw, etc. as soon as they fall into the water. The tourists and foreigners who visit the place are amazed at this exploit. This story is about Aabhi.

Aabhi has been busy for ages. Eons have passed but her work is still not over. Instead, it has only increased in the twenty-first century. She wakes up before sunrise and sits on a rock beside the lake. She dips again and again into the water and flutters her little silken wings. After finishing her bath, she sits singing for a while. The sweet music of her song descends somewhere deep into the pure azure waters of the lake and frolics in the ripples, as if trying to awaken the sleeping lake. Aabhi feels the lake stir languidly from its deep sleep. Then she flies to the threshold of the ancient temple at the bank of the lake. She pecks at the door and sings as if to wake Budhi Nagin Ma reposing inside. Her melodious music permeates the entire jungle. The other aabhis and birds also join her in the dawn chorus.

As Aabhi completes her tasks, the sun creeps over the glaciers to step into the lake. Its rays mingle with the water in such a way that innumerable diamonds seem to glide on the surface of the lake. Aabhi is dazzled by their brilliance. She swoops down again and again to try and pick up the diamonds with her beak, but nothing other than water drops fills her mouth. This game goes on until the sun leaves the lake and moves along, gathering up its rays across jungles and hills and crosses over the snow-clad mountains. Aabhi heaves a sigh of relief and relaxes on regaining the pristine waters of her lake. All of a sudden, a stray bit of straw or leaf drifts with the whispering breeze and falls into the lake. Aabhi picks it up in a flash and throws it to the side.

Aabhi can do all her work only when the snow has melted on the mountains and the lake. She does not like the snowy season. Aabhi's home, where she lives with the lake and Budhi Nagin Ma, is more than eleven thousand feet above sea level. There is no trace of any village for miles around. The roads are frozen with snow. The lake freezes into an ice skating rink and wild animals often wander across it. Aabhi has seen snow leopards and their cubs turn it into their playground. Once the leopards leave, the musk deer and tahr crisscross the frozen lake in rows. At times, she has also spied a swamp deer with long antlers run across the surface with its mates. Aabhi loves to perch quietly on its antlers. The bears are cheerfully content. A mother bear comes along with her little soft cubs and lies down for hours on the frozen lake. The little cubs never tire of romping on the lake.

In winters, the lake often disappears completely in a snowstorm leaving Aabhi bewildered. She does not know where to go! To whom to turn! She keeps wondering where her lake has vanished. But Aabhi stays there resolutely. Her only refuge is the temple of Budhi Nagin Ma. Grumbling to herself, Aabhi perches on one of the temple's pointed wooden purlins. She flaps her wings and chirps but no one hears her call. There is no movement in the frozen waters of the lake, nor rustling in the deodar or baan oak trees, nor pealing of the bells in Budhi Nagin Ma's temple.

Aabhi has borne this weight of nature's white kingdom for ages. For almost six months every year, this kingdom of snow grinds life to a standstill. Everywhere one looks, jungles and mountains huddle under enormous blankets of snow. Even the temple is buried under heavy snow. The sacred trees in the jungle also stand with their heads bowed as if smitten by a deadly curse for their sins. These are the worst days for Aabhi. Dismayed and sad, she continues to circle the lake and the temple.

When the clouds bring shade, the branches of the trees set amidst the blinding whiteness are able to open their eyes briefly. They can breathe easy only when the snow slides off them. In the harsh sunlight Aabhi is annoyed by the hustle and bustle all around her. There is a cacophony of sounds ... as if thousands of soldiers are sounding the bugle of war. This is the season of the thawing, melting and dripping snow, but nobody heeds Aabhi. In her state of separation from the lake, she swings between sad silence and loud wailing. The anguish of parting is an ever-present undercurrent in her songs; but who recognises her pain? Aabhi again goes to Budhi Nagin Ma's doors to make her plaint but no one hears her pleas– not even Budhi Nagin Ma; it seems she too is hiding from the cold wave, deep in the inner sanctum of the temple.

When the snow melts, the frozen layers on the lake begin to split open. It seems to Aabhi as though the lake is trying to make its presence felt from beneath those stretched swathes. The lake has woken from deep slumber. The frozen white sheet of snow gathers slowly and slips off it. Glass-like frozen pieces of ice begin to float on its surface. Aabhi perches on one and experiences extreme bliss. For long, she sings and glides on the surface of the lake. Deodars, baan oaks, and rhododendrons too lift their heads towards the sky as if thanking God after finishing their penance. Then one morning, when the temple bells ring out or the piercing horn of a vehicle on the road reaches Aabhi's ears, she gets all set to take charge of her work.

Sometimes Aabhi feels that Budhi Nagin Ma weaves this entire weft and warp of winter for the sole purpose of giving Aabhi rest from her labours. It is she who brings the snow. She who freezes the lake and makes it like an ice rink so that for six months not even a whit of straw or twig falls into the lake. No one comes to throw litter into it. The lake, the deodars, and the residents of the forest are at peace in their solitude. It is she who causes such heavy snow to fall far and wide that the roads are blocked and no one can reach there. Budhi Nagin Ma too gets to spend some days in peace. No one solicits her with petitions of prospering the market of their selfish desires.

Aabhi does not want anyone to dirty her lake, to throw anything in the lake that would muddy or spoil it. She is busy from dawn to dusk for these six months of the year. She quarrels with the tourists who come there, wrestles with the wind, and stands up to the trees of the forest to keep the lake crystal clear. As soon as a sprig of straw falls into the water, she swoops upon it with her beak and throws it to the side of the lake. People have started to throw all kinds of things into the lake now. They do not know the value of the waters of lakes and rivers. They do not know the freshness of the breeze. They have not witnessed the penance of the deodars. They are untouched by the fragrance of the red rhododendrons. They do not know what havoc they wreak by throwing around litter that they bring with them from the plains.

Aabhi is now more afraid of human beings than of the falling leaves. She is upset with the behaviour of people. The whole day so many people come to visit there. Some sit and eat in the shade of the trees–and leave the place strewn with plastic bags, empty chips packets and water bottles. Some behave indecently in the bushes a little way below the temple and leave behind all manner of garbage. They do not fear the divinity of the deodars. They do not care about the origins of the baan oaks. They are not even chastened by the presence of Budhi Nagin Ma. Aabhi watches all of this. The solutions to these problems are beyond Aabhi. These new-fangled ways of the world bewilder and trouble her. She finds this intrusion into her solitude unbearable. Yet, what can she do? She only knows her duty.

For Aabhi, the plastic trash has become an evil. The empty plastic bags and bottles that float on the pure waters of the lake are not fallen leaves or bits of grass. These do not grow on any tree of her jungle. These are not shed from the branches of deodars, pines, baan oaks, or rhododendrons. These are also not straws from the swaying grass in the meadows spread over the hills, in whose dens Aabhi builds her nest and lays her eggs. This refuse, which comes out of human beings' bags, is from another world or from an alien jungle.

Aabhi wails loudly. She is distressed. Many aabhis gather around on hearing her cry. They know why she has called to them. Although they all clean the lake in different places, they know that now they must work together. They fly over the lake in twos and fours. They join their wings together and try to lift the waste. But despite their best efforts, they fail to do so. They sit atop the domes of the temple and begin to chatter. This chattering is not ordinary. It bears their anguish at the pollution of the pristine lake.

The people who come here do not realize for how many long centuries these tiny aabhis have served the lake and Budhi Nagin Ma. They do not know that their actions are destroying the jungles and the hills. They do not know that the noise of their vehicles has destroyed the solitude of the wild animals; and in fear they crouch in their several caves far away. They do not know that Budhi Nagin Ma's eyes are being blinded by the smoke of diesel and petrol. They do not know that these deodars, deep in penance, are at the final leg of their lives and at any time they would end their lives and fall to the ground. They do not know that the baan oaks no longer ornament themselves as lushly as before. To them, the flowering of the rhododendrons has no worth. They do not know that the milkmaids no longer come to fill their baskets with rhododendron flowers because they are afraid of falling prey to the savagery of beasts in human form.

Aabhi's problems are growing now. It was all right as far as picking up straws and leaves off the lake, but what of the strange men who come into the darkness of the jungle with sweeping lights. The sharp axes and sharp-toothed saws on their shoulders frighten the entire jungle. Trees tremble at the sight of the gleaming axes and the dark evil in the hearts of the barbaric jungle mafia. Winds cower, hidden behind the clouds in silver valleys. It seems that the terrible darkness would destroy the whole jungle. No one is around at that time. God is invisible somewhere in the heavens.

Budhi Nagin Ma, the mother of a myriad snakes, too is afraid of the keen edged axes and sits holding her breath quietly inside her temple. Mothers in the jungle take their children and crouch deep in their dark dens. Birds do not sing; they sit beak to beak on treetops in dismayed and fearful silence.

Aabhi watches the mafia rule the deep dark jungle. In a moment, the jungle is petrified by the fearsome sounds of axes and saws. Many deodars die at once. The baan oaks writhe in pieces. Far from these heartrending cries of death, the jackals let out long howls; the snow-leopards raise a tremendous yowl as if pleading with Lord Shiva on Mount Kailash: Oh Shiva! Where is your Trishul? Why are you not angry now? Why don't you dance the tandav and annihilate this evil jungle mafia?

Aabhi hears loud heart-wrenching laughter ring out in the wilderness. And a strange putrefying smell permeates the air–of gunpowder, cannabis and tobacco; of poisonous country liquor; of rustling currency notes. Aabhi runs hither and thither to escape this foul smell but it dogs her everywhere. She pecks at the threshold of the temple in the deep darkness of the night, she cries out, but Buddhi Nagin does not respond. She seems to be in deep sleep. Or her arms are debilitated. Or her divine powers have waned. Then Aabhi circles the lake several times in the darkness. All of a sudden, it seems as though innumerable glow worms have descended on the lake. Aabhi is familiar with the glow worms. She lives and cohabits with them. She wonders why they have come to the lake so late in the night. She goes close and realises that these were not glow worms. These were half-lit butts of cigarettes and biris. She tries to pick up the butts in her beak in the thick darkness but ends up scorching her mouth.

Aabhi sees many strangers swaying and staggering together in the shelter of the deodars. They are carrying the long and thick pieces of the dead deodars and baan oak trees on their shoulders to the road. They are loading them onto the trucks. Aabhi does not sleep the whole night. The lake also does not sleep. Deodars, baan oaks and rhododendrons too stay awake. Wild bears, goats, snow-leopards, peacocks, partridges, cocks, and monals also stay awake. They crouch in silence at a distance. But troupes of lemurs and monkeys are impatient for the morning. They rummage for leftover food near the empty liquor bottles.

Aabhi does not know how to write an application. She doesn't know how to file a complaint. She does not know the guard or chowkidar of this jungle. She doesn't know the range officer of this reserved forest area. She doesn't even know the pradhan of the panchayat. She is not familiar with the inspector or thanedar. She doesn't know the forest minister of the state. All that she knows is that she will bathe before daybreak in the pristine waters of the lake. After cleansing herself she will sit and sing at Buddhi Nagin's door. And then the whole day she will pick up leaves and twigs off the surface of the lake so that the water does not become dirty. When Budhi Nagin Ma is thirsty she will have clear cool water to drink. With dawn's help the sun will hide his jewels in the water. The moon will come and dive into it. Innumerable little stars of the sky will bathe in it. Leopards, bears, and other animals will come to it with their young ones and drink to their fill.

Budhi Nagin Ma is helpless. She feels herself chained by hundreds of shackles. She has begun to dislike the incense smoke and the lamps. Praise and worship of the people vex her. Their prayers and supplications irritate her. She is frightened of the devils hiding inside the minds of her devotees. She has begun to fear the desolations of the night. Nevertheless, she holds on to the hope that her people, the aabhis would never give in. They would never allow the purity of the lake to be lost. They would pick up every speck of straw or leaf and keep it clean.

Aabhi is greatly troubled today. She has witnessed a petrifying incident. Both Budhi Ma's temple and she have seen some people assault a female snow leopard. The deodars have also heard the loud reverberations of this attack. Her companion aabhis too have heard them. The leopards, bears, musk deers have also heard them. The peacocks, monals and jujuranas too have heard them. And the valleys and hills have heard them. They are all bewildered and worried like she is. They have woken fearful and terrified. Aabhi is aware that one day or the other this calamity would fall on each one of them.

Groaning and writhing, the mother leopard has dragged herself to the edge of the lake. It is pitch dark here. Aabhi sees that she is drawing short shallow breaths and her four or five cubs are suckling her teats. They do not know that humans have attacked their mother. They do not know that their mother is about to die. That streams of blood are pouring out of the wound on her back. A few of the kids are soaked in her blood but secure in the proximity of their mother they are free from fear. Aabhi approaches the leopard quietly and checks her breath. The leopard's eyes brim with excruciating pain. This pain does not stem from the fear of her own death but from the fear for the life of her babies. Aabhi sits between this life and death. Helpless and dismayed.

A number of people have set about in search of the leopard. There are axes and guns on their shoulders. In the darkness they do not see where the leopard is lying. Aabhi knows that they will drag the mother away if they find her. Her courage fails her. She wants to scream but her beak seems to be clenched shut. She wants to flap her wings but her feathers seem to have been plucked. She agonises on how to save the leopard. How to give a lease of life to the little ones? She braces herself. Opens her beak with great difficulty. Spreads her wings. The rustling of her feathers is the silent voice of her soulful entreaty. Slowly and gradually a number of aabhis gather there. Aabhi takes the lead. She wants to conceal the leopard. She picks up a twig and places it on the leopard. And in no time hundreds of twigs and leaves are heaped over the leopard, covering it. But Aabhi does not know what to do with the cubs. They are running all over the place.

Aabhi's eyes can see in the dark. She has seen a couple of men come there and then return. They did not see the leopard. Then a fat dark man staggers forward. He carries a filthy backpack and an axe on his shoulder. His dishevelled hair bristle like a bush scorched by fire. Beneath his grey brows his deep-set eyes appear like that of a statue. He has tied his long unkempt hair to his forehead with an ugly black muffler. His mouth is hidden behind a thick moustache and beard. The hair of his moustache quiver slightly as he breathes. His stomach hangs out. Instead of a belt, he has held up his unwashed jeans tightly with a string, which divides his paunch into two. His pockets balloon with things crammed into them. He wears black rubber shoes. He has stuffed the bottom of his jeans into them.

His feet fall on the dry leaves as he steps forward. A strange crackling sound is heard, as though there weren't leaves under his heavy shoes but a creature groaning in deep agony. He lifts his foot to clear the leaves and twigs stuck to his shoe but slips and falls. His axe falls away from him. His torchlight tumbles down the slope as if someone is running away with stolen light. He is bereft of both the axe and the light. He is now unarmed like Aabhi. He steadies himself for a moment but slips again and skids down on his back to the edge of the lake. Once again, he regains his balance and starts to climb back up. He pants. His pungent bitter breath fouls the air, gagging the aabhis. He walks a few steps and leans against a deodar.

He now removes a biri and matchbox from his pocket. He is so intoxicated that he cannot light a match despite striking it several times. After a long time, a blue flame spreads on the heap of twigs with a frightening sound. In the flare his face looks like the burnt stump of an oak. He takes a few quick drags on the biri before tossing the half-burnt stub aside and begins to look for the leopard again. He has barely walked a few steps when he hears a crackling sound.

The dry leaves and straw are on fire. He wants to run back but his legs are weak with drinking. With great difficulty he returns and tries to stamp out the fire with his right foot. But the fire does not die down. The breeze gradually spreads its blaze. He tries to put out the fire again but falls down.

Instantaneously, his clothes begin to flame. His companions rush to the spot on hearing his cries. They try to extinguish the flames but retreat on seeing them rage. He cries out for help but they have all gone. The breeze blows towards him. All of a sudden, the man turns into a ball of fire. Desperately, he jumps into the lake with a loud splash. There is an upheaval in the lake. Budhi Nagin Ma has awakened from her slumber and watches the man bobbing in the water from behind her doors. The flames float on the surface of the lake for a while. The aabhis see that the burning man has gone deep into the water. From the whorl of a whirlpool several circular waves dart from one end of the lake to the other. After some time, bits and pieces of his burnt clothes are seen to float on the lake.

The companions of the dead man are still running. They do not care for the death of their mate but only for their own lives. They want to save themselves come what may. They want to live. But they feel the inferno hot on their heels and it is difficult for them to escape.

Then Aabhi breaks into a song. Her companion aabhis also join her in singing. Deodars, oaks, pines, and rhododendrons begin to stir. Animals emerge from their dens. Birds leave their nests. They all think that it is morn and begin to sing the dawn chorus.

Aabhi busies herself picking up the burnt pieces of cloth strewn on the lake.

Translated by Meenakshi F. Paul

CONTRIBUTORS

R. K. Shukla is former Professor of English, Banaras Hindu University. He specialises in Modern and Contemporary Literary Theory, Indian Writings, Comparative Literature and Translation Studies. Prof. Shukla has translated and published several articles, short stories and books, including *Edward Said: Varchshav Aur Pratirodh* (collection of essays); *Eric J. Hobsbawm: Itihas, Rajniti Aur Sanskriti* (2015). His forthcoming translations are *Derrida's Spectres of Marx,* and twelve essays by Jacques Derrida.

Manjari Tiwari is an Assistant Professor of English at Sant Gadge Maharaj College of Commerce and Economics, Mumbai. She teaches literatures and interpersonal skills, and has translated several texts into English. Dr. Tiwari has contributed several articles in national and international journals. Her areas of interest are Indian Writing in English, Modern Literary Theory, Indian Literature in English Translation, and Communication Skills.

Ira Raja is Assistant Professor in the Department of English, University of Delhi, and Postdoctoral Fellow, La Trobe University, Australia. She has co-edited *The Table is Laid: The Oxford Anthology of South Asian Food Writing* (OUP 2006); and *An Endless Winter's Night: Mother-Daughter Narratives from India* (2010). Her book *Grey Areas: An Anthology of Contemporary Indian Fiction on Ageing* (OUP 2010) brings together a range of stories and poems from across Indian Languages. In addition, she is the Associate Editor of *South Asia: Journal of South Asian Studies* (2011-)*;* and *Journal of Commonwealth Literature* (2005-2008) and poetry editor of *Postcolonial Text* (2006-2010). Her areas of interest include Postcolonial Literature and Theory, Cosmopolitanism, Globalisation Studies, Twentieth Century Novel and Poetry, Dalit literature, Indian Literature in English Translation, Literary Gerontology, and Urban Cultures.

Ravi Nandan Sinha is Head, Department of English, St. Xavier's College, Ranchi, Bihar. He is the co-founder of the *Writer's Forum*, an organisation of creative writers in English. Prof. Sinha is the editor of *The Quest* (1985-). His books include *Dayspring, Wanderlust, Blossom, Horizon, Rendezvous,*

Rhapsodies, Essays on Indian Literature, The Poetry of Keki N. Daruwalla, Harbour Lights, and *Three Women Novelists.* He translates texts from Hindi and Oriya into English. His *Exuberance and Other Poems* is a translation of noted Hindi poet, Mahendra Bhatnagar's seventy-five poems. Sinha has translated Oriya poet Hara Prasad Das' award-winning collection of poems, *Garbhagriha* into the English as *Dark Sanctum* (Sahitya Akademi). The *Great Hindi Short Stories* (2013) is a translation of classic Hindi short stories penned over the last hundred years.